OWN IT
A Wolfshead Whiskey Novel

ELISABETH BARRETT

COMPLETE BOOKLIST

Wolfshead Whiskey Series
Own It
Want It
Need It

West Coast Holiday Series
Christmas in Tahoe
New Year's in Napa
Rendezvous in Point Reyes

Return to Briarwood Series
Once and Again
The Best of Me
Anywhere You Are

Star Harbor Series
Deep Autumn Heat
Blaze of Winter
Long Simmering Spring
Slow Summer Burn

ACKNOWLEDGMENTS

So many incredible people gave their time and energy to help answer my questions about distilling and brewing. In particular, I want to thank Mark Hall, Cameron Wong at Sonoma County Distilling Company, the folks at Anchor Steam Brewery, and the team at St. George Spirits.

You'd think that after ten books I'd know everything there is to know about publishing. Yeah, no. Not even close. Joan Swan, thank you for talking me through this process and for telling me I could absolutely do this. You are an inspiration. Marina Adair, goddess, thank you for your friendship and support. There is no way I would have had the courage to do this without you.

Thank you also to Anne Hearn, Marni Bates, Claudia Connor, and my Friday morning writing crew: Jina Yoo, Sue Sbardellati, Layla Reyne, Alyson Charles, Gayle Parness, Rachel Scheuring, and Kristina Wright.

Jessica Scott, thank you. You are an incredible human being and a first-rate problem solver. Erin Crum, thank you again for your copyediting expertise and assistance. Jeff and Johanna, thank you for all the bus stop brainstorming.

Jennifer, you rock. Jonathan, thanks for your continued belief in me (and your editing and your suggestions). Your pride in my work means everything, and I love you. Also: Bop it..

CHAPTER 1

"Mmm, Voodoo. I *love* Voodoo."

Emma Crandall's eyes lit on the array of pastries on the conference room table and she quickly picked out her favorite—a maple-bacon doughnut almost as long as her forearm. If she had to drag herself to downtown Portland at eight thirty on a Monday morning, she might as well be fed for her troubles.

Taking a big bite of the pastry, she let out a little moan as the sweet, salty, savory goodness practically melted on her tongue. Immediately, her day became a little brighter. Good things really did come in pink boxes.

The only other occupant of the room, Philip Lewis, attorney—the senior Lewis in Lewis & Lewis LLP—had his face practically buried in a stack of papers and ignored her expressions of ecstasy. Not only had he barely spoken to her since she'd arrived fifteen minutes ago, he'd also ignored the tasty Voodoo doughnuts.

Suspicious behavior, indeed.

Emma frowned at the top of his bald head, which was gleaming under the fluorescent lights, realizing she still had no idea why he'd asked her to come in.

Delicately, she wiped her fingers on a napkin and cleared her throat. "Mr. Lewis?"

"Yes?" he said, head still down, flipping through his papers.

"Could you at least tell me what's going on? And maybe also

why you couldn't have given me more information over the phone?"

She had been decidedly unhappy about the vague phone call she'd gotten last week. Emma liked knowing what she was walking into, and it was only because the law firm was reputable that she'd even shown up.

Still refusing to look at her, Lewis made some noncommittal noise.

Emma cleared her throat again. "Perhaps we should reschedule. I've interrupted my very busy day to come downtown and talk to you."

Lie. Since opening her own freelance business Emma Crandall Marketing and Branding—ECMB for short—a couple of months ago, she'd had only two clients, both of whom had hired her for one-off jobs. But time spent at a lawyer's office meant time not spent hustling for her next gig, so she shifted in her seat, subtly intimating that she might actually leave.

Lewis finally acknowledged her unspoken threat, then sighed and looked up. "We're waiting for another party. Then we can begin."

"I see." Emma slid her doughnut onto a white plate, conveniently located in a stack next to the pastry box. "And exactly when is this other party supposed to arrive?"

"Any moment now," Lewis said, and returned to his papers.

Emma pressed her lips together and smoothed down her pencil skirt as she rose to pour herself a cup of coffee. If there was anything positive she could say about law firms, it's that they were always well-stocked with amenities—pastries and good, strong coffee being two of them.

But the positives ended there, as almost every dealing she'd had with lawyers in the last few years had been distinctly unpleasant. Unfortunately, this encounter was rapidly following suit.

She was stirring a bit of cream into her mug when she heard the door open.

"Ah, Mr. Phelan," Lewis said. "You're here."

Her back still to the door, Emma froze. Surely it couldn't be, it *wouldn't* be, him.

"Lewis," a familiar voice growled.

Oh God, she'd know that deep, low rumble anywhere.

There was a telltale thud in the vicinity of her chest, and an answering throb in her core. Slowly, inexorably, she turned around, and there he stood.

Aidan Phelan, in the prime, glorious flesh.

The room wasn't small, but somehow he seemed to fill it, all muscle and masculine attitude. He'd always been a big man, but in the two years since she'd last seen him, he seemed to have gotten bigger, his chest and shoulders broader.

His hair was the same—a rich dark auburn that he wore too long and pushed back off his face—but he'd grown out his beard. He'd always liked to do that in the fall, but it was early spring now, and he hadn't shaved. Maybe this was a new thing for him.

He had on worn jeans and giant boots, steel-toed no doubt, for added protection in the warehouse. A long-sleeved Henley shirt stretched over his shoulders, emphasizing his strength and power. He hadn't bothered to tuck it in, but he had shoved the sleeves up his arms, displaying forearms rippling with ropy muscle.

And then there were his hands. Large and scarred. Capable. Talented.

She missed those hands.

Even now, even after all the time that had passed, she remembered how good it was between them. Until…it wasn't. Until all there had been left was arguing and sex. The arguing got old, fast.

The sex hadn't. It had been crazy good, right up to the bitter end.

Do not *go there.*

She dragged her gaze from his hands back up to his face.

Aidan was staring at her, his blue eyes hard, his lips curled in a sneer. "Oh, *hell* no." He turned back to Lewis. "Tell me what that bastard did. *Now.*"

Lewis stood. "If you'll just calm down, we can—"

"Calm down?" Aidan laughed, a harsh, grating sound. "I've been waiting three fucking months to find out and now *she's* here." He tossed his hand in her general direction.

"Yes, about that," Lewis started.

Aidan's eyes narrowed. "Don't like being played."

"I understand, but—"

"Six feet in the ground, and I'm still being jerked around." He stood to his full height and crossed his arms over his massive chest—Aidan's digging-in-his-heels stance, one she knew all too well.

It was the same stance he took when he'd unilaterally decided to buy an extra warehouse property even though the rest of his family had hated the idea. The same stance he took when he told her that her marketing ideas were okay, but they were sticking with the way they'd always done things. The same stance he took right before he'd signed their divorce papers with a blank expression, then left and never looked back.

It had been two years, but she hadn't forgotten. How he'd been stubborn as a mule with everything until the end…when he'd let her go without so much as a whimper.

She thought she'd put it all behind her. But all it took was one glimpse of his handsome face and every emotion she'd suppressed came roaring back with a vengeance. Hurt, betrayal, failure.

And desire, so acute it almost took her breath away.

Not that. Not now.

Coffee. She needed coffee, stat, if she was going to deal with this, so she took a big gulp, burning her tongue, but it didn't matter. Because now she knew *exactly* what she was doing here, and so did her ex-husband.

Hot-tempered as ever, Aidan was beyond pissed off and making no bones about sharing that fact. He didn't yell. He never yelled. He simply demanded, in unequivocal and oftentimes colorful language.

"Explain this," he bit out to Lewis. "Explain *her*."

"*Her* is standing right here," she interjected tartly, by now fed up with his attitude. Plus, the sooner she got the information she needed, the sooner she could get out of here. "If you'll just let the man speak instead of acting all lumberjacked up, we both might get some answers!"

She strode across the room, intensely conscious of his eyes on her hips.

He'd always loved her curves, had made no bones about the fact that they turned him on, and her form-fitting skirt was exactly the kind of thing he'd loved her wearing back when they were together.

But they weren't together anymore. Hadn't been for a long time.

Ignoring his gaze, she slid back into her seat and turned to Lewis. "Now, if you wouldn't mind, could you please tell us what's going on?"

Lewis looked relieved that Aidan had stopped grilling him. Nervously, he glanced at Aidan, who remained standing, and for a moment, Emma actually felt sorry for him. He'd always hated feeling out of control, and right now, that's exactly what he must be experiencing.

Then he glared at her, and any sympathy she had quickly vanished.

"Yes, well," Lewis said, "as I was unable to explain to you over the phone due to the fact that things were still being finalized on our end, this meeting concerns the last will and testament of Patrick Phelan."

Aidan's expression went hard. Closed down in that way he always got when he'd been pushed too far.

Before Aidan lost his composure again, Emma jumped in. "It's been months since he died. Shouldn't this have all been sorted out earlier?"

An uncomfortable expression crossed Lewis's face. "There were some…complications which have now been resolved."

"Paddy's still yanking my chain," Aidan translated.

Emma raised an eyebrow. "From the grave?"

"Something like that," he said, his voice a snarl.

Emma tried to wrap her head around that information. Okay, clearly Paddy had left her something in his will, something to anger Aidan, even though she wasn't a Phelan anymore, a fact Paddy brought up during every one of their monthly lunches since the divorce. Unfortunately, this didn't surprise her.

Patrick Phelan, Aidan's grandfather and the patriarch of the Phelan clan, was known for three things: his legendary ability to hold his drink, his love of fine-looking women, and his heavy-handedness with his family. He'd been in everyone's business until the day he died.

To some extent, she understood why Paddy felt the need to control everything, because for a while, he hadn't been able to control *anything*. Losing his twin sons in the prime of their lives had twisted him, morphing him from an ornery old man to a tyrant. When he'd regained control over Wolfshead, the family brewery and distillery, the task had been monumental. Not only was he taking on the company, he was also taking on his seven grandsons, who could not agree on anything to save their lives. Even simple decisions ended in fights, and Emma had been with Aidan long enough to see how dysfunctional the entire family was.

It was Aidan's stubbornness that had attracted her to him in the first place. Unfortunately, that same stubbornness had destroyed their marriage.

Aidan had always been intense, but after his father died it was like he'd become a different person. His obsession with controlling Wolfshead had grown until it was the only thing he cared about. Instead of spending time with her, developing their relationship, allowing her to be part of his life, he'd spent almost every waking hour at the damn company, locked in some insane power struggle with his grandfather. He rarely came home, preferring to spend nights out with his brothers and cousins. And the nights he did come home?

Those were typically spent…*not* talking.

Then he'd leave, and she'd be alone, loathing herself for simply being available to him on his schedule. Hating that the only time she saw him was in bed.

Lewis made a harrumphing sound. "I know you and your family have been waiting a long time to hear about your inheritance," he said to Aidan, "but given your grandfather's bequests, we thought it would be more comfortable for you to hear this one-on-one instead of with your entire family present. And as this also concerns Ms. Crandall, I invited her too. Please bear in mind that I was only trying to make this as easy as possible for the two of you, given your…history."

"Please," she said to Lewis. "Just tell us what's going on."

Lewis cleared his throat. "As you suspected, Mr. Phelan, your grandfather divided Wolfshead up into shares, with each beneficiary inheriting an equal portion."

"Tell me that every one of us inherited a share," Aidan said through gritted teeth.

Lewis scanned the papers in front of him. "Yes. According to the will, you, your brothers, and your cousins will each inherit a share of the company."

Aidan let out a breath. "Thank God."

"But that's not all."

"We inherited something else?" he asked sharply.

"Yes, yes—some property, including the cabin up at Mount Hood, the land around the cabin, and your grandfather's Beaverton home. All of which will be detailed at the formal reading of the will next week."

"That's fine," Aidan said, as if all that didn't signify. "As long as there are seven equal shares of the company."

"Ah, yes. Well, that's what I need to talk to you about," Lewis said, his voice quavering. "You see, your grandfather didn't divide Wolfshead up into seven shares."

"What?" Aidan growled.

"There aren't seven shares," Lewis repeated.

"Then how many fucking shares are there?" Aidan's voice was low. Dangerous.

"Eight," Lewis said quickly. "There are eight shares."

"Eight?"

"That's right."

"If every cousin has one share," he started slowly, "then who the hell owns the eighth share?"

Lewis paused for what seemed like an eternity. Swallowed audibly and shuffled papers around before turning to her and giving her a weak smile.

Oh no. Oh *God*.

"Congratulations, Ms. Crandall," Lewis finally said. "You own the eighth share and are now a part owner of Wolfshead. This comes with its own share of rights and responsibilities, including voting, a seat on the board of directors, and of course a share of the profits. Once the will is finally executed, we can—"

Lewis went on, but Emma barely heard him because there was a strange growling sound coming from the vicinity of Aidan, which was drowned out only by the roaring in her ears.

She owned part of Wolfshead.

Aidan's company, his inheritance. His *life*.

She forced herself to look at him, her chest tight, as if her rib cage were pressing on her lungs.

He'd composed his face into a mask, a terrible mask without so much of a flicker of warmth. He could have been carved out of stone for all his hardness. A beautiful stone statue of the man she'd once loved. The man she'd had to give up because otherwise he would have destroyed her.

"Get out of here, Lewis," Aidan said, his voice eerily calm. "I need a few minutes alone with my wife."

CHAPTER 2

Alone in a quiet room with Aidan Phelan, the man who'd broken her heart, the man whose company she now partly owned, Emma didn't know whether to laugh or to cry.

There was definitely some twisted irony in there—her coming back into his life thanks to one of the primary reasons they'd gotten divorced in the first place.

Their beginning had been so easy. They'd met freshman year just as she was about to enter a fraternity party. The house had been packed. She and her best friend, Sara, had been walking in and Aidan had been walking out.

Emma had noticed him right away—the huge man with the spark of humor in his eyes—and apparently, he'd noticed her, too, since the next thing she knew, he'd pulled her and Sara aside before they'd even set one foot in the door.

Don't go in there, he'd said. *Not your scene.* Then he'd smiled, daring them to contradict him.

So presumptuous. So bossy. And in retrospect, so Aidan.

She hadn't known he was the captain of the college baseball team, hadn't quite understood the power he'd wielded even then, and she'd challenged him right back. *Do you have a better idea?*

Yeah, he'd said with a cocky grin. *Come hang out with me and my friends.*

Aidan's cousin Brody had been there. Some other guys and girls who'd all seemed friendly. Emma had looked at Sara, who'd simply shrugged. So they'd ditched the frat party and gone with

Aidan's crew instead.

It had been the best decision of her young life.

They'd spent the evening talking, joking, and laughing. For Emma, who'd grown up in a quiet house with a quiet family, the interactions between Aidan and his cousin were amazing to watch. They were rowdy and funny and completely at ease with each other.

At some point, everyone else went home to crash, and it had been just her and Aidan, talking about their hopes and dreams for the future. She'd never felt so comfortable just *being* with someone before. They'd gone for tacos at Uly's and talked until dawn.

And then they'd kissed, one of those kisses that only happens after you've stayed up all night with someone exciting and new and everything's off-kilter but perfect all the same.

She'd already fallen half in love with him.

But what sealed the deal was when he'd shown up the next day at her dorm room for a study break with a fresh cup of coffee and half a dozen doughnuts from Voodoo because she'd mentioned in passing that she was stressed about her history midterm. It was then she knew what kind of person he was.

Falling in love had been so simple, so uncomplicated.

Falling out of love? Not so much.

Now this. This…drama. Like something out of a bad rom-com movie, with the lawyer and the mystery inheritance and being forced back together with her angry ex.

But this was real life, not the movies, and somehow she just knew this story wasn't going to have a happy ending.

Warily, she watched him watching her.

He didn't move. Barely breathed as he sized her up. Her chest got tighter. More uncomfortable.

She swallowed, desperately trying to get some moisture onto her dry tongue. "Ex," she finally managed to get out. "Not wife." Not anymore.

Aidan didn't flinch. Didn't even blink.

Slowly, he stalked around the table, pulled out the chair directly next to hers, and folded himself into it.

He was close, so close, which only served to emphasize his immense size. One hand gripped the armrest, knuckles white on the black leather. The other hand was clenched into a tight fist. There was a new scar on his forefinger, a recent one—raised, red, and angry. Dimly, she wondered if his tetanus shot was up to date.

"I want your share," Aidan rasped into the quiet. "I'll pay double what it's worth."

Emma froze, the tightness in her chest amplifying tenfold.

Aidan didn't want her. He just wanted Wolfshead.

"You could use the cash," he reasoned, oblivious to her inner turmoil. "I know about your new freelancing gig. It'd be nice to have the money, give yourself a little cushion while you ramp up your client list. I get what I want, you get what you want. We put all of this"—he gestured between the two of them—"behind us. Simple. Easy."

Not simple and not easy. At least not in her mind.

Paddy had really done it, hadn't he? When he died, she thought she was done with Aidan, done with all of the Phelans. And then this. A share of Aidan's company, dropped in her lap, designed to…what? Confuse her? Complicate her life even more?

"Well?" he demanded, giving her no time to process anything. "What's it going to be?"

"Aidan—"

"I'll give you triple," he said, not even bothering to wait for her response. So typical.

She took a deep breath, trying to keep calm. *One* of them had to be. "It means something to you, I get that."

"It means more than just *something* to me," he said. "It means *everything* to me."

"Right. I know. But Paddy left it to me, so he must have had some grand plan."

"Yeah," he said, his voice bitter. "To screw me over."

"It's not always all about you." But of course, it always was. It always had been.

"Sell me the share, Emma," he said slowly.

God, he was so beautiful. And so stubborn. She shook her head. "I can't."

"Can't?" he growled. "Or won't?"

Her head was beginning to throb, so she rubbed her temples with her fingertips. "I just found this out. I need time to think."

He leaned back. "Fine. What do you want? You must want something, so name your price."

What *did* she want? Not money. She could definitely use the cash, but having him pay up so she could walk away would just make her feel cheap. And she didn't want to be around him, either, but the thought of a new project was too enticing to pass up. Especially a project that could help her in the long term.

An idea began to form in her mind—a brilliant idea that might actually serve both their purposes while she sorted things out.

"I want to work with Wolfshead," she told him.

"That can't happen." He said this with conviction.

"Just hear me out," she said. "Despite the little you think I know, I truly understand your company, inside and out. I already have relationships with your family. You're launching a new whiskey, right? I can help you brand and market your new product, arguably better than anyone else. And you have a tasting that's coming up soon." Paddy had mentioned that the last time they'd had lunch. "I can help you get that organized."

She took a breath. "I won't lie—working with Wolfshead to launch the new brand would definitely help me kick-start my business. Doing a good job for you would mean raising my profile, more clients, and more work. But it would also mean that you would have the benefit of my expertise at a time you need it the most. And given that I'm now a part owner of the company"—Aidan grimaced, but she went on—"I have a stake in the outcome, too. I want Wolfshead to do well. I want *us* to do well."

"There is no *us*," he said bluntly. "You threw that away when you walked out the door."

What was left of her heart felt like it was imploding, but outwardly, she showed nothing, not even a blink.

"As far as I'm concerned, this would be strictly business. You can count on me to do an incredible, professional job, same as I would for any client."

"But I'm not just any client, am I, Emma?"

A challenge if ever she heard one. "I can handle anything you throw my way."

Grabbing the arm of her chair, he swiveled it so it was facing him, then pulled her close, trapping her knees between his. He leaned forward. She leaned away, but could only go as far as the seat back allowed. He was close now, so close she could feel the heat emanating from his skin, could smell his masculine scent—earth and grain and that spicy maleness she could only identify as pure Aidan.

She caught her breath. Held it.

His lips curled up in the semblance of a smile, but without any warmth. "You sure about that?"

Emma tilted her chin up just a fraction. "Absolutely."

"Funny, I seem to remember you divorcing me."

"Funny, I seem to remember you giving me a reason to," she retorted.

He tipped his head to the side and regarded her carefully. "Forgot what a firecracker you are," he said, sounding almost…playful. Oh, that was so not good. Because playful Aidan was sexy.

And sexy Aidan was dangerous.

She stiffened. "I'm not a firecracker."

"Forgot how riled up you get."

"I am not riled up!" she said, definitely sounding riled up.

He was still staring at her, and he was still so very close. Unconsciously, she licked her lips. His gaze dropped to her mouth.

And then it happened—a full body shiver swept over her, from head to toe and back up again. She couldn't stop it, and that was bad, so bad. Because she knew exactly what it meant, and so did he.

She still wanted him despite everything they'd been through. Despite the fact that he didn't want her.

"There's just one little problem with your plan," he said gravely.

"What?" she whispered.

He leaned in even closer, making her feel it *everywhere*. "Things can never be just business between us."

The strangest look was on his face, but only for a moment. Abruptly, he pushed her away and stood, his expression harder than ever.

"Are you going to sell me the share or not?" he demanded, looking down at her.

It was as if she'd been doused in a bucket of ice water. She crossed her arms over her chest and looked up at him defiantly. "No!"

"Then this isn't over," he vowed.

He stalked toward the door, wrenched it open, and strode out.

Scenes from their entire relationship flashed in her mind. Aidan holding out a single red rose on their first Valentine's Day together. The two of them laughing as he pushed her on the rope swing near his family's cabin higher and higher until she begged him to let her come back to earth. Her wedding day, when she was so damned happy and full of hope. Kissing him good-bye at the airport when he went off to spring training. Burying Aidan's father and uncle on the same day. Sobbing while Aidan delivered the most beautiful eulogy. The jagged pain as she signed the divorce papers. The long, lonely nights she spent wondering how things had gone so very wrong, and wishing somehow she'd had the strength to stay, just to see if she could make things better between them.

"With you," she whispered into the stillness, "it never is."

Emma extricated herself as quickly as she could from the lawyer's office, and when she stepped onto the street, she found that it was raining, unsurprising for spring in Portland. Only tourists used umbrellas, so she steeled herself and walked briskly to the light rail stop near Pioneer Courthouse Square. She'd missed the Max by two minutes, so she had to wait another fifteen. Finally, when she was good and cold, not to mention wet from standing in the rain, a train arrived.

She was feeling edgy and raw when she found a seat. It wasn't even lunchtime, and she'd already been through the wringer. Thankfully, it was warm in the train car, and the soft white noise of the wheels on the tracks helped make her mind a blessed blank.

When she'd mostly recovered from her encounter with Aidan, she checked her email. She had one new message from her dad about planning a boating trip, but that was it. Dad ran a hardware store in Cannon Beach on the coast where she'd grown up, and he was pretty bad at returning phone calls while he was at work. There was no point in leaving a message he probably wouldn't even listen to for hours.

Feeling a bit at loose ends, she called Sara. Unsurprisingly, it went straight to voicemail.

Sara called her back just as she was getting off the Max. She tucked her phone under her chin to protect it from the elements, and her friend's brisk, no-nonsense voice came through the line.

"Hey!" Sara said. "You busy?"

Emma kept walking, heading in the direction of her Laurelhurst neighborhood. "I should be asking that of you."

An oncologist at Providence Portland hospital, Sara's schedule was pretty much jam-packed from the time she got to work to the time she dragged herself back to her house at night.

She and Sara had been best friends since the ninth grade, when they'd been assigned to be lab partners in biology for their frog dissection. Sara had been a shy, tiny girl interested in science, while Emma, though no less academic, had been outgoing and sporty. But the two of them bonded over that dead frog, so much so that when Arnie Arbuckle made fun of Sara's thick, plastic glasses, Emma had tipped a tray of dissected frog parts reeking of formaldehyde directly onto his lap. Sara had laughed, they'd gotten detention, and that had been the beginning of a lifelong friendship.

They'd both ended up at University of Oregon, still best friends, and became roommates. Over the years, even the ones when Sara was at med school in San Francisco, they'd remained tight, and when Sara had finally moved back to Portland to do her residency, Emma had been thrilled. Sara hadn't gotten married—hadn't even had any kind of real relationship, actually, despite Emma's prodding, mostly due to her crazy work hours. It was Emma's goal this year to get Sara to date someone. *Anyone.*

"I have a few minutes between patients, and you didn't sound so great on your voicemail message," Sara said. "What's up?"

"I had a meeting with a lawyer this morning," Emma said, stepping over a big puddle and continuing down the sidewalk. Knowing she had a decent walk, she'd swapped her heels out for the flats she'd stashed in her giant purse. Smart move, especially since her next step was directly into a puddle she hadn't seen, which completely soaked her left foot. *Crap.*

"For what? Your business?"

"No," Emma said, shaking out her wet foot. "Something else. Aidan was there."

Sara inhaled sharply. "How'd that go?"

"Not well."

"Par for the course with that man," Sara said with a snort. "His way or the highway, I suppose?"

"You suppose correctly."

"So he's still as bossy as ever?"

"Oh, yes."

"Arrogant."

"Definitely."

"Hot?"

"Unfortunately," Emma said with a sigh. "Bearded, too."

"Damn it. I was hoping he'd look like a troll. That his body would have gone to seed by now."

"No. The man just gets better with age," she said, wishing it weren't true. In fact, he looked trimmer and tighter than he did at the peak of his ballplaying career. "And it gets worse."

"How could it possibly get worse than seeing your bossy, arrogant, hot, bearded ex-husband?"

"It can when you now own a part of said bossy, arrogant, hot, bearded ex-husband's company."

There was a shocked silence on the other end as Sara took in that information. When she spoke, her voice sounded thin, as if she were straining to get the words out. "I'm sorry, what?"

Emma broke it down. "The lawyer told me that Paddy left me a share of Wolfshead in his will. Specifically, one-eighth." She'd regaled Sara with many tales of Paddy over the years, so she knew exactly who he was and what kind of shenanigans he enjoyed.

"An eighth? So it's you and the seven Phelans?" Sara surmised.

"Exactly."

"That is…" Sara paused, casting around for the right words. "That is…just…*whoa.*"

That pretty much summed it up. "Yeah."

"Leave it to Paddy to pull a stunt like that. I'm guessing that Aidan did not take that well."

"Nope. He offered to buy my share from me on the spot."

"Did you accept?"

"I told him I wanted to work for Wolfshead while I thought about it."

"And have you? Thought about it, I mean?"

Sara knew her all too well. "A little. I know this sounds weird and I just found out a little while ago, but my gut tells me to keep it. I won't lie—I have a ton on my plate right now since I just went freelance, but I'm not desperate for the money, and long term, it might actually help me. This might be an incredible opportunity for me to flex my brain, get my head around the whole business instead of the small piece of it that I've seen so far doing branding. Even better, Wolfshead is about to launch a new product—a whiskey apparently—and I know a bit about branding and marketing beverages of that nature thanks to my work with that vodka distillery I did when I was still with Stroud & Thistle, so I'd be able to lend my expertise there, too. Plus, I feel like now that I have a vested interest in seeing the company do well, I'll do an even better job."

"You're forgetting one thing," Sara said quietly. "This windfall comes with a curse."

Emma bit her lip. "Yeah. I haven't quite figured the dealing-with-Aidan part out yet."

"Look, I'm saying this as a friend—"

"My *best* friend."

"Right. And you know this comes from a place of love, so don't get angry with me—"

"But?"

"But when you're thinking about what you're going to do—really thinking about it—maybe you should think about selling the share back to him. Not because I don't trust you do to an amazing job," she quickly went on, "but mostly because I don't want you to get hurt again."

Emma sighed. "I know."

Sara had been there from the beginning. She'd been the first person Emma had called after Aidan proposed, and had been the maid of honor at their wedding. And when their marriage started crumbling, Sara had been there, too, talking her through the aftermath of the worst of their fights, helping her try to rationalize Aidan's behavior, and finally holding her the night she'd asked for a divorce while she sobbed for the loss of her marriage and the man she thought she'd have kids and grow old with—the one she'd once considered to be her other half.

She could understand Sara's reluctance to give her blessing to this insane scheme, especially since lately Emma had been doing really well.

"But…I just can't," Emma said. Not now.

Sara let out an audible breath. "Okay, if you think you can handle this, I have faith in you. You can handle anything. You're strong and fierce and—"

"Sara," Emma said, now crossing Sandy Boulevard and continuing on as the commercial area gave way to residential. "I'm pretty sure this is the same exact pep talk you gave me when I quit my job a few months ago."

"Yes, well, the same principles that applied to you opening your own marketing consulting practice apply to dealing with this situation. You have strength. You have guts. And you can face anything thrown in your path, including your ex."

"I sure hope so."

The wind picked up as Emma turned onto her street, noting the soggy, muddy gardens of her neighbors' homes, as well as of her own, the second house on the left. The spring rains had been brutal this year, and while that was part of the deal in living here, sometimes she wished for a bit less. Some days—today, for instance, when she was being soaked by the driving rain and she was chilled to the bone—it felt like she was battling a monsoon just to get to the coffee shop and back.

Her snug little Craftsman surrounded by hydrangeas and crepe myrtle sat a few yards back from the street. When she'd bought it a year ago, she'd painted it lemon yellow with a royal-blue trim. Her sanctuary after her divorce. No matter the weather, it always cheered her up to look at it.

"What are you going to do for the rest of the day?"

"I have a little bit of work," Emma said, shaking out her wet foot under the overhang and leaving her shoes on the porch to dry. "And I need to do some research on whiskey." She unlocked her front door with a silver key.

"Need some help with that?" Sara asked, her tone hopeful.

"Paper research. Not drinking…yet."

"Let me know when you get around to the drinking bit."

Emma laughed. Sara was a bit of a whiskey fiend. "Will do."

"Hang on." There was murmuring on Sara's end of the line, but she was back on fast. "Gotta go, but are we still on for dinner next Friday night?"

"Definitely. Late?"

"I'm on call until six, so maybe seven thirty or eight? Pambiche?" The hip Cuban restaurant was one of Sara's favorites. "After these crazy two weeks of nonstop call, I'm going to need a mojito."

"Should I call Robin, too?" Robin was another good friend of theirs from college who was mom to almost-one-year-old twin girls. Her husband, David, had also been at University of Oregon, but a couple of years ahead of them. He was in sales, and seemed to be on the road constantly.

"Definitely. If anyone needs a night out, it's her."

"Cool. I'll send you a reminder to text me when you're done." Sometimes Sara got held up writing her final reports of the day—not a problem, but it always helped to know so Emma could plan.

"See you soon."

Emma clicked the phone off and let herself into her thankfully dry house, pushing her mail out of the way with her damp foot. She took off her coat, dropped her bag in the hall, and went to the kitchen to put the teakettle on. Some tea and a couple of cookies would set her right again, especially because she hadn't had the stomach to finish that doughnut after everything that had transpired.

While the water was boiling, she pulled out the big guns— Mallomars, the best cookie ever—grabbed one from the cellophane-wrapped package, and took a large bite, making sure that the flavors from the chocolate, marshmallow, and graham cracker layers melded on her tongue. Chewing thoughtfully, she went back down the hall to collect her mail.

She needed space and distance…from the law firm, from the will, and from him.

Definitely from him.

She'd given up too much of herself trying to love Aidan, and she was not for one second about to be drawn back down that path. Not again, after all of this time.

It had taken months, years, really, but she'd finally weaned herself of thoughts of him. At least during the day.

But at night…well, that was a whole different matter. In the stillness, alone in her bed with only her memories—unfortunately she thought about him a whole damn lot. Too many midnights she'd woken up in the dark, damp and unsated, wishing things were different. Wishing he were there lying next to her.

Of course, he never was.

Work. That always did the trick to get her mind off of him, and she had that client meeting coming up and a lot to review now that Wolfshead was on her radar.

When mail was sorted and the water was boiled and her tea was steeped just the way she liked it, she took her mug and went to her office to get started.

But when she flicked the switch, there was a sharp crack, an audible *poof*, and the distinctive sound of electronic devices turning off. Several beeped, including her printer, indicating they were now offline.

And there went the rest of her workday.

Maybe Sara was right. Maybe her Wolfshead windfall *had* come with a curse.

Except Emma had already experienced the worst possible curse of all…giving all your love to someone who didn't know how to love you back.

CHAPTER 3

The crowd was thick tonight, people swarming all over the tasting room in Wolfshead's brewery. Aidan's grandfather had moved into the warehouse space fifty years ago when their operations had expanded and they'd run out of room at their old warehouse, which was located in the back of the property and was now being used as their distillery.

The space was vintage Portland—exposed brick walls and steel beams crisscrossing overhead, virtually unchanged from the way it looked when it was built in the early twentieth century. Over the years, they'd done a few things to get it up to code—fire sprinklers and exit signs, to name two—and had made some modifications, such as walling off the production floor from the tasting room, installing a huge brushed-steel bar, and adding additional lighting. Still, the place had character, especially tonight, with the lights down low, the music playing…and all the Phelan men strategically dispersed throughout the room.

Except Aidan and his cousin Connor.

His back against the side of the metal staircase that wound up to the catwalk on the second floor, Aidan spared a quick glance over at Connor. The tall, bearded man was holding up a full glass of amber-colored IPA with a thick head of foam, eyes practically gleaming as he admired the rich, hoppy bounty in his big hand.

"Cheers," Connor said, in a voice quiet, but so deep it was definitely audible over the din of the room.

"What are we toasting to?" Aidan asked. "Your killer

whiskey? Though you're not even drinking it."

Connor shook his head. "To Paddy's will finally being settled. To a new Wolfshead."

Bitterness lanced through him, sharp and fast. New, his ass. Wolfshead was the same company it had always been with one exception—it wasn't fully theirs anymore. He'd gritted his teeth and borne the ridiculousness of the official reading yesterday. His brothers and cousins seemed pleased that it was over, but not him. For him, it was just beginning.

But now wasn't the time to get into that. Instead, he offered up a strained smile and forced himself to clink his tumbler of whiskey against Connor's glass. "Cheers."

Connor smiled, then downed a quarter of his beer in one long swallow.

Watching his cousin carefully, Aidan took a small sip of his own drink, letting the fiery liquid rest on his tongue before sliding down his throat. It was silky smooth, with a rich, caramel aftertaste, the product of years of experimenting. Connor had done incredible work. Better than even Aidan could have imagined. Which had made all the agony worth it.

Their dads would have been proud that they'd done it—that they were on the cusp of releasing this whiskey that had been eight years in the making, over a century in the dreaming—the pride of his great-great-grandfather, old John Phelan.

And now it wasn't even theirs anymore.

Aidan shook his head. He needed to stop picking at old wounds and rehashing what could have been. This was Connor's night, and he needed to support his cousin.

Unfortunately, Connor was now frowning into his glass. "Nervous?"

The big man looked down. "Yeah."

Connor was huge—six seven in his bare feet with a muscular build and scary-as-shit tattoos adorning his skin—but beneath that giant exterior lay a shy man with a gentle heart. His cousin was clearly freaking out about this tasting event—the first time anyone outside the family would try the whiskey. Plus, Connor hated talking to almost everyone except family.

"Don't be."

"Easy for you to say. It's not your ass on the line."

"All for one, man," Aidan responded. "Always." The Phelans ate, slept, and breathed this company, and when one of them succeeded, they all did. When one of them screwed up, well, they all did that, too. "When you told me you wanted to start distilling, what was the first thing I said?"

Connor's lips twitched. "You said, 'Hell yes.'"

"That's right," Aidan said. "Because I believed in you. I believed in *this*." He held up his tumbler, and Connor's eyes lit up at the dark amber liquid shimmering in the dim lights. "This was our dads' dream. Our legacy. And you made it happen."

"No, Aidan," Connor said quietly. "*You* did. You were the leader we should have had all along. You stood up to Paddy. Insisted that we do this despite the obstacles he threw in our way. Put everything aside to focus on the company."

Namely, his dream to play professional baseball.

Except it hadn't been a dream. At twenty-two, Aidan had been drafted by the New York Mets. He'd been doing well in the farm system, had worked his way up from Single-A to Triple-A in three years, and had decent prospects. His game plan was simple: make it to the majors in under five years, play for a decade, and retire before forty so he could start the next chapter in his life—returning to the family business.

That never happened.

He remembered it like it was yesterday. He'd been playing ball in New Orleans—one of those hot summer afternoons where the air was so heavy and humid that no amount of cold water could wash away the stickiness. He'd been about to take the mound when the coach had called for a conference. He'd thought it was going to be about his pitching, a couple of last-minute instructions. But then the GM had come out.

That's when he knew something was very, very wrong.

They'd pulled him from the game, told him that his father, Patrick Jr., had been killed along with his twin brother, John, in a Jeep accident near Mount Hood.

It was the last game he'd ever pitched, because with the Phelans, family always came first. They needed him. So he'd cut his baseball career short and come back to Wolfshead.

Little did he know that his frustrations were only just beginning. By the time he'd untangled himself from the Mets, Paddy had already retaken control of Wolfshead as the senior Phelan. At the time, it made sense. Aidan had been young—only twenty-five with zero real-world business experience—and the rest of the Phelan boys had been even younger.

Unfortunately, Paddy had very different ideas about running the company than his sons did. Whereas Aidan's dad and uncle had wanted to grow Wolfshead and expand operations to distilled spirits, Paddy insisted on maintaining the status quo. "If it ain't broke…" he was fond of saying, and just like that, Wolfshead was back in the dark ages.

Aidan was the oldest, and he'd been way too similar in personality and temperament to the old man. Which meant that he and his grandfather had had more than their share of fights, especially once Paddy had run roughshod over Patrick Jr. and John's plans for expansion.

Worst of all, Paddy had done his best to snuff the fire out of all seven of his grandsons, to break them down, make them drones, dutifully carrying on the Phelan name. He'd tried to mold them, shape them the way he wanted, which meant that son of a bitch had controlled everything.

And damned if he wasn't still trying.

He'd thought when his grandfather died, that'd be the end of it. That he'd be free to run the company the way his dad and uncle had envisioned.

Wrong.

Leaving a share of the company—*his* company—to Emma had been one of Paddy's mind-fucks, pure and simple. And seeing Emma again had rocked him to the core, and not in a good way.

He'd screwed up his marriage to her, big-time. But it was too late. He'd already made his choice.

What had Paddy thought he'd do? That he'd take one look at her gorgeous face and fall in line? Forget about his plans for expansion and beg her to come back to him? Tell her how badly he'd fucked things up the first time?

No. He couldn't, because nothing had changed between then and now. He was still the head of this company, and more than his livelihood was on the line. It was his reputation, his family's reputation, and the whole future of Wolfshead. He wouldn't let his family down, and damned if Paddy wouldn't have known that.

So he buried his emotions, shoved his need aside, and did what he did best—led. Except the company wasn't completely family-run anymore.

As if reading his mind, Connor clasped a big hand on his shoulder. "Everything's going to be okay. She used to be a Phelan, too. She'll remember how it is with us. And I trust her not to mess with the company."

His brothers and cousins had been surprisingly calm about what Paddy had done. Of course they'd been disappointed that Wolfshead wasn't solely family-owned, but they'd always liked Emma and had been pretty vocal about the fact that they thought he was crazy for letting her go so easily.

They wouldn't be so happy when she came in like gangbusters and tried to change everything. When it came to the company, they were as dedicated as Aidan was to pursuing their fathers' dreams.

He took another sip of his whiskey, but it tasted like sawdust on his tongue.

Damn Paddy. He'd spent the better part of two years trying to exorcise Emma from his life. Now she was back, her passion and intelligence enticing him, those dark eyes seeming to see through his very soul, just like they always used to.

"Look, we still own a majority of the company," Connor said. "If we need to, we can outvote her, right? And you're still the CEO."

Aidan gave a snort.

"What's so funny? The way I see it, you're the only one with balls for the job."

Aidan shrugged. "Eh, Brody would be okay." Brody was Connor's older brother, just a year younger than himself, and he dealt with all of Wolfshead's financials. "Or you."

"I'd be shit. And everyone knows it." Connor took another long draw on his beer.

"Everyone knows what?" Aidan's brother Gabriel had materialized by his side.

Gabe was the youngest Phelan, and growing up, they'd all been protective of him because he'd been a tiny thing. Although he'd topped out at six one, he still had the distinction of being the smallest Phelan. But what he lacked in size, he made up for in looks and personality.

With his bright red hair and scruff to match, not to mention his piercing blue eyes, Gabe didn't exactly blend into the crowd, and tonight was no exception. He stood out like a beacon, drawing everyone around him into his orbit.

Gabe was charming beyond belief and infuriating as hell, but he knew how to hustle, and as head of sales for Wolfshead, hustle was most definitely required. His one weakness?

Women.

More than once his plans had been screwed up because of a pretty face or a sweet ass.

"The fact that Aidan's CEO and I'm not," Connor said.

"Oh, yeah," Gabe said, eyeing Connor. "You'd be shit."

"Told you," Connor said cheerfully and took another long pull of his beer.

Maybe Connor and Gabe were right. Connor certainly had the temperament to be CEO, but he was way too soft-spoken, not to mention that most people were scared witless of him.

"Okay you two, genius-in-the-corner time is over now," Gabe snapped at them. "Get out there and mingle. Even Ed's talking to people, and you know what a stretch that is for him."

Aidan smiled. His younger brother Ed was pretty intense, and party talk wasn't really his thing. But he'd also noticed that in all the time he'd spent talking with Connor, no one had come up to chat. Not a surprise. People tended to give them and the other Phelan men a wide berth. Aidan chalked it up to their size and their attitude. Especially his.

Gabe narrowed his eyes at him. "Everyone wants to hear the big baseball star talk about the company and the new product. And you," he said, turning on Connor. "You're the chemist, and this whiskey is your baby. This is a friendly crowd, and they all want to hear the story, how you found Great-Great-Grandpa's recipe for sour mash in his old journal, how we all thought it was some weird Belgian beer but then you realized it was really a starter for rye whiskey, how our dads wanted to distill again and once they died, how you pushed Paddy to make it happen. I've told you a million times, the story is what sells the product. And you need the practice before we go public."

Connor shook his head. "No one wants to hear me talk."

"Who's the sales guy here?" Gabe snapped. When Connor

merely raised an eyebrow at him and placidly took another sip of beer, Gabe gave an annoyed snort. "Fine. If selling product isn't enough incentive, how about this: a lot of people in this industry would be thrilled to see us fail."

On this point, Gabe was right. Paddy Phelan had a reputation for doing whatever the hell he wanted, consequences be damned, which had rubbed many the wrong way. But for Aidan and his brothers and cousins, it had always been substance over style. Lots of folks were watching them, seeing what their next move was…and what kind of competitor Wolfshead would turn out to be.

"Still not enough to get you off this wall? Okay. How's this— there are some seriously hot women here tonight."

"I'm sure you invited half of them," Aidan said. His little brother wasn't known for his monogamous ways.

"Half?" Gabe retorted. "Try *most.*"

"I'm sure you've slept with *most* all of them already, too," Connor said with a smile.

Gabe simply shrugged. "I like women." And the women most definitely liked him. Liked all the Phelan men, actually, but Gabe seemed to have the easiest time of it, mostly because relationships weren't his thing.

"Come on, seriously, guys, you're killing me," Gabe moaned. "This is our dry run, and it needs to go well. Stop with your shit and go talk to them."

Aidan sighed and pushed himself off the wall. "I'll go."

"Finally, the man does his job," Gabe said, sarcasm infusing his voice.

Aidan ignored his kid brother's attitude. "Where do you want me?"

"Anywhere, really. The entranceway so you can greet people as they come in, or maybe over by the tasting bar where…" Gabe stopped, his eyes appearing to pop out of his head. "Lord have mercy, who is that?" He clenched his fist and bit it. "Mmmph. My God, her ass is a thing of beauty."

Connor glanced over and gave a low grunt. Then he lifted his chin in the direction Gabe was goggling, indicating that Aidan should have a look.

"I'm not in the mood for that shit tonight," he growled.

Truth was, he hadn't been in the mood for a long while now.

There'd been women—way too many who'd thrown themselves at him after his divorce—but there had been no one like Emma. Unfortunately, *hate* was probably too weak a word for the way she felt about him, especially after that scene at the lawyer's office. Controlling his temper had never been his strong suit, which is why he'd steered clear of her at the reading of the will. She'd been in and out like a flash at the lawyer's office anyway.

"Trust me, Aidan," Gabe insisted. "You'll be in the mood for this one."

Reluctantly, Aidan redirected his gaze to where Gabe and Connor were staring.

"The blonde?" Gabe liked blondes.

"No," Gabe said. "The one next to her. To the left."

Aidan shifted his gaze, and then he saw her. A tall brunette, her back toward him, with hair that fell in soft waves past her shoulders.

She wore a skirt cut just above her knees, sexy enough to show a lot of leg, but demure enough to leave him guessing as to what lay underneath. Her sweater was of the long-sleeved variety, and therefore was less interesting. But when he followed the long, lean line of her legs down to where they ended in a pair of sky-high stilettos, he felt something deep inside him stir.

Then the woman leaned onto the tasting bar, just a fraction, and the material of her skirt pulled over her rear, revealing generously molded curves capped off with taut thighs. He'd know that ass anywhere. *Jesus.*

"Told you," Gabe said, his voice smug. "Doesn't she look like…"

"Emma."

"Tell me about it," Gabe said. "Sure looks like her from the back, yeah? Don't know who she is, but I'm guessing she's a friend of one of the bartenders. If you don't go over and talk to her, I will. But if you want to make a move, do it now because Finn's already in there and you know how fast he likes to——"

"Idiot," Connor said to Gabe. "That *is* Emma."

Gabe's face went white. "Oh, shit, man. I'm sorry, I——"

His little brother was saying something else, but Aidan didn't hear the rest. Of their own volition, his feet were moving toward her. He cut a path through the crowded room, aware that people were parting to make way for him.

In a matter of moments, he'd reached her.

"Emma," he said, rewarded when she quit talking to Finn and her eyes snapped up to his.

She blinked once, very quickly, and her lips parted in surprise. "Aidan," she said, her voice a little breathy, and damned if his name alone didn't hit him right in the groin. Her expression was soft, the way she used to look at him…before things went to hell.

"What are you doing here?" he growled.

Emma went rigid and that soft expression evaporated faster than the angel's share in an oaken cask. "I have a perfect right to be here."

Yeah, that whole part-owner thing was a bitch.

"You sure you want to play it this way?" he asked, his voice low.

"I don't want to play at all," she said. "Though I'm sure you could have figured that out. Here." She pulled a small stack of papers out of her handbag and thrust them at him.

"What's this?" he said, keeping his gaze trained on her face.

"A PowerPoint presentation about me. I prepared a short deck last night for you and your family to review. Just to remind you of my qualifications and my work. What I can bring to the table. You know," she said, looking up at him with those big brown eyes, "highlights from what you've missed over the past couple of years."

There was a slightly sardonic look on her face, and damned if he didn't know whether he wanted to kick her out or kiss her. As that internal battle waged, Gabe walked up.

"Emma!" he exclaimed. "It *is* you."

Immediately, her expression softened. "Hi, Gabe," she said, accepting a hug from him.

Gabe held her longer than was strictly necessary, his hand lingering on her shoulders even after he'd pulled away, completely checking her out. "Damn, you look good. Your new business must agree with you."

Emma's gaze warmed further. "I'm just getting started, but it's going well so far."

"So you're here to scope things out?"

"Mostly to say hi." She shot Aidan a quick glance. "I haven't been here in a long time."

"And you've been missed," Gabe said, trailing his hand down her arm.

Aidan was going to kill his little brother. Slowly and painfully.

Now Gabe had his hand in hers. Emma made a big show of giving it a squeeze, then artfully extricated herself from his grip to tuck a stray lock of hair behind her ear. "Thank you, Gabe. I appreciate your warm welcome."

He raised one eyebrow suggestively and dropped his voice. "It could be warmer."

"Oh?" she said, a smile playing on her lips. "In that case, where do you think I should start getting reacquainted with Wolfshead? I always like to know what I'm dealing with before I start a project."

"Right here," he said, pointing at his lips.

Emma laughed. "Still an incorrigible flirt, I see."

"Only with you," Gabe said, giving her a smoldering look.

"Knock it off," Finn said, shooting daggers at Gabe. Good thing, because Aidan was about to smash Gabe's face in. Quickly, Finn poured a tumbler full of whiskey and presented it to her with great flourish. "Start here. Welcome back, Emma."

"Thanks, Finn," she replied, gifting his cousin with a sweet smile that transformed her beautiful face.

She took the tumbler from the bar and held it up. "Cheers." Then she raised the glass to her mouth.

Aidan hadn't anticipated how erotic it would be, watching her taste his alcohol, her face flushed and her eyes closed. She swallowed, her delicate throat doing a little shimmy, then exhaled once, very deliberately. When she finished, she licked a stray drop of liquor from the corner of her lush red-tinged lips.

The same lips that he'd loved having wrapped around his cock.

His body stirred again, slowly coming to life after being dormant for so long. Trying to stop the desire was futile, so he embraced it. Let it wash over him as a perverse kind of penance.

After what seemed like an eternity, he finally tore his gaze away from that maddening mouth and moved it back to her eyes. He'd always been able to tell what she was thinking, just by looking in her eyes, and what he saw there now nearly blew him away—surprise, excitement, and a healthy dose of awe.

That alone made him hard as a rock.

"Whoa," she breathed. "That's just…" She stopped. Shook her head. "Do you even know what you have here?"

"We know," Gabe assured her.

"Seriously, it's amazing. Now *that*," she said to Gabe, "was an excellent place to start."

Her voice didn't waver, but as she put the tumbler back onto the bar, he noticed her hand was shaking—not hard, but just enough to see she was affected by something. Maybe by the alcohol.

Maybe by him.

From behind the tasting bar, Finn cleared his throat. "Uh, Aidan?"

"Yeah?" Aidan turned his gaze to his cousin, not sure why he felt so murderous.

Finn scowled at him behind his trim strawberry-blond beard, his expression saying without words to lay off her. His youngest cousin, Brody and Connor's little brother, had always had a soft spot for his ex-wife. Had seen her like the sister he never had.

"Before you got here, Emma suggested that we have all the sampling bottles on display, and since they don't have labels yet, that we write up short descriptions of our methodologies and the taste spectrum."

"She did?" Aidan asked, surprised at how quickly she was able to jump in.

Finn nodded. "And she also suggested we sample some of the un-aged rye, so that people can see the difference in taste and depth."

Slowly, he turned back to her. "I see you're already hard at work."

She gave an elegant little shrug. "I want this place to succeed as much as you do."

"Those ideas are brilliant," Gabe said, reaching for her once more.

Aidan angled his body in front of Gabe's before he could lay hands on her again. "You say you're here to help, so help," he barked, before jerking his head over to where his giant cousin still stood. "Start by getting Connor off that wall."

The words had come out more gruffly than he intended, probably because Gabe's flirting was driving him nuts.

A less assured woman would have blinked. Freaked out. Gotten angry. Or more than likely, jumped to do what he demanded.

But Emma didn't show a single ounce of emotion on her face, nor did she hop to do his bidding.

Instead, she crossed her arms over her chest and assessed him coolly. "Now's probably a good time for us to clarify a few things."

"What things?" he asked, narrowing his eyes.

Her eyebrow arched. "First, we're not married anymore. We're not even friends, so you don't get to order me around. Period."

"Emma—" he started, his voice a warning note.

"Next," she said, continuing straight on as if he hadn't spoken, "I know you don't like it, but I'm a part of Wolfshead now. If I know you, and believe me, I do"—she give him a significant look—"our working relationship will be as contentious as our marriage was. But I'm not your wife, or a member of the family, so you need to treat me like you would a business partner—with respect." She took a deep breath. "This isn't going to be easy, and I'm sure there will be many times we disagree, but you need to know that I'll stick to my guns if I don't think what you're doing is good for the company, and I won't be shy about telling you that. And *when* I do, you will not belittle my opinion or tell me there's only one way to do things and that it's your way."

He set his jaw. "Anything else?"

"Actually, yes," she said, her voice calm. "Despite what you said before, this is not going to be personal. I can promise you that."

She uncrossed her arms and shook them out. "There. I've said my piece, and you know where I stand."

Carefully, she picked up her glass and drained it in one long swallow, gave a pleasant little shudder, then licked her lips, which of course made him even harder. She smiled brilliantly at Finn, that bastard. "Too delicious to waste a single drop. See you soon."

She turned back to Gabe. "Let's go."

And with that, she strode off toward Connor, her perfect ass swaying with every step, Gabe trailing behind her like a lovesick puppy dog.

Finn leaned his elbows onto the bar and let out a long, low whistle. "Ho-ly shit," he breathed, admiration in his voice.

"Yeah," Aidan agreed, unhappily. Holy shit was right. She'd lost none of her spark, none of her bite, and damned if that didn't turn him the hell on.

"Guess she's not selling her share."

"Guess not."

Finn shook his head. "Emma is the ultimate whiskey chick. Why'd you let her divorce you again?"

It was a question all the Phelan men, not to mention his mother, were going to ask—one he most definitely wasn't prepared to answer.

"Do what Emma said," Aidan told Finn. He might be stubborn, but he sure wasn't stupid, and her suggestions were gold. "And get back to work."

A smile tugged at Finn's lips. "Touchy, are we?"

Aidan snarled at him, and then Finn surprised him by holding up his hands in supplication. "All right, all right, I hear you. I'd be touchy too if my hot ex strutted in here all feisty and fiery and handed me my ass on a platter."

At that, Finn turned away to talk to Rick, a Wolfshead employee who was helping him out behind the bar.

Aidan narrowed his eyes at his cousin's back. He knew why Finn had given in so easily.

Emma.

Shit, she'd been here all of five minutes and already had Finn and Gabe wrapped around her little finger. It would be the same for the rest of the men, he was sure of it. When they'd been married, his brothers and cousins had worshipped her, and it was a safe bet that they would have done anything for her. They'd been as devastated as he'd been when she'd left him.

He clenched his fist, fighting for the control not to follow Emma, haul her off to the nearest corner, and kiss her senseless. See if she lit up for him the way she used to do.

Jesus, where was his restraint? There was a reason he'd shut down the first time, and mauling his ex-wife wouldn't help him regain control over Wolfshead. He'd have to rein it in, and fast.

Forget that he still wanted her. Forget that even looking at her made him hard as a fucking rock. He had a job to do and a company to run. Anyway, he'd already blown whatever they had to hell.

And with a woman like Emma, there were no second chances.

CHAPTER 4

The day after the party found Aidan with a massive headache. Not from drinking too much (because he never drank too much), but from the strain of keeping his hands off his mouthy, curvy, delectable, frustrating-as-hell ex-wife who at this very moment was waltzing around his factory, scoping out the joint as if she owned it.

Which of course, now she partially did.

Last night she'd been an unstoppable force, talking to his brothers and cousins, tasting the new product, getting the lay of the land, and charming everyone in sight. She'd fended off Gabe's ridiculous advances and made Ed laugh—typically an impossible feat. Hell, she'd even gotten Connor off that fucking wall and talking to people.

She could be exactly what Wolfshead needed.

No. That share belonged to the Phelans, not her.

Damn Paddy for screwing him over. He'd been doing all right, keeping his head in the game, keeping his family on track. Then Emma had come back into his life, reminding him of everything he'd given up, everything he'd lost…and everything he still had to fight for.

And having her close once again was pure, unadulterated torture.

He'd barely been able to get anything done this morning, and the work he *had* been able to get through was only because he'd locked himself in his office with a strong cup of coffee from Coava, far away from her.

At his feet, Ulysses, the family's golden retriever, lifted his head and let out a little whine. Technically, Dylan and Ed shared ownership of the dog, but they'd all claimed him as their own. Ulysses made the rounds throughout the day, wandering all over the property. He was allowed everywhere except onto the production floor, which was a safety hazard, but he usually made his way up to Aidan's office this time of day to get a treat and take a walk. Ulysses was particularly perceptive, and was remarkably canny at sensing when Aidan was frustrated.

When Aidan didn't immediately respond, Ulysses whimpered and rubbed his furry cheek on the leg of his jeans.

"I'll take you for a walk soon, boy," he said, giving the dog's head a scratch. Ulysses gave him a searching look, then yawned and smacked his lips before settling back down.

Aidan rubbed his eyes, bleary from staring too long at his computer screen. He'd have to deal with Emma later, but right now he needed to finish up the work piled in front of him. Or try to.

He had bills to approve, supplies to order, that new branding plan to work on, and a huge pile of regulatory mumbo-jumbo that Brody had insisted he review.

Whiskey production was heavily regulated in the United States—much more so than beer. The government required manufacturers to keep track of every drop of liquor they produced so that it could be properly taxed, even before it went on sale. In fact, the whiskey that Wolfshead made was taxed as soon as it was placed into the barrel, which is why it was such an expensive proposition— they were paying taxes on alcohol they hadn't yet sold. The barrier to entry into the industry was high, mostly because of those costs, which could take years to recoup.

Wolfshead's beer production had been floating them while they ramped up the whiskey production. As far as business plans went, it was a fair one, but ultimately, their ability to make up their losses depended on how quickly they could sell their first-run whiskey. It was Aidan's hope that once the stuff went on sale, they could start earning back the money they'd sunk into starting up the distillery arm of the business. Maybe break even, which would justify the costs.

This was turning out to be more complicated than he'd anticipated.

Beer to him was easy. He'd grown up making it, and when he was old enough, drinking it. As far as craft breweries went, they were somewhere in the middle of the pack. Wolfshead produced approximately 100,000 barrels of beer per year—not huge, but not insignificant, either. Last year they'd had revenues of more than $20 million. Aidan had been doing this long enough to understand the market and Wolfshead's place in it decently well.

Whiskey, not so much. Their output, at least to start off, was only fifty barrels, which put them into microdistillery status. And Aidan knew the rudiments of the industry, but didn't pretend to understand much else, including all of this regulatory stuff.

Now Brody had deemed it time for Aidan to get up to speed. Aidan had put off learning the program for way too long, and wasn't thrilled about spending the time to figure it out, but Brody was right. As CEO, he needed at least a working knowledge of not just the regulations, but how they were implemented.

Unfortunately, the whole thing had just been a huge pain in his ass.

It wasn't as though he was technology-illiterate, but every time he tried to get through the tutorial for the computer program, he got a headache. And it was easier to do the million *other* things he had to take care of than to sit for hours and figure the damn program out.

If only Brody weren't off today, he could get help to wrap his mind around this shit, but the big man was up in the mountains, working on the old car he was refurbishing at their cabin near Mount Hood. He wouldn't dream of ruining Brody's vacation by phoning, but damned if he didn't wish his cousin were around, because he was getting nowhere, fast.

Ulysses lifted up his head, and then all at once the dog's ears went back. Aidan raised his gaze to find Gabe in the door.

"You called, my captain?" Gabe said, a sardonic look on his face.

"Come in," he said, motioning for his brother to enter.

As Gabe sauntered over, Aidan closed the program and pulled up the other document he'd been working on earlier in the week.

His brother flung himself into the seat directly in front of Aidan's desk, reaching down to scratch Ulysses behind the ear in that spot he liked. The dog made a happy rumbling noise and licked Gabe's hand.

"What's up?" he asked.

"I have a job for you."

Gabe raised an eyebrow. "What is it? Wait, let me guess. There's a hot distributor you need me to woo. Or a bartender you'd like me to sweet-talk into carrying our beer?"

Aidan frowned. "No. You've screwed up enough lately."

"What are you talking about?"

"I seem to remember a certain brunette distributor telling you in no uncertain terms to shove that bottle of ale where the sun don't shine."

"Oh, that." Gabe waved his hand as if that weren't important in the slightest. "Like I said before, a total misunderstanding. She thought I said *ass*, when what I really said was *assets*." He shrugged. "It was noisy in that bar."

"Uh-huh," Aidan said, believing him not one whit. "Well, her not hearing those three extra letters cost us nearly a hundred grand in placement. You can't keep making mistakes like that."

Gabe looked bored. "Get to the point, brother."

"Fine. Remember before Paddy died how we talked about branding the new whiskey?"

"You mean making it an extension of our branding for the beer with a similar feel for the labels, similar marketing plan? Targeting the same drinkers?"

"Right. And then when he died, we dropped the ball for a while."

"I thought that was for the best," Gabe said. "I mean, sales are my thing, not as much marketing and definitely not branding, but I don't think lumping in our whiskey with our beer is a good direction for us to be taking."

"It is," Aidan said, in no uncertain terms.

"How do you know? I don't think we've done enough research to draw that conclusion. And you heard what Emma said. It's excellent stuff. Better than our beer. Shouldn't we be branding and marketing it differently?"

"No. All we need is to break even, and to do that, we're going to brand and market it the way Dad and Uncle John wanted. It's good enough for me, and it should be good enough for you."

Gabe shuttered his gaze. "We're here. They're not."

"I don't need a fucking reminder of that."

"My point is that times have changed," Gabe said. "The craft distilling movement has been on the rise, especially in the past few years. It's not all frat boys and bros anymore. There are some seriously discriminating connoisseurs of fine alcohol out there, and the level of education, even among the most casual drinkers, is high. We need to capitalize on that, get our whiskey in the right hands. Influential hands."

"Or we stick to Dad's plan," he said.

Gabe knew when he was being shut down. He crossed his arms over his chest and gave Aidan a petulant look. "I'm not as stupid as you think."

"I don't think you're stupid." *Just irresponsible.* "But I'm in charge. If you don't want the job, I'll give it to Dylan." Ed's much more outgoing twin.

Gabe made a rude noise. "At the tail end of snowboarding season? Forget him. I'll deal with it. What do you need?"

"Drag out our old plans, the ones we started on a while ago. We'll update them, get a proposed label ready to go, and start reaching out to distributors, see how interested they'd be in carrying Wolfshead whiskey. The goal is to have a branding plan up and running in time for the next board meeting."

"Fine."

"Oh, and one more thing. This all has to be kept under wraps. I don't want Emma finding out."

"Why?"

"Emma does things in a certain way," Aidan said, doing his best to be diplomatic. Otherwise Gabe might go running. "She had no power before, but now she does. And unless we're careful, she's going to start instituting changes."

"Maybe she's right to want to make changes," Gabe said, his tone defensive. "Maybe we should listen to what she has to say. I mean, it's not like everything you say is always right on the money."

"True, I'm not always right. But in this case, I know what Wolfshead needs more than she does."

"And when she presents her ideas? Ideas that are probably going to be good?"

"We'll listen. And then we'll make our own decisions about

what happens to *our* company." He needed Gabe to see that despite her fractional ownership, the company was theirs and always would be. Emma might want to help, but really, he knew what was best. After all, he was a Phelan.

Gabe shifted in his seat, clearly uncomfortable. "It's just that I think we should all keep open minds about her suggestions."

"I'm not going to roll over for her," Aidan said, his tone fierce. "None of us are."

"I'm not saying we should. All I'm saying is that we shouldn't do this behind her back."

Aidan gave him a level look. "We're just protecting what's ours."

"I don't like this," Gabe said tightly. "Not one fucking bit."

"You don't have to," Aidan snapped. "All you have to do is your job."

Gabe rose in a jerky motion. He stalked over to the door, muttering something unintelligible but probably very, very filthy.

"And Gabe?"

His brother paused at the door frame and turned back with a frown.

"I'm counting on you, so don't screw this up."

Gabe scowled at him and left.

Aidan was about to turn back to his papers, but a moment later his mom appeared, an expression of concern on her beautiful face.

Time had been kind to Christine Phelan. Even at fifty-eight, she looked better than many women half her age. Her skin was still mostly unlined, though she had a few wrinkles around her eyes because she liked to be outside during the summers. She kept herself fit by long walks and longer hikes, sometimes joining Dylan on his epic ones. The only sign that she might be older than she looked were the streaks of gray in her dark auburn hair. She steadfastly refused to dye it, insisting that with her, what you saw was what you got.

Christine favored jeans, boots, and lots of silver jewelry. She was real. Uncompromising. And gorgeous. Which is why she made the perfect brand ambassador for Wolfshead. Sometimes she worked with Gabe, and sometimes she didn't, but she mostly spent her days talking with customers, chatting up distributors, and generally representing their products at hundreds of meetings and events per year.

Why Christine hadn't gotten remarried after his father died was a mystery, but whenever he asked her if she would consider dating again, she always just smiled a sad kind of smile.

"What was that all about?" she asked in her rich, husky voice. "Something wrong with Gabe?"

"No. He's just being himself."

His mom sighed. "You're too hard on him."

"Maybe he should try not screwing things up, then," he told her.

She glided into the room, took one look at the pile on his desk, and let out a soft *tsk*. "You're struggling."

"Is it that obvious?" he asked.

"I'm your mother. I can always tell when things aren't going your way."

"Yeah." Par for the course over the last forty-eight hours.

"Want me to get Fiona?" His aunt, who was a CPA. Both his mom and Fiona remained close to Wolfshead, helping their sons to run it when their husbands had died. Christine was one of the public faces of the company, while Fiona assisted Brody behind the scenes with anything number-related, something that perfectly fit with Fiona's quieter, gentler personality.

"No," Aidan said. "It's not accounting stuff. It's this new regulatory junk, and Brody's off the grid."

"So wait until he gets back," she suggested.

"That's what I'll have to do, since figuring it out on my own will take too much time."

He rose and crossed the room to the window. Rain was coming down outside, shades of gray darkening the sky. Across the lot and the highway, he could just see the Willamette River, a snake of water dividing his city.

And shit, those Costas were at it again, parking their delivery van on Wolfshead's side of the lot.

The Costa family owned an Italian food and dry goods import company that operated out of the warehouse next to Wolfshead, but they were anything but neighborly. Every month, like clockwork, they'd do something to tee him off. Whose turn was it to go this time? Oh, yeah. Connor's.

His mom came closer and placed a hand on his shoulder. "Something else on your mind?"

The look in her eyes went way beyond *concern* and had begun to approach *worry*.

"Yeah."

"It's the will, isn't it?" she said with a sigh.

"Among other things."

"Did you ever read the letter that Paddy left for you?"

Lewis had handed him the handwritten letter at Monday's will reading. Aidan had been hanging on to his temper by a hair, and he knew without a doubt that reading anything Paddy wrote would have sent him over the edge. So he'd shoved it in his desk drawer as soon as he'd gotten back to his office, and there it sat, unopened.

"No." He wasn't in the mood to read it now. Maybe not ever.

"You should," she said. "Maybe it'll shed some light on why he did what he did."

Aidan grunted, but didn't answer. He knew why Paddy had divided Wolfshead—because he was a bastard who needed the last word.

"Look, I know you're not happy about it, but it could have been worse. Paddy could have left you and Fiona's boys nothing. Honestly, Emma's owning a share isn't so bad. I trust her. I always did. And I think you did, too, once upon a time." His mom cocked her head at him. "Right?"

Aidan set his jaw. They needed that share, but if they couldn't get it, there were other ways to handle it.

His mom frowned. "I don't like that look on your face."

"What look?"

Christine's hazel eyes met his. "That look that says you're plotting something."

His mom was way too perceptive, but he simply shook his head. "Don't worry about it, Mom," he told her. "I'll take care of it."

"You have nothing to prove to anyone, understand?"

His mom was wrong. He'd been waiting years to prove to himself—and his family—that he could run this company the way it was supposed to be run. The way his dad and uncle wanted.

Yes, he had a plan, but Christine would definitely not be involved. She had been strong enough already, fighting tooth and nail for him, his brothers, and his cousins when Aidan's dad and uncle had died. Never stopped trying to get Paddy to give up control. He was proud to call this woman his mom, but she didn't need to add her sins to his.

When he didn't answer, Christine gave him a significant look. "Whatever Paddy did to you, however he's still trying to jerk you around, don't forget that Emma's innocent in all of this. And as far as I can tell, she's already been through enough with you."

"Emma can take care of herself," Aidan said. She always had.

Christine frowned again and looked like she was going to say something else when a soft voice broke in.

"Excuse me, I hope I'm not interrupting anything."

Aidan jerked his head to the door. Emma was standing there, wearing another one of those sexy pencil skirts and an uncharacteristically uncertain expression. Her brown eyes flickered over to his mom, then back to him.

His mom spoke first.

"Emma, hi!" Christine looked pleased as punch to see her former daughter-in-law. "You're looking well." She crossed the room to give Emma a kiss on the cheek, which Emma returned, albeit decidedly less enthusiastically. "I didn't get to talk to you at the will reading, you disappeared so fast. How's your family? How's your work going?"

Emma didn't blink at the rapid-fire questions. "Everyone's okay, thank you for asking," she answered. "Dad's still down in Cannon Beach plugging away. He keeps saying he's going to retire, but I think it's just talk. Ryan's still a sports agent in LA, and he just switched firms. He says he likes the new one better. And my work's going well. I don't know how much Aidan told you, but I recently left my old company to open my own branding and marketing consulting business."

"How wonderful," Christine said. "And now you're back in the fold. Part of the family, as it were." She gave Aidan a meaningful look that could only mean one thing: trouble.

"Emma and I have some things to talk about," he said, hoping his mother would get the hint to leave.

"Oh, but I'd love to catch up."

"Later," he ground out.

"Then I'll leave you to it," Christine said smoothly, as if he hadn't just practically ordered her out. "Emma, lovely to see you, as always." She turned to him. "We'll continue this conversation later," she promised. She snapped a finger. "Come, Ulysses." The dog leaped up and padded over to her. "Good boy. Bye for now."

Emma had been smiling at his mom, but as soon as Christine left, her smile faded.

Since she'd arrived that morning, she'd kept a healthy amount of distance between the two of them, so he wasn't surprised when she chose the seat in front of his desk instead of the one next to him.

Emma removed a pad of paper from her bag. "I made some notes," she said, all business.

Aidan shrugged. "I already know about the company. It's mine, remember?"

"And mine," she said, uncowed in the slightest.

He had to admire her pluck, walking right into the lion's den, head held high. God, she was beautiful. The hair—up in a gentle twist, but just a little messy. Glossy lips. Dark eyes. And a big brain to match. She was the full package, and to this day, he'd never found her equal.

Not that he'd been looking too hard. Or at all.

When Emma crossed her legs and her skirt rode up her thigh, Aidan jerked his gaze away and cleared his throat.

"Fine. Let's talk about last night. What did you figure out?"

"Aside from the fact that Gabe hasn't changed in the slightest?" she said, giving him a wry smile.

Despite himself, he smiled too. "Yeah. I wouldn't say he's evolved any."

"But the party he planned was a huge success. You had the right amount of influencers, bartenders, and friends—people who will really help to get the word out. That being said, while I think Gabe has a strong sense for how to sell and market Wolfshead's beer, I'm not convinced he has his head wrapped around what will be required for the spirits. I'm going to need to do more research on your product and then figure out how it fits into the existing market, but what I do know is that continuing the way things are is not going to work. Craft spirits are different from craft beer, and they need to be marketed accordingly. And if you're giving the wrong message to your influencers, that's going to result in less-than-optimum sales."

"Mmm," he mumbled, only half listening.

"Anyway," she went on, "I also talked to Connor, oh, for

maybe an hour or so."

Now *this* he was interested in hearing. "Connor actually talked to you for an hour?"

"Yes, of course," she said, as if Connor's stringing together more than two words at a time to someone who wasn't a Phelan was the norm. "He had a lot to say about his vision, the recipe and his tweaks, the distilling. He's both the chemist and the production manager, and his knowledge as to process is immense. This kind of information is *exactly* what buyers are looking for in craft spirits, so I'm taking his ideas for the branding very seriously."

Back up a second. "Connor has ideas for branding?" He'd never shared them with *him*.

"Sure. He had some general thoughts about overall marketing, as well as more specific ideas about what he'd like to see on the label, how we're pitching the product to the public…that kind of thing. Of course these are just ideas and he hasn't fleshed it all out yet, which is exactly where I come in."

Huh.

He must have made some kind of face because the corners of her mouth went down, hard.

"It seems," she said, giving him a significant look, "that you are seriously underestimating your family."

He didn't respond.

"It also seems that you are seriously underestimating me."

He crossed his arms over his chest. "You're here talking to me, aren't you? And I'm listening."

She pursed her lips, then snapped her notebook closed and shoved it into her bag with force. "Look, I get paid to facilitate this process for companies. Help them come to some sort of agreement on what would be best. You have this resource at your disposal for free, so I'd appreciate your cooperation."

"I'm cooperating."

Emma snorted. "You're tolerating me. It's not like we see eye to eye on, well, on pretty much anything these days."

"Maybe it's because I don't agree with anything you say."

"Or maybe it's because you're a stubborn ass," she shot back.

He grasped at his control, which was rapidly slipping through his fingers. "You're playing with fire."

"Am I?" she asked, arching her eyebrows. "Good. Maybe it'll

snap you out of whatever rut you're in."

"You think I'm in a rut?"

"Absolutely. Especially when it comes to your PR. It's the same old stuff in the same old way. You need something different. Incredible."

Time to put his plan into action. "Why don't you put your money where your mouth is?"

"How?"

"Prove that your ideas are better than mine."

A crease formed between her brows. "What, like, share them with everyone?"

"Exactly. We have a board meeting coming up soon. We'll each work on a proposal, and we'll present our ideas then. Whichever proposal gets the most votes will be the winner and what we'll adopt as our branding and marketing plan."

Emma cocked her head at him. "That…actually sounds fair."

On its surface, yes. They'd each present their proposals. But his brothers and cousins were as determined as he was to see their dads' dreams through. There was no way in hell they would ever vote for Emma's ideas over his.

"And you'll swear to abide by the results of the vote?" she demanded.

He held up his hand like a Boy Scout. "On my father's grave."

A strange expression crossed Emma's face, but only for an instant. "Then I accept your proposal."

She held out her hand for a shake, and he took it. A jolt of electricity coursed through him, and her eyes widened. She'd felt it too.

But instead of going all soft on him, she went hard.

Carefully, she withdrew her hand, her eyes glittering brightly.

"I'm sure you realize by now that I have serious professional reasons for being here, and I'm not going to let you intimidate me in any way, shape, or form. I'm going to prepare the best damn proposal you've ever seen, and I promise you this: I'm going to win."

She was tough, and damned if he hadn't missed this—this heat simmering between them, this game of tug-and-pull where neither would give any quarter. And truth be told, the thought of Emma challenging him, fighting him, was fucking hot. He wasn't stirred up before, but he damned sure was now.

"Bring. It. On."

Fire flashed in her gaze. "Count on it."

She grabbed her bag and slung it over her shoulder, gripping it tightly as she stood. Then she turned, giving him a prime view of that luscious ass, and left.

God, she had bite. A fierceness that had only gotten stronger with time. Yet there was something still so vulnerable about her, something that dredged up all his protective instincts.

Which didn't matter in the slightest. Things with Emma were over. Done. And had been for a long time. He'd best remember that, even if she still turned him on without even trying.

All he knew is that she'd better keep fighting him.

Because if she didn't, he knew exactly where they'd end up—in bed, with Emma under him, giving up everything the way she used to do.

This was something that could not happen.

He'd made his choice long ago, and he'd worked too hard to shut down the idea that he could have her again. Shoved aside the memories of them together and buried them deep inside. Emma was his past, and that is where she had to remain.

Wolfshead was his present—and his future. His choice was clear. The company came first. No matter how tempting the alternative was.

CHAPTER 5

When Emma returned to Wolfshead the next morning, Aidan was nowhere to be seen. However, Gabe spied her almost the moment she walked through the door and sauntered over.

"Good morning, Emma," he said, giving her a hug, gently brushing his lips against her cheek. "You look amazing today."

His words had the ring of sincerity—the mark of the ultimate smooth operator. Which is exactly what he was with his artfully tousled red hair and his heavily lidded eyes and his clothes that hung elegantly on his lean body. Of course, she was older now, and if not entirely immune to his charms, at least able to appreciate what he had to offer.

"Thanks, Gabe," she said. "So do you." That elicited a big grin.

"So what are you hoping to get accomplished today?" he asked.

"A tour, perhaps? I feel like I've only scratched the surface, but I want to learn more about Wolfshead."

When she'd been married to Aidan, she'd had a full-time job and plenty of her own work to do. Not to mention the fact that he'd tacitly discouraged her from getting too involved in the company. Now there was nothing stopping her from learning all she could.

"Ah, I see," Gabe said, at once all seriousness. "I can definitely help you. You'll want to see production, of course. And maybe afterward I can talk you through what we've been doing on the sales side. You'll probably also want to speak with my mom. She's a great ambassador for the brand, and will probably have some insight as to the way customers and people in the industry view Wolfshead and its products."

"Yes. Yes, that sounds great. I—"

She stopped. Stiffened. The skin prickled on the back of her neck, and permeating every inch of her body was a strange sense of awareness. *He* was here.

Gabe leaned in close. "My brother's watching us, isn't he?"

She lifted her gaze and spied him. He was up on the second-story catwalk, looking down at her with an inscrutable expression. How long he'd been there, she had no idea. She gave a little shiver.

"Yeah," she breathed back.

Gabe leaned back, his eyes slightly hooded. "Good. Let him watch. Stick close and I'll give you the tour to end all tours." His lips curled up. "By the time we're done, smoke'll be coming out of his ears."

She was liking Gabe more and more.

Ignoring Aidan, she laughed, took Gabe's arm, and gave him a huge smile. "Sounds like a plan."

Gabe was in sales, so it was no surprise that he was an excellent guide. First, he started with a quick refresher on Wolfshead's history, starting with his great-great-grandfather John, who'd immigrated to the United States from Ireland, making his way from New York to California, and finally to Oregon. He'd worked in a couple of factories, making illegal moonshine in his spare time, before experimenting with beer. Even early on, his beer was in hot demand, and he'd soon opened his own brewery. A wife and children followed.

"Any questions?" Gabe asked.

"No," Emma said. "That was the best history lesson I've ever gotten on the place." Aidan had given her a bare-bones description, but nothing in such detail. "My only question is why it isn't on the website."

Gabe gave her a grim smile. "One guess."

"Aidan."

"Actually, it was Grandfather. He didn't want anything negative about his own grandfather put up on the Internet."

"What, the illegal moonshining enterprise? Surely the statute of limitations has expired on that one."

"All I know is that he and Aidan got into a fight about it, updating the website got pushed off, and now no one wants to deal with it."

"I'll deal with it," she told him. "That is, if you'll help me."

"Of course I will, if only to tee off Aidan. He still watching us?"

She glanced up at the catwalk. "No, he's gone."

"He'll be back," Gabe said, guiding her through a pair of double doors with a strong hand on her waist. She let herself be led, knowing it was for show, but aware that she could handle him all the same. "We'll tour the brewery first."

Emma found herself in a familiar warehouse, one she'd visited maybe half a dozen times. The place was huge—several hundred yards long and just slightly less wide. A black metal catwalk was situated on the second story of one wall, a mirror of the one in the tasting room area, with a metal staircase leading down.

"When was the last time you were here?" Gabe asked.

"In the production area? I don't know. A couple of years ago?"

"I'm sure you remember a lot, but some things have changed. Let me give you a quick rundown. First, we get the grains. Our shipments come in at the far side of the warehouse, get inspected, and are stored there." He pointed to a corner where there lay many large bins and burlap sacks. "We start with the hops—those are the flowers from the hop plant—which impart different flavors to our beers. We mix those with hot water and put them into the lauter kettles," Gabe said, indicating three enormous silver vats, each approximately ten feet high, that were lined up to her left and bolted to the warehouse floor. "We cook the mash in those for about ninety minutes to get the grains to release those oils and enzymes, get everything nice and sugary and ready to react with the yeast." Gabe pointed to another huge vat, a bit taller in size and also bolted down to the floor. "Then we go to—"

"Fermentation."

Gabe gave her an approving look. "That's right. The mash goes into the fermenter, where we mix it with yeast, which eats the sugars and starts to transform the hops. Primary fermentation takes place in that open vessel, and then we move it to a closed vessel for secondary fermentation. Depending on the kind of beer we're making, we'll mix up the yeast we're using. We have ale-yeast strains and lager-yeast strains. If the yeast gets too chilly, it's not as active, and different types of beer get fermented at different temperatures. For example, ales are fermented at seventy degrees Fahrenheit, but others are fermented at—" He stopped and gave her an apologetic look. "Sorry, I'm getting carried away. I just can't help myself with the details."

"No, it's perfect. I like hearing the technical stuff."

Gabe looked relieved "Great. So after fermentation, we go to aging, where we let the flavors mellow out. It's here that the carbon dioxide gets reabsorbed back into the beer, which makes it naturally fizzy. We age our beer in chilled stainless steel vats, but we've been experimenting with aging the beer in old whiskey barrels, just to see if we can get a different flavor spectrum. I like the smoother taste of the steel-aged beer, but Finn loves the new stuff. It's just personal preference, and you'll have to try it to figure out what you like.

"When the beer is aged to our liking, we do a flash pasteurization, then go to bottling. You'll see our operation over there." He pointed to the far corner, where several huge machines were connected with a silver conveyor belt that was currently operational. "It's all automated now, but we still need staff to ensure that everything runs smoothly and nothing gets gummed up." As she watched, workers in white uniforms milled around, poking here, checking there. "So many of our peers are experimenting with cans now, but Aidan says it's more 'authentic' to stick to bottles and tap."

Gabe spoke briskly and authoritatively, giving her just the right amount of information and lacing it with a dollop of humor. When she wanted to know more, he went deeper. When she seemed to have had enough, he backed off.

"You know so much about this!" she said after he'd answered yet another question.

"I know a lot about other things, too," he said, his voice deepening suggestively.

Emma rolled her eyes at his lame attempt at seduction, and knowing when his audience wasn't biting, Gabe laughed.

"See, that's what I love about you," he said, giving her an affectionate squeeze. "You're one of the only women who doesn't put up with my shit."

"What about your mother?"

"Her, too," Gabe said wryly. "In all seriousness, you shouldn't be surprised I know so much about this stuff. Beer's in my blood. I grew up around the company, and I even apprenticed with Finn and Connor before I realized that sales were more my speed. Plus, in order to sell it, I have to know this product inside and out."

"You should give tours. People would eat this up."

Gabe gave her a rueful smile. "I asked. Many times."

"Let me guess. Aidan doesn't want to?"

"You got it."

"Aidan can be such an ass."

"Agreed. And fair warning, that ass is watching us again."

Emma clenched her hand in a small fist. "If he's trying to intimidate me into leaving, it's not going to work."

"I know." Gently, he took her by the elbow. "Come on. Ed's got to be around here somewhere. Let's go find him."

They found him crouched behind one of the giant vats, his back toward them.

"Hey," Gabe said, greeting his older brother. "I'm just showing Emma around."

Ed didn't look up from what he was doing. "Give me a minute."

Ed had always been intense, which is why his job as stillhouse manager was perfect for him. Safety was of primary importance, as there were way too many things that could go wrong at every stage in the process.

Gabe leaned close to her ear. "As you can see, my brother hasn't changed."

As far as she could tell, no one had changed, but she kept her mouth shut.

Ed finished what he was doing, checked something off on a clipboard, and came over. She hadn't seen much of him the night of the tasting event, just a few words exchanged over the noise of the crowd.

He was six four and lean, with reddish-brown hair, a neatly trimmed beard, and intelligent brown eyes. It was uncanny how much he looked like his twin Dylan, but their resemblance was all superficial, as the two men couldn't have been less alike. Whereas Ed was serious, Dylan was much more lighthearted, and this difference was manifested in almost every facet of their lives.

She took Ed's offered hand, and he gripped it tightly. "Emma," he said, his voice low. "Come to check out your property?"

That was Ed. Always cutting right to the chase. Of course she understood. Ed was a reserved, deliberate man, and anything he thought might upset his status quo would be perceived as a threat. But she wasn't there to mess with whatever he—or anyone else—was doing. She was only there to help.

Squarely, she met his gaze. "That's right. But I'm not here to interfere with your operation. I just want to get a sense for what you've been working on since I was last here."

Ed sized her up for another uncomfortably long moment, then, seemingly satisfied, gave her a nod and released her hand.

"Not much has changed on the brewery side," he said. "As you can see, we have expanded production by adding two more fermenters and an additional still, but that's about it. You'll see most of the new stuff in the distillery."

That made a lot of sense, given that from what she knew, their beer-making operation had grown marginally over the past few years. She glanced around. Except for the new equipment, the warehouse still looked the same. There was the machinery on one side, bolted to the concrete floor. And on the other side was the bottling equipment and the storage area.

"I don't see the distilling operation. Are you doing it somewhere else?"

"Yes," Ed said. "Even though we have our beer mash fermenting in closed-top fermenters, we were worried about contamination with the open-top stills on the distilling side." At her confused look, he clarified. "Bacteria and yeast from the beer mash could make its way into the whiskey mash, creating a different flavor spectrum than what we want and potentially spoiling the mash during the fermentation process. So we have the other stills at the site of the old brewery on the other side of the property. Connor or Finn will give you a rundown when Gabe takes you over there later."

"Great," she said.

"And Emma? I don't need to remind you that you shouldn't be wandering around the production area without a guide. This place is dangerous. I'd never forgive myself if anything happened to you."

"Neither would I," a deep voice said. Aidan had joined them and was now giving Ed a significant look. "You check the valves today?"

To his credit, Ed's expression didn't waver in the slightest. "And every day."

"I didn't see them on the log last night."

"They were there," Ed said.

"Uh, thanks again for the info," she said, doing her best to break up the stare-down currently going on between the two brothers. "I promise I won't come in without a guide."

Ed finally dragged his gaze away from Aidan. "Good. Catch you later, Emma." He gave her a nod and disappeared back between the vats again.

Emma turned back to Aidan, who had his arms crossed over his chest.

"Back for more, I see," he said.

"Of course," she told him. "There's a ton I have to learn." *That you didn't teach me.* She gave the smaller man a fond look. "But Gabe's doing an amazing job so I'm guessing I'll be up to speed pretty soon."

"I'm going to take over the tour from here," Aidan said.

"Oh, I'm doing just fine with Gabe," she said.

"Gabe's busy."

"With what?" Gabe demanded.

"The Farleigh account."

"But I dealt with that yesterday!" he said, sounding irritated.

"They need you to call them back. They have a few more questions…"

"…that can be answered later."

"Now, Gabe."

Gabe's eyes narrowed, and Emma was sure that if he could have burned Aidan to a crisp with his gaze, he would have. "Fine, I'm going, I'm going. I'll see you later, Emma."

He brushed his lips against her cheek, and then he stalked off.

Emma put her hands on her hips and turned back to Aidan. "Nice job. Not only did you chase away my tour guide, but you made him feel about two inches small."

Aidan snorted. "He'll get over it. Besides, he has to get on this client or I'll have to clean up another one of his messes."

"Maybe if you stopped treating him like a kid, he'd stop acting like one," Emma threw back. Not that Gabe needed defending, but the way Aidan simply made assumptions was starting to grate on her.

He set his jaw. "Do you want to see the distillery or not?"

"Yes," she said, by now exasperated by the turn this conversation had taken.

"Follow me."

Emma bit her lip. Displeased at this turn of events, but still dying to see the distillery, she took another long look at the brew-making equipment and machinery before trailing after Aidan.

It wasn't until they were out of the warehouse and walking across a short stretch of blacktop that she broached a question she'd been dying to ask. "Was Ed a little on edge? I mean, more than usual."

"Yep," Aidan agreed. "For good reason. The guys over at Birdhouse had a bad accident last month—fire in the warehouse."

"Fire?" She hadn't paid much attention to the goings-on in the brewery community recently, but she knew that Birdhouse made a great craft beer and enjoyed a strong local following.

"Yeah. I heard through the grapevine that their manager forgot to double-check the valves before closing. The whole kettle went up in flames. It took out the entire production operation. It's going to set them back big-time. Too bad. They were doing some great work over there. From what I know, their financials are solid. I hope they get back on their feet soon. We need the competition."

About a hundred yards away sat the old warehouse. It wasn't as big as the new warehouse, but it was built in the same style, with the same metal siding, the same signage on the outside.

Aidan held the door open so that she could walk into the large tasting room. It was what she'd describe as modern-rustic, with wood walls and drop lighting hanging over a pounded-copper bar. A huge picture of a wolf's head was prominently displayed on one wall. This was a space for men to come, to congregate and drink and talk.

"Whoa," she said.

Aidan let out a soft breath behind her. "Beautiful, isn't it?"

"It is," she agreed. "Who redesigned the interior?"

"I did."

She was impressed despite herself. "Really?"

"Yeah. I hired someone to build it, but the lines and the vision were mine. Finn helped some, too." He pointed to a bass guitar on the wall. "It was his idea to incorporate things we loved into the design."

She looked closer, and saw that there were meaningful objects woven seamlessly into the decor that made the place truly theirs.

A couple of old Oregon license plates graced the wall behind the bar—those must be Brody's from the vintage cars he loved to restore. One of Ed's old fishing poles was back there, too, along with a trophy he'd won fly-fishing. Near the main entrance, a glass display case with an unlabeled bottle of whiskey held some of Connor's more intricate wood carvings. And one of Dylan's old snowboards soared below the rafters, as did one of Gabe's old surfboards, riding an invisible wave.

"Where's yours?" she whispered.

"There." He nodded to a small alcove. An old baseball glove, worn from age, was displayed behind the glass, along with a signed baseball and a folded uniform. "I needed to have some of me in here, too."

Of course. Senior year, he'd not only been captain of the college team, but their star pitcher, which had brought him to the attention of professional scouts. She'd been thrilled when he'd been signed by the Mets, because she always thought she'd head to New York City after graduating with her degree in marketing. But that never happened. He'd come back to Portland, she'd stayed with him, and that had been that.

"You gave up a lot, didn't you?" she murmured.

"I did what I had to do," he said. "Anyone would have done the same."

That baseball gear was a shrine to what could have been. His old idealism, his youth, moldering away in a curio cabinet.

She'd tried countless times before to put herself into Aidan's shoes. Tried to see why he'd acted the way he had. But it hadn't hit her until this very moment exactly how much he'd lost by abandoning his dreams, not to mention the strength required to just walk away from everything he'd always hoped for.

"No," she said quietly. "Not anyone."

"That's what you—" He stopped in midsentence, looking stunned. Then he reached out and ran his finger over her collarbone, pulling her necklace up and over the edge of her cardigan.

And then she realized what it was. The only piece of jewelry he'd ever gotten for her, aside from her engagement and wedding rings—a small bronze disk hanging from a simple chain stamped with a single word: *forever.*

Emma looked up at him, but his gaze was riveted to her throat.

"You kept it."

Yes, she'd kept it. She remembered the day he'd given it to her as if it were yesterday. Right after his graduation before he'd left for summer league training. *Wait for me*, he'd whispered.

She'd loved him, so she had.

Emma rarely wore the necklace these days. In fact, she couldn't remember wearing it once since they'd split. But for some reason, she'd put it on today. A trick of her subconscious, no doubt.

Still, she wasn't ashamed. She couldn't erase the past, and even if she could, she wouldn't want to.

Aidan was still staring at the necklace. "I can't believe you didn't throw it away."

"I didn't," she said, her mouth inexplicably dry. *I couldn't.*

His gaze met hers.

Slowly, he stepped back. Pinched the bridge of his nose. "Look, Emma, I know I've been a dick, but you've got to understand. This isn't easy for me. *You're* not easy for me."

"You're not easy for me, either."

A complicated look crossed his face, and for a moment it seemed as though he were going to say something else.

Then it passed, and the moment was gone.

"Come on," he said, indicating the door to the production area. "I'll take you in."

He placed a hand on her waist to usher her through. His touch was different from Gabe's—heavy and warm. Proprietary.

Before she could think too hard about it, they were inside.

This production room space was larger than the tasting room, but smaller than the brewery's production area. It was almost a twin of the other warehouse, complete with second story and catwalk. On the floor of the warehouse, just like in the brewery, the heavy equipment was bolted to the floor. Some things she recognized. A kettle. A fermenter. But other equipment was completely different.

"What's that?" she asked, indicating the big, unusually shaped machine gleaming in the center of the room.

"It's an alembic still," Aidan said into her ear. "It's a slower and older method of distilling that captures more flavor. And since we're all about the flavor, it's a good fit for us."

Connor and Finn stood in a corner, deep in discussion.

Finn was big—about six three with strawberry-blond hair styled in an undercut and a thick but closely cropped beard. An obscure indie band's logo was printed on his long-sleeved T-shirt, and his jeans were held onto his lean hips with a grommet belt. Except for their size—Connor was a lot taller and broader—the resemblance between the two men was striking.

Connor's hair was slightly redder and it was a bit longer in length, including his beard, which was definitely more lumberjack than hipster. Like Finn, he wore jeans and boots, but his T-shirt was plain, black, and long-sleeved, which served to hide the tattoos on his arms.

Connor could be really intimidating—unless you knew him and knew how kind and gentle he truly was.

Finn spied her first. "Hi, Emma," he said. "Welcome to the distillery. You like?" He definitely noticed Aidan touching her, but he chose not to comment.

"It's amazing." She pointed to a door on the far side of the spacious warehouse. "Where does that lead?"

"To the rickhouse, where we age the whiskey in barrels," Finn said.

"Oh, I'd love to see that. Would you show me?"

"With pleasure," Finn said. "But I think Connor would be the best one to talk you through the distilling process."

"Are you okay with that?" she asked the big man softly. It had taken a long time for Connor to get comfortable with her, and even though she believed he still was, she never wanted to presume anything when it came to him.

"Yeah," he said, meeting her gaze briefly. "'Course. You'll find it's similar to beer-making…up to a point. We start out by cooking the mash and letting it ferment, same as with the beers. Then the process diverges. Instead of just aging the mash, we run it through a still, and we age the distillate."

"You doing the double distillation today?" Aidan asked.

Finn nodded and turned to her to explain. "We're

experimenting by running one batch through two cycles of distillation. See what that does to the texture and flavor. I think it'll make it smoother, but will take out some of its character."

"We'll see," Connor said.

"Call me when you're going to taste so I can weigh in," Aidan demanded, then leaned down to her. "I've got work to do," he said, "but I'm leaving you in good hands." He looked deep into her eyes and offered her the ghost of a smile. "Catch you later."

Emma frowned at his departing back. His cold-then-hot routine confused her. Muddied the waters between them, especially when it came to her body. Damn it, she didn't want to want him again. That would lead to nothing but heartache.

Good thing she'd already shut him down in her mind. If only she could keep reminding herself of that...

She turned back to Finn and Connor, only to find that they were watching her carefully. Not wanting to show how much Aidan had affected her, she pasted on a big smile.

"Please," she said. "Keep going. I want to see and hear about everything."

Thankfully, that's exactly what they did.

CHAPTER 6

It turned out that Emma's traipsing around his factory, waltzing into his office, and generally being everywhere, all the time, was a little more to handle than Aidan had counted on. And watching her watch him in those little pencil skirts with a wary smile provoked his imagination like nobody's business.

Knowing that seeing her was just going to end in an argument like it always did, he'd shut himself in his office for hours rather than deal with her. He'd even skipped lunch, pretending he couldn't hear her heels clacking around downstairs, or her laugh, which snaked its way up the stairwell and seeped through his closed door.

When he'd finally bitten the bullet and emerged, he'd found her with Gabe. He hadn't enjoyed that feeling of jealousy as his brother talked to her, smiled at her, *touched her*, not one tiny bit. He'd acted like a caveman, but he couldn't help himself.

Admit you want her.

Easily. But that had never been the problem. He'd never stopped wanting her. And it was high time he came to grips with that.

Because it seemed that she'd never stopped wanting him, either.

Case in point: she was wearing the necklace. *His necklace.* The one he'd given her as a stake, a claim for their future.

Now, a relationship with Emma wasn't really compatible with his plans for Wolfshead given that she had very different goals, and he wasn't certain he could separate their relationship from his professional life like he'd done during their entire marriage.

Because this time, it was different.

She was different.

Maybe he was, too.

As he was stewing, Brody strode into Aidan's office, dropping his big body onto the couch. Ulysses, who'd been camped out underneath Aidan's desk, picked himself up and padded over to him, then lay down at his feet.

Most people just saw Brody as Wolfshead's finance guy. While he looked similar to the other Phelan men—that was to say big and bearded—personality-wise, he was as different as could be. Brody was the family's peacemaker, calm and cool in almost every situation, the perfect yang to Aidan's yin. Aidan rarely saw him ruffled, even when everyone and everything else was in an uproar.

Although Brody had been off work for the past week, taking a long-overdue break from Wolfshead, his moss-green eyes, an unusual color he'd inherited from his mother, sat at half-mast. He gave Ulysses a few gentle pats before scratching his reddish-blond beard and letting out a huge yawn. As if sensing naptime on the horizon, Ulysses lay his head on his paws and closed his eyes.

"Didn't you just get back from vacation?" Aidan asked.

"Yep," Brody answered.

"So why are you so damn tired?"

"Finally finished the Torino," he said on an exhale.

When he wasn't keeping Wolfshead in the black, Brody lived, ate, and breathed classic cars. On his days off, he'd hightail it out of town and head up to their cabin where he'd spend hours in his garage—really a large, converted shed—working on one of his many projects. He'd even done jobs for his brothers and cousins. Connor had asked him to renovate an old Ford truck, while Finn had sweet-talked him into restoring a '67 Mustang hardtop that he drove to all his band gigs.

Brody was generous with his time and talent, but that meant he'd put off work on his own car—a 1968 Torino. He'd bought the car off a family friend almost two years ago, and it had sat outside the shed since then, protected from the elements under a heavy tarp. A couple of times when they'd been up at the cabin together, Aidan had seen Brody lifting the tarp and staring at the car longingly before covering it up once again. Finally, just before Christmas, Brody had moved it into the shed and had thrown himself back into working on it like a man possessed.

"Sweet, man. I know you put a ton of effort into that car. I'm glad she's finally done."

Brody scrubbed a hand over his face. "Yeah. But I stayed up for two days to finish. It was worth it, though."

"How's she running?"

"There's a small hitch when I shift. I think I may replace the gearbox next time I'm up there and have some more time."

"You're going to drive her around?"

"Hell yeah I'm going to drive her. I'm sure not going to let her gather dust in the shed." Brody was pretty vehement about his dislike of car collectors who simply had cars on display. He was a firm believer that cars were meant to be seen on the road, in their natural habitats.

Aidan held up his hand in supplication. "I hear you. I'm just concerned she might not be street-worthy yet. Plus, you already have a killer ride." Years ago, Brody had restored a '71 Camaro, which he used to make his daily commute from the West Hills area of Portland to the warehouse. It had been his first big solo project, and the car still seemed to run as well as ever.

"She's street-worthy, but you're right about me figuring out what to do with my other car. They both need to be driven weekly." He shrugged. "I'll figure it out."

"You could always give one to Gabe. He's been after you for a while to fix something up for him."

Brody snorted. "He can't handle the power."

"Don't tell him that."

"Already did. Loudly and repeatedly. Which of course he denied." Brody gave him a tired smile. "So what's been going on while I've been out of the office?"

Brody hadn't technically been due back at Wolfshead until the next day, but Aidan had asked him to come in early as a favor.

Aidan rubbed his temple. "A bunch of things. I can't figure out the regulatory software."

"So we'll go through it together, step by step," Brody said decisively. "By the time I'm through with you, you'll have it down cold. Next?"

"The Costas are parking on our lot again," Aidan informed

him.

"For how long?"

"A week. Like they knew you were gone and just wanted to fuck with us."

"So go talk to them."

"Nope. I sent Connor."

Brody blinked. "Jesus, Aidan, why'd you do that? That's like a declaration of war."

Aidan smiled grimly. "I know."

"Shit," Brody said, massaging his head. "I bet they did not take that well."

"Nope."

"Well? What the hell happened?"

"What do you think happened? They called the cops."

"Escalating everything yet again," Brody groaned.

"Nah, it's cool. The cops were big fans of Wolfshead and backed off. In fact, they told those assholes to keep their van on their own side of the lot."

"Being dicks isn't good for our image," Brody told him. "I thought you were going to let me handle things with the Costas since that last time when you almost beat the shit out of…what's his name…Tony?"

"No, the middle one. Gio."

The Costas had four kids—three sons and a daughter. The daughter usually minded her own business, plus she was gorgeous—lots of dark hair and eyes of obsidian—which always helped to improve relations. The sons, on the other hand, went out of their way to make life miserable for their neighbors…big, loud, and argumentative, a complete recipe for disaster.

A couple of months ago, the Costas had a whole pallet of imported canned tomatoes delivered to the Phelan side of the lot and refused to remove it for half a day. Not only did Aidan not want to look at the stupid thing, but it had also blocked multiple parking spots on a day when they'd had a tasting event at the brewery.

"Whoever," Brody said. "I just wish you had waited for me. Or sent one of our moms."

"They already do way too much shit around here."

"Yeah. I see your point. So what's the plan now?"

"It's Ed's turn next." His younger brother's intensity might just freak the Costas out even more than Connor's stare-down had.

"No," Brody said quickly. "Just…just hold off. Don't send Ed in. I'll go myself. Get them off our side of the lot, okay?"

"If you really want to."

"I don't," Brody said. "But it's better than going on the way we are."

"I'm kind of enjoying myself," Aidan said. He always did love a good fight.

Brody just shook his head. "You're sick, you know that?"

"Yeah."

"Okay, what else?"

Aidan took a deep breath. "Emma's here."

At this, Brody blinked. "Your Emma?"

"She's not mine anymore, but yes. Since she actually owns a share of the company, I can't just kick her out."

"Riiight," Brody said on an exhale. He'd come back from Mount Hood for the reading of the will, so he knew the score. "So she's going to be around all the time?"

"It appears so."

"Not that I don't like Emma—we all did, *do*, I mean—but that's going to be a problem. What if she wants to change shit? We're finally free of Paddy"—Brody paused to give the sign of the cross—"and now we have someone new breathing down our necks? That's not going to be good for anyone."

"Tell me about it." Though the thought of Emma breathing down his neck didn't sound so awful. In fact, it actually sounded kind of pleasant. Except for the fact that afterward, there'd been the inevitable argument about it.

"Is there any way to get the share back?" Of course Brody knew Aidan would be doing everything he could to figure a way around the problem.

Aidan ran a hand through his hair. "We can't undo the will. I checked, and not just with Lewis." With another lawyer he'd specifically retained as an unbiased third party.

Brody thought for a moment. "Maybe we can buy her out."

"Already asked."

"And?"

Aidan simply gave him a look. "This is Emma we're talking about."

"So she said no. Maybe you should try again."

"She won't change her mind. In fact," Aidan continued, "I'm pretty sure she means to give us her input about the way we run things, about our marketing and branding strategies.

"Well, she does that for a living, right? So she probably knows what she's talking about."

"She does," Aidan confirmed. "Problem is, I think her ideas are very different from ours. I worry that she'll try to push Wolfshead in a direction we're not going to like."

"Look, I'll be honest," Brody said. "I always respected Emma. Liked her, too, but respected her a hell of a lot. She was the only woman I know who could give you a run for your money. The best damn thing that ever happened to you and then..." Brody stopped and shook his head. "Well, we all know why things went south."

"Yeah." *Me.*

"And nothing's changed since then? I mean with her? She still the same?"

He nodded. Still gorgeous, brilliant, and infuriating. Still not falling for his shit.

"Okay, well, on the positive side, Emma's sharp. I assume that if she's well-informed about the company, she'll have some halfway decent ideas about strategy, so it won't be a total hardship to hear her out. On the negative side, she's pretty persuasive, and thanks to that share, now she has some power. We'll have to be careful."

"You think she'll make things difficult?"

"Maybe," Brody said. "She's clever. And she's not afraid to burn bridges. Hell, she divorced you, didn't she?"

"I can handle her."

"I'm not so sure you can," Brody said, all seriousness. "Trying to handle a woman like Emma is like trying to ski in an ice storm—slippery, dangerous, and too easy to head right off a cliff."

"Thanks for the visual," Aidan said, his tone wry.

"Seriously. She didn't put up with your shit when you were married. What makes you think she's going to put up with it now?"

"If she wants to play with the big boys, she's going to have to." Whether she liked it or not. "We still have the majority vote, and we're going to do what's best for us. I already have Gabe working on the whiskey branding."

"You have a plan," Brody said slowly.

"Don't I always?"

"And you got Gabe to help you? You think he'll be able to pull it off?"

A vision of Gabe's arm wrapped around Emma's waist made him see red. "Yeah. If he can manage to keep his fucking hands off her."

Brody blinked once, very deliberately. "Oh *shit.*"

"What?"

"You still want her, don't you?"

For the briefest moment, he thought about lying to Brody's face. Saying no, he didn't want her anymore. But Brody would see through his ruse in a hot minute.

"Yes," he gritted out.

To his credit, Brody didn't laugh. He didn't even smile. Just scratched his beard and looked serious and thoughtful. "Well, this complicates things, doesn't it?"

"I know," Aidan said darkly.

"What are you going to do about it?"

"Nothing." On this, he had to be firm.

"Bullshit."

"I told you I'm not going to do anything, and I meant it."

Brody shook his head. "That's not the way you're hardwired. She's back in your life, and it'll be all you can do to keep away." Aidan started to protest, but Brody held up his hand. "Don't bother to deny it. You're two of a kind. You work hard, you love hard, and yeah, you fight hard. But if you guys go to war again, we'll be the ones caught in the crossfire. Wolfshead is in a fragile place right now. We've got ninety-nine problems, and I don't want this to be one more."

"It won't be," Aidan vowed.

"Good. Because I can't handle putting out any more fires." Brody rose, stretching his arms above his head. "Damn, I'm tired. I need some coffee and then I'm heading to the Costas."

"Good luck," he said as Brody disappeared out the door.

Aidan leaned back in his seat and sighed.

Brody was right. He was between a rock and a hard place when it came to dealing with Emma and Wolfshead, because handling Emma was virtually impossible. He'd been able to do it when they were younger, but this tough-as-nails Emma, the one who saw right through him, would be even tougher to manage.

Forget Gabe—keeping his own fucking hands off her was proving harder than he ever anticipated.

She'd lost none of her warmth, none of her passion, the kind of passion that a man was lucky enough to have once in a lifetime, let alone twice. Only now it was coupled with a gravity, a depth of experience she hadn't had when she was younger.

God, he wanted her. He could no longer deny it. They'd be quite a pair, the two of them. He lived for the fight, and she'd been the only one who'd ever been able to match him, in bed and out.

But as tempting as it would be to seduce her, Wolfshead came first, now and always. So he'd just have to suck it up, play nice, and give Emma the illusion of control while really keeping it all for himself.

Nothing could jeopardize the plans he had for his company, not even the woman who'd gotten away.

CHAPTER 7

"Oh, yessss," Emma said as the server placed the dish of yam fritters on the table. "Thank you!"

She took one, still piping hot, and bit into it. "Mmm…" Her tongue would be singed, but she didn't care. There really was nothing like this—buttery, nutty perfection—and Pambiche was the best place in town to satisfy her craving.

In addition to having great food, the restaurant was fun and vibrant. Its bright red-and-yellow-painted walls were decorated with Cuban art and kitsch, and its character was evident from the colorful serving plates to the funky craft beers to the incredible desserts in the glass display case. The clientele was the usual mixture of Portland folks—foodies, hipsters, and intellectuals—the eclecticism of the city reflected in the patrons who'd come out to enjoy the evening.

Plus: fritters.

"What is it with you and fried food?" Sara asked with a smile.

"It's delicious," Emma said, swallowing the last of the fritter and reaching for another. "Rich and greasy and crispy and…oh God, I'm just working myself up again." She took another bite, loving the crunch of the exterior. "So good," she mumbled, shoving the plate closer to Sara and Robin.

Robin eyed them hungrily. "Oh, I shouldn't," she said.

"Why on earth not?" Emma asked. Robin was carrying a few extra pounds, but it had settled in all the right places—her hips and ass—and was accentuated by a stretch wrap dress that hugged her curvy body. She didn't look at all like a new mom, let alone one who'd had twins.

"I just stopped nursing the girls, so no more free-calorie pass for me."

Sara explained. "Nursing expends approximately five hundred more calories per day, in essence to make food for the baby. Or in your case, babies."

"With twins it was closer to seven hundred calories, which was great. I ate whatever I wanted." Robin sighed. "Nothing lasts forever. But I do get to drink, so I'm not complaining at all." She held up her own mojito and took a long drag.

"Huh," Emma said with a frown. "So drinking but no eating? I think I liked Nursing Robin better."

Robin gave a rueful laugh. "So did David."

"Because there was always so much food in the house?" Emma asked.

"No, because my boobs were bigger. I went up a whole cup size. As soon as I stopped nursing, they shrank," Robin said mournfully. "Now I think they're smaller than before."

"So eat something and get them back," Emma said with a laugh. She nudged the plate toward Robin again.

"The calories will just go straight to my ass."

Emma rolled her eyes. Robin was a lost cause. "Come on, Sara, how about you? You know you want one."

But her friend merely shook her head no and took another sip of mojito. Lean as a whippet with smooth skin stretched over her narrow frame, Sara was *definitely* more into drinking than eating, and had been since college. All this meant was that when they went out, Emma and Robin usually got whole dishes to themselves, and it'd be even worse now that Robin wasn't eating, either.

Tonight, both Robin and Sara had started drinking early. Both women were already on their second drinks, and Emma hadn't even ordered her first.

"This place is perfect for us," Sara said, eyes a little too bright. "We drink, you eat."

"Oh, I'm drinking too, but I have to catch up. You got the jump on me." She hailed a passing waiter. "A Wolfshead amber ale, please."

The server nodded and went off to tell the bartender.

When she turned back to the table, Sara gave her a strange

look. "Tell me you did not just order what I think you did."

Emma shrugged. "It's good. Besides, it's my job now. Gotta sample all the offerings."

"Mmm-hmmm," Sara said, as if she didn't believe her.

"Come on. It's just a beer."

"Like I said before, I don't want you to get hurt."

"I'm not going to get hurt by drinking a beer."

"You're already invested. I can tell."

"I'm invested in the company, not in him."

Robin was looking back and forth between the two of them. "What is going on?"

Quickly, Emma filled her in as to the whole inheritance situation, as well as the tension between her and Aidan at the company.

"Oh no, Emma," Robin said when she was through.

"I've told her repeatedly to sell that damn share back," Sara said.

"But if I do that, I'll feel as if I'm just giving up."

Sara gave her a look. "He's giving you a hard time, isn't he?"

"Ye-es," Emma reluctantly acknowledged.

"Tell us," Robin breathed.

"Okay. Well, I went to the tasting, he was cold as ice. I showed up at the warehouse later that week, he was down my throat. The day after that, he actually followed me around while I was touring the factory with Gabe." It was too confusing to get into what he'd said to her after dismissing Gabe. And telling her friends about the weird sexual tension she'd felt would only freak them out. Still, it felt good to unload a little bit. Give a voice to her confusion.

"What'd he do today?" Sara asked.

"Nothing because today I stayed home and did some work. Oh, and I started calling around to see how to get the fixture repaired."

"What a pain. And I don't just mean the fixture," Robin said.

"Aidan's the least of my worries right now." Emma's voice dropped. "I talked to my dad yesterday. I don't think he's doing so well."

"His diabetes?" Robin asked.

Emma nodded. "I grilled him about it, but I'm not sure he's taking his medicine. And I'm just worried that even if he does, the damage is already done because his eating and exercise habits didn't change at all. At the rate he's going, it looks like insulin is going to be in his future."

"I can't believe your dad was this forthcoming," Sara said. "He usually plays his illness down, doesn't he?"

"Oh, he did," Emma said. "I just got the information from another source."

"Who?"

"His neighbor." After her dad's call, she'd immediately dialed Suzi Richardson, a lovely fifty-year-old who lived next door with her husband, Merv. The Richardsons had been their neighbors ever since Emma could remember.

"Sneaky," Robin said.

"I know." It sucked that she had to resort to subterfuge to get the information she needed, but if her dad wasn't doing a good job of taking care of himself, she was going to figure out another plan.

"Send me his files, okay?" Sara said gently. "One of my friends is a diabetic specialist. I can have her take a look. See if there's anything else she can recommend for him."

Emma let out a grateful breath. "I'd appreciate that," she said. "I mean, there are doctors near him, but I've been trying for a while to get him to come up here so he can see a specialist. If mom were still alive, she'd have dragged him to every doctor in a hundred-mile radius already, but he's just being stubborn."

Emma's mom had died of breast cancer when Emma was in high school. The disease had been so advanced by the time they caught it that she'd lasted only seven months after the initial diagnosis. That time had been one of the darkest in her life—and she, her brother, and her father had clung to one another for support.

"Let me see what I can do, okay?" Sara said.

"Okay," Emma said gratefully.

"So," Sara said, sliding her short fingernail into a small groove in the wooden table. "I invited someone to have dinner with us."

Emma immediately sat up straight. "What? Who?"

"Johann."

"Wait, Johann? *The* Johann?" Emma asked.

"What do you mean by *the* Johann? There's more than one?" Robin asked.

"I mean the hotshot Swiss surgeon." Sara had mentioned him a couple of times, but only in the context of work.

"Ooooh." Robin was suitably impressed.

"This is the one you told me about who did the complicated spinal cord operation with the giant tumor, right?" she asked Sara, looking for confirmation. "The one everyone at your hospital worships?" Sara nodded in the affirmative, so Emma turned to Robin to explain. "Apparently, the man's a surgical god. And because surgeons are already at the top of the hospital hierarchy, that means that Johann is a god among gods."

"Kind of like the head god?" Robin supplied.

"Zeus," Emma agreed.

Sara merely rolled her eyes and took another sip of mojito.

"I thought surgeons only hung around other surgeons," Robin said. "That they're all kind of jerky."

Sara had informed them on numerous occasions that surgeons had reputations for being obnoxious and entitled, and thought themselves above the other doctors in almost every way.

"That's not…exactly true," Sara said, hedging.

"Sara?" Emma prompted. "Tell us."

"Well," she said, turning a little pink, "Johann isn't like that. Maybe it's because he's not originally from here, but he doesn't have the same attitudes. I don't know. Anyway, we met when we collaborated on a pretty tricky case involving an advanced brain tumor and a patient who was…you know what? The specifics don't matter," she said, waving her hand a little. "He was smart and polite and really very funny. So we'd work, and then have lunch together in the cafeteria sometimes, if we were still talking. I mean, you know me. I like to eat at my desk, but if I can kill two birds with one stone and get some work in, I will."

"We know," Emma said.

Sara gave her a look. "I thought our relationship was just professional, but earlier this week, he asked me if I was free for dinner tonight. Rather than tell him no or try to reschedule, I told him he could join us."

Emma blinked, hardly believing what she was hearing. "But he asked you out! And usually that's kind of a one-on-one thing."

"I couldn't cancel on you two. Besides," she said, "I'm sure he just wants to talk about the case. We're working on another tricky one together. But we're both so busy at work."

Emma and Robin gave each other significant looks, then turned their gazes back to Sara.

Outwardly, Sara seemed so confident. She was beautiful, with light brown hair cut in a long bob, wide-spaced blue eyes, and a killer figure. But her beauty was so much more than skin-deep. She was loyal and generous and brilliant, an incredible doctor, and an incredible friend. But despite her successes, she still thought of herself as that nerdy little girl with the thick, plastic glasses.

Sara was open with her and Robin—the product of years of acquaintance—but with new people, she wasn't as relaxed. In fact, she could be downright nervous, especially in social situations.

"Oh, *honey*," Emma breathed.

"You got this, sweetie," Robin said.

Sara looked at Emma and Robin with a tremulous gaze. "I…I haven't done this in so long," she confessed. "I don't know where to start."

"First," Emma said, taking the drink out of Sara's hand and placing it on the far side of the table, "you stop drinking alcohol on an empty stomach."

Robin plucked a fritter from the basket and held it out. "Eat."

Sara took the fried dough ball. "Fine." She took a bite, then cocked her head and really looked at the tasty nugget. "You know, this is actually pretty good."

"Told you!" Emma said, grinning.

"Ugh, don't say that," Robin groaned.

"Next," Emma said, "calm down. Take a deep breath. You can do this, I promise you."

"Just like that international studies class, remember?" Robin said.

Even though she'd majored in biology, Sara had taken several humanities courses, including one class that required an end-of-year oral report. Emma and Robin had coached her through everything, and after much stress and many tears, Sara had emerged triumphant in the end.

Sara nodded. "I remember. Hardest A-minus I ever earned."

"If you can tackle an analysis of capitalism in modern China, you can handle making small talk with one hotshot Swiss surgeon." Emma handed Sara another fritter and was rewarded when she ate that, too. "Now," Emma said, "tell us all about Johann."

Johann turned out to be a complete gentleman, not at all obnoxious or entitled. Though, by rights, he could be. He was obviously extremely well-educated and intelligent—this, Emma expected. What she hadn't expected was that he'd be totally charming, not to mention *very* handsome.

He was tall and long-limbed, with golden hair, dark blue eyes, and a strong nose. By his own admission, he was bookish, and in addition to volunteering his time and expertise to those who wouldn't otherwise be able to afford his pricey services, he trained for marathons. But by far, the most attractive thing about him was that he was so clearly into Sara.

Johann asked lots of questions deliberately designed to draw Sara out, and more than once when Sara was talking, Emma caught him staring at her friend.

Emma was pleased. Very pleased.

For the first time in a long while, she found herself happy. Over arroz con pollo and more cold beer, she talked and laughed with her friends.

Hours later, when the last crumb of coconut-lime cake had been consumed and the check was settled, Johann excused himself to go to the bathroom.

As soon as he was gone, Emma turned to Sara and raised one eyebrow. "Told you," she said.

"Was it easier than international studies?" Robin teased.

"Only because you two were here to help. So do you guys like him?" Sara asked, looking genuinely hopeful.

"Sweetie, I *love* him," Robin said. "Especially for you."

Emma nodded emphatically. "He's lovely, Sara. Really."

"There's nothing wrong with him," Robin said. "Like *nothing*."

"I wasn't sure at first, but I think so, too," she said quietly. "Thanks again for letting him crash our girls' night out."

"No thanks necessary. I had a lot of fun."

"Me too," Robin said.

"Maybe we could do it again another time?"

Emma slowly shook her head. "If there is a next time, I think we're going to bow out."

"No!"

"Yes," she said gently.

"I told you before that you got this, and you totally do," Robin said. "He's so clearly into you."

Emma nodded. "What we're saying is that you need to go out with him on your own."

"I don't know, guys. I—" Suddenly, Sara's eyes went wide and she gripped Emma's forearm. "Ohmigod."

"Oh, come on," Emma said. "You can do it. You were laughing and talking and, dare I say it, even *flirting* a little."

"No, not that," Sara whispered. "Behind you."

Emma craned her neck to follow Sara's gaze. The restaurant was tiny, so it wasn't difficult to spot what her friend was staring at.

Aidan, standing at the entrance of the restaurant, Connor by his side. As always, Connor looked immense, but it was Aidan who sucked all the air from the room.

He wore a blue plaid shirt rolled up his forearms and slightly darker blue jeans fastened with a thick leather belt, and he'd trimmed his beard enough to emphasize his strong cheekbones.

Damn, the man looked way too good.

She knew the instant he saw her. Through the dim light, his eyes met hers. Flared in recognition. Flickered with heat. Or was that last bit her imagination?

He said something under his breath to Connor and then he was coming toward them, stopping right in front of their table before she could even think to rise.

"Emma," he said, eyes never leaving her face.

"Hi," she said back.

"I missed you at Wolfshead today."

She doubted that very much, but she offered up a brief smile all the same. "Sorry. I had work to do."

"Did you get it done?"

"I did," she said.

"When are you going to be back?"

"I'm not sure," she demurred. She needed more information to prepare her branding proposal, but she wasn't keen on stepping into the ring with Aidan every time she showed up.

"Soon, yeah?" he said with a slight smile.

"Okay," she found herself agreeing. "Soon."

He was gazing at her intently, and all at once, she was conscious that there were two additional pairs of eyes on them—her friends watching them with what seemed like fascinated horror.

She cleared her throat. "Aidan, you remember Sara and Robin, don't you?"

Aidan slid his eyes sideways to her friends. "Hey," he said. "Long time no see."

Sara muttered something that sounded suspiciously like *not long enough* under her breath, then forced a smile. "Hi, Aidan." Nope. No love lost between these two.

"Hi," Robin said, in a slightly less hostile manner. "It's been a while."

"Have you met my cousin Connor?" Aidan asked.

"Once," Sara said, looking up at him in a squint. "He's kind of hard to forget."

Connor gave her and Robin a brief nod.

"Sorry you caught us at the tail end of our dinner," Sara said, sounding not sorry in the slightest. "We were just about to leave."

His gaze swung back to her again. "Were you?"

"Yes," Robin supplied. "You can have our table if you want."

"What I want," he said slowly, "is—"

At that moment, Johann chose to return. When it was clear that Johann belonged to their party, Aidan's gaze darkened, for what reason Emma couldn't be sure. It wasn't as if Johann posed any physical threat. Granted, he was almost as tall as Aidan, but he didn't have the same musculature, making him look slight compared to Aidan and downright small compared to Connor, who still stood there, silent. But the look on Johann's face was one of determination.

Seemingly unfazed by Aidan's glower, he held out his hand for a shake. "Hello," he said cordially in his crisp, clear voice. "I'm Johann Wyss."

The tension was unbelievable as Aidan glared and Johann simply stood there, his politeness unwavering.

Aidan finally extended his own hand. "Aidan Phelan." He nodded to his left. "This is my cousin Connor."

The giant man gave Johann a chin lift.

"It was nice meeting you," Johann said before turning back to the three of them. "Shall we move on to the next part of our evening?"

All three of them rose.

"Emma, wait," Aidan said.

Sara gave her a look. One that said *no way in hell am I leaving you alone with him.* Johann must have picked up on Sara's unease, since he inclined his head. "We're happy to wait."

Aidan stared at Johann and went still, a strange expression on his face.

"It's okay," she told her friends, wanting to defuse the situation as quickly as possible. "I'll be out in a minute."

With what seemed like great reluctance, Robin and Sara went outside, followed by Johann. As soon as Johann was gone, Aidan immediately relaxed, thank God.

Never taking his eyes off her, Aidan half turned to Connor. "Give me a minute?" he asked the big man, who simply nodded and went to the bar.

Then they were alone, standing way too close together in the crowded restaurant.

"Are you okay?" he asked.

"Fine. Why wouldn't I be?"

"You look at little…" Aidan pressed his lips together and gave a shrug.

"I'm okay. Just tired. Work and house stuff." *And you.*

Aidan cocked his head. "What house stuff?"

"Oh," she said, "my office light fixture blew. I just haven't had the chance to deal with it yet and…" She stopped talking, not really sure why she was explaining it to him. "Anyway, Connor's waiting for you and I'd better go catch up with my friends."

"You'd better go then."

Then he did something shocking. Instead of walking away, nodding and saying good-bye, he wrapped a big hand around her waist, leaned in, and brushed his lips against her cheek as if they were old friends.

Or old lovers.

"Enjoy the rest of your night, Emma," he murmured.

Instantly, her body reacted, nipples hardening, sex clenching.

So that was all it took for her these days? Primed only by a touch. If it had been any other man, she would have kissed him back, invited him home.

But this wasn't any other man. This was Aidan, her ex-husband, and God, she was pathetic.

It had been stupid of her to think she'd been done with him. The reality was she hadn't ever let him go.

After a long, tense moment, her self-preservation mechanism finally kicked in.

She pushed him away, grabbed her bag, and without even bothering to say good-bye, practically fled.

She burst out the door into the cool, damp night and took several deep, cleansing breaths.

Sara and Johann were on the street talking quietly near the corner, their heads close. They looked good together—him, tall and angular, her, small and lithe. At least *something* good had come of this night.

"You okay?" Sara asked the moment she spied her, concern in her voice.

Emma nodded. "Yes." No way was she going to spoil her friend's evening. "Totally."

Sara seemed to accept her answer. "Robin went home, but we were planning to head across the street to Migration Brewing for a beer. Won't you join us?"

"I've had a long day," she said. "I think I'll call it a night."

"Please come, Emma." Sara's eyes were pleading.

Emma reached out and gave her friend's hand a squeeze. *You have this.* "I have a lot of work to get through this weekend. Big client meeting on Monday, but please go and enjoy yourselves."

"May we walk you to your car?" Johann asked.

"That'd be great," she said. "I'm just around the corner."

It didn't take long for them to get to her vehicle, and as Emma watched Sara walk off with Johann, she found herself envying her friend.

Sara and Johann had no baggage between them, no insurmountable wall. Nothing but the unencumbered future to worry about.

While she still struggled to shut down her feelings for a man she'd never stopped loving.

CHAPTER 8

Emma took a deep breath, making sure to look every single executive team member directly in the eyes as she finished her presentation.

"…so the new color scheme, coupled with tailored and modern prompts, alongside the other specific branding and marketing suggestions that I've detailed, would be my recommendations for your new campaign. I think this would be a way to distinguish Younger Beverages from other companies in the space and would gain you some serious traction as you planned the international launch for your electrolytes line."

Emma closed her folder, signifying she'd reached the end, and offered up a smile to the group. "Do you have any questions for me, about my previous work, or about any of my recommendations? I'm happy to give you a few minutes to talk, if you need it."

Several of the seven men and women in attendance began to speak among themselves, so Emma took the opportunity to slow her rapidly beating heart.

Younger Beverages, a locally based company, was her first pitch outside her existing client base since she'd started freelancing.

The company's story was fascinating. Its founder, Burt Younger, was an endurance runner and had started out preparing special electrolyte-laden drinks for himself to drink during his competitions. After he started winning, he began making bigger and bigger batches, which he'd sell to friends and family. He'd made the leap to commercial only five years ago, but the company was doing gangbusters, in large part to the rise of extreme sports and ultraathletes over the same period of time. Now they had national distribution and were thinking of going international in the near future.

Younger was playing in a completely different league from her other clients and had the finances to match. She knew for a fact they could afford to pay her quadruple what she was currently getting, which would make a huge difference for her bottom line. If she got this account and did a good job for them, it would raise her profile considerably, too, garnering her even *more* big-name accounts.

Emma had been prepping for weeks for this opportunity, and she'd done a ton of research on the company and the space, drawing up a game plan on how best to set Younger apart from others in the same arena.

She wasn't sure yet whether she'd nailed the presentation, but there'd been lots of nodding and murmurs of agreement throughout her spiel.

Then the executives began with their questions. One lobbed a softball at her, which she answered with ease. A few others had some more detailed questions about timing and focus, which she also felt she handled well.

"I don't have any more questions at this time, Ms. Crandall," said the lead executive, a well-built man with dark brown hair named Enzo Voglia. "But it truly was an excellent presentation. You have a clear grasp of Younger Beverages and the image we're trying to create, especially your proposed slogan: Push Harder. That's exactly what we want our consumers to do when they compete, and why they'd choose Younger products."

"Thank you," she said, trying not to get too pleased. This was only round one, after all.

"Then again," he continued, "I'm not surprised you really know your stuff, given that you came highly recommended by Mike Sutherland."

Mike was the owner of a company that had invested in several high-end restaurants in and around Portland. He—or rather one of his restaurants going through a branding crisis—had been one of her first clients at Stroud & Thistle. Over the years, they'd built up a rapport, and she was now his go-to branding expert. When she'd left her company, he hadn't wanted to lose her expertise, and ended up hiring her freelance.

"Mike's great. I've been working with him for a while now, and always enjoy the projects he brings me. By the way, how do you know him?"

"He's a friend of the founder's."

"Ah," Emma murmured, making a mental note to call Mike ASAP to let him know how the presentation went.

Before she knew it, they were all shaking hands and saying good-bye.

"We'll call you soon," Enzo promised, and she believed him.

With a smile on her face, she practically skipped out of the downtown office building onto the brick sidewalk. She was still antsy, a bit jittery, in that zone she got into when she had to keep a laser focus for too long.

What time was it? Only eleven? Too early for lunch. Feeling restless and filled with nervous energy, she called Sara. Unfortunately, it went straight to voicemail, so she left a message.

Next she called Mike Sutherland, and had to leave a message with him, too.

"Mike, hi," she said. "It's Emma Crandall. I want to thank you again for referring me to Younger Beverages. I had a meeting with them this morning and…well, please give me a call and I'll tell you how it went. Maybe we could meet for coffee? My treat."

She clicked the phone off and shoved it back in her bag. Now what?

She was on top of the world. She could do anything, conquer anything, and damn it, no one was around to share in her exhilaration!

She could go to Wolfshead.

Now, with the adrenaline riding high, would be the perfect time to show the Phelans that she couldn't scare. Aidan couldn't get rid of her that easily. She should go there, stake her claim like a boss, figure out exactly what was going to work to get that new whiskey branded.

Then her phone rang.

Quickly, she reached into her bag and picked it up.

"Emma, hi," a pleasing baritone voice intoned. "It's Mike Sutherland."

"You got my message."

He chuckled. "Yes, I was just in a meeting, but it's over now.

You still up for coffee?"

"Definitely. I'm downtown."

"Same. Case Study Coffee Roasters?" A local favorite.

"I'll meet you there."

Fifteen minutes later, Emma was perched on a wooden stool at Case Study. Several tattooed baristas busied themselves behind the wood-paneled counter. Their movements were elegant, scripted, like dancers in a ballet, as they prepared the drinks.

Like many small-batch roasters and brewers in Portland, the staff at Case Study really knew their stuff. One of the baristas was educating an interested customer on the difference between single-origin and multiple-origin beans, while another was carefully brewing what would undoubtedly be a perfect shot of espresso.

Although her bourbon caramel latte looked like a work of art with its cloud of white milk foam and its light brown drizzle, Emma took a sip anyway. It was completely addictive, with a nutty, burnt-sugar, faintly alcoholic flavor. Though the adrenaline from her successful meeting was waning, it was rapidly being replaced by the sweet, sweet caffeine, which was going straight to her brain.

"Good?" Mike asked, smiling as he sat down on the stool next to hers.

"Delicious," she said, smiling back. "How's yours?"

Mike took a sip of his cold-brew coffee and nodded in satisfaction. "Excellent, but it always is. Thanks for buying."

Michael Sutherland was a tall, good-looking man in his early forties with dark hair, only slightly graying at the temples, and warm brown eyes. Today, he had on jeans and a collared shirt, over which he'd thrown a blazer. He dressed a little more corporate than many in the city, but then again, so did she. Emma had long thought of him as attractive in a polished way.

"It's a small way for me to thank you for the referral," she told him sincerely. "I'm not a big operation like Stroud & Thistle, and currently, I'm not doing any advertising for my new business. The way new clients will find me is through word of mouth, and I truly appreciate your support as I get ECMB off the ground."

"As I told you before," Mike said, "I was glad to recommend you for the Younger account. You'd be perfect for the job, and I think you could quickly get up to speed on what they need." He gave her a wry smile. "Of course, if you get the gig, you might not have time for my work."

"I'll always have time to help you, Mike," she said.

He took a sip of coffee. "I hope so. Because you're the best." She blushed at his praise. "I'm serious. I credit you with Harvest's turnaround. They were floundering. Lost. And then you came in and completely revamped the plan."

Harvest had been one of her first solo accounts at Stroud & Thistle. The restaurant had been around for a couple of years. It was doing fine, but when the place changed hands, things started to go downhill. The way it was originally branded didn't make sense in the current market, and the new owners and the old staff didn't see eye to eye. She'd pointed out the differences in what the restaurant actually was and what it hoped to be, then did a complete overhaul of their branding to reflect their new direction. This had directly led to an 80 percent increase in profits over the next two years. She'd been proud of her work, and it had earned her praise and a promotion.

"There's something I've been meaning to ask you," he said.

"Another restaurant project?" She smiled. "You know I'm in."

Mike leaned a little closer. "I was actually thinking of dinner."

"To kick-start the discussions? Sure."

"No, Emma," he said gently, taking her hand in his. "For us. To get to know each other on a more personal level."

"Oh." *Oh.*

He was asking her out. And as she looked at him, *really* looked at him, she realized how easy it would be to fall for someone like him. He was handsome, successful, and completely appreciative of her work. They'd complement each other well. But there was one small problem.

He wasn't Aidan.

"Mike—" she started.

He withdrew his hand. "Let me guess," he said, his voice resigned. "You don't mix business with pleasure."

About a year ago, she'd mentioned in passing that she was recently divorced. Mike had clearly waited until he thought she was ready to date again, which elicited both respect and regret.

"I try not to," she told him gently. "But the real truth is that

I'm not ready."

As if that desperate wanting for her ex-husband wasn't evidence enough that she still had some issues to work through.

Mike looked surprised, then nodded in understanding. "I see. I only brought it up because…" He paused. Shook his head. "It doesn't matter. I only hope this doesn't change anything between us. You're extremely good at what you do, and I'd hate to lose your expertise because you felt uncomfortable around me."

"I don't. I won't," she promised. "You've been nothing but a gentleman, in every way."

"I won't lie," Mike said. "I think we'd be good together, but I'm willing to wait. And when you're ready, you know where I'll be." He glanced at his watch. "Look, I've got another meeting in twenty minutes, so I'd better be going. Thanks again for the coffee."

"Thanks again for the referral."

"It was well-deserved. Good-bye, Emma. Have a productive day, and I'll be in touch soon to talk about a new project I have coming up for you."

After Mike left, Emma sat there for a while, thinking. His admission had definitely come as a surprise. He must have had those feelings for a while, and he'd hidden it well. She'd never even gotten an inkling that he'd been interested. He'd been nothing but professional, and she knew he'd remain that way, no matter what.

The more she thought about it, the more she realized that she could use Mike as a model for her own situation. If Mike could separate out his emotions from his work, she could, too. Especially with respect to Wolfshead and Aidan.

Simply because she felt uncomfortable around Aidan was no reason not to go to the company and make sure she was keeping tabs on her new investment. Starting now, she would sort out her head, act like a professional, and keep her work life and her personal life separate, just as she should have all along.

She'd gotten something else from her meeting with Mike, too—namely a reminder of what she was dealing with in Wolfshead. There were many parallels to be found between Harvest and Wolfshead. Like the restaurant, Wolfshead had just transferred to new ownership and now seemed to be suffering from an identity crisis with no clear brand or marketing plan. Emma pulled out her laptop.

Then, coffee in hand and computer fired up, Emma got to work.

CHAPTER 9

Emma spent most of Saturday at a coffee shop near her house, working on pitches and proposals and smartening up her website. Just after 6:00 p.m., over-caffeinated and practically brain-dead, a very weird combination, she finally dragged herself out to head home and make dinner. Good thing she left when she had, since it was obvious from the dark gray sky and the increased wind that there was a big storm on the horizon.

A tree branch skittered past her on the sidewalk, narrowly missing her ankle, and the wind whipped her hair. Emma picked up her pace.

Aside from the Younger account—which she was by no means guaranteed to win—her business wasn't going as well as she hoped. She still had no actual new clients, though she had a handful of meetings lined up over the next few weeks.

Truth was, although she wasn't desperate for it in the short term, in the long term she needed to earn a living. She'd set aside a decent amount to live on while she got her new freelancing business off the ground, but her savings wouldn't last forever. She still had bills to pay, a mortgage, a car…and she needed to eat. Portland was no Seattle or San Francisco, but it was still expensive.

And it was all on her to make it. Emma was way too old and independent, not to mention proud, to ask her dad or brother for help.

If she was going to make a go of this new business, it was going to be on her to make it happen. It was good for her, this independence, and she thought she'd done a pretty decent job of it since her divorce.

The last time she'd been completely solo was the first few months of college before she met Aidan. Since then, except for the three years he'd been on the road playing baseball when they'd dated long-distance, they'd been together.

When she'd graduated, they were still dating seriously. Because she'd assumed that they'd end up in New York due to his career, that's where she'd done her interviewing for post-college jobs. To her surprise, she'd received an offer at one of the fanciest PR firms in Manhattan. They'd said they specifically wanted her for her West Coast aesthetic. She'd already accepted the job when she found out that Aidan was coming back to Portland.

Even then, she thought she still might go to New York. It was a huge dilemma, but compared to the tragedy playing out in Aidan's family, it seemed less important. So she'd agonized solo for weeks over the offer before she finally had the guts to tell Aidan about the choice she'd have to make.

His answer was swift: *marry me*.

She'd loved him, so she had said yes. Trading a high-powered career for love seemed fair. After all, hadn't Aidan made a similar choice when he'd chosen Wolfshead over baseball? Except things at Wolfshead turned out to be harder than either of them thought.

Then Aidan began to shut down, and she realized she'd traded one type of loneliness for another.

She made it home just as the wind was reaching gale proportions. Her cheerful yellow house beckoned her in from the cold. The heaviness around her heart lifted a bit. At least she still had enough to pay her mortgage…for now, anyway.

Emma dragged herself inside, flicked the light switch and got…nothing.

Crap.

She flicked it again, hoping that it was just a fluke, but nope. No power at all. She crossed to the parlor and flicked another light switch. Nothing again.

Either the wind had knocked it out—not an unusual occurrence—or the electrical short she had in her office had affected the rest of her wiring. Damn. She shouldn't have waited this long to get the fixture repaired, but there was no one to call at this hour.

So she'd order takeout and deal with it in the morning, probably paying double the rates for a Sunday call. The price of doing things on her own.

With a sigh, she went to the front closet, where she kept a couple of spare flashlights, just for emergencies such as this.

She grabbed one and turned it on. There. Much better. Now she could see the dimly lit hallway, the small table, and the antique mirror that further reflected the narrow beam of light, casting shadows on the wall in all the wrong places.

She placed her purse on the hallway table, kicked off her heels, and scooped up the mail. Her path illuminated by the flashlight, she slowly made her way down the hallway to the back of the house.

Just as she reached the end, the door that led to the back staircase opened and a beam of light emerged.

Someone was in her house!

Before she could think about what to do, the figure moved forward. She cocked her arm back, waiting for whomever it was to emerge so she could hit him on the head.

And ready…set…

All at once, the lights came on, temporarily blinding her.

Emma blinked once, then twice, trying to make her eyes adjust, and when they did, she found herself looking up into a familiar face.

"Aidan! Wh—what are you doing here?" she sputtered, and focused her eyes on his form.

In one big hand he held a flashlight and a power screwdriver. He was wearing a black T-shirt, dark gray jeans, and a murderous expression.

"Jesus, Emma, give me that!" With embarrassing ease, he plucked the flashlight from her raised arm and flicked it off. "You almost nailed me!"

"You're skulking around my house in the dark and I thought you were a burglar! That looks like a gun!" She lifted her chin at his power tool.

"So you come after me with a flashlight?" he asked, his jaw clenched behind his beard. "Do you have a death wish?"

"It was the only thing I had on hand!" she retorted. "And I'm not apologizing for trying to defend myself."

"Woman," he growled. "The only thing you do in a situation like that is run like hell."

Caffeine and adrenaline still coursing through her, she pointed a finger at him. "You don't get to lecture me when you broke into my house. And you still didn't answer my question. What are you doing here?"

"Replacing your damned office fixture," he said.

That was…nice of him. Very nice. But then Emma shook her head. No. He'd busted into her place, scared her half to death, and put her on the defensive.

"I appreciate the work, but I could have handled it."

"But you didn't."

"But I could have."

"You're crap at electrical stuff, Emma. You always were."

She frowned at him. "I don't need your help."

"Yeah, you do."

"No, I don't," she ground out. He wasn't budging, and arguing with him was an exercise in futility. "Ugh, just forget it. How did you get in, anyway?"

"Babe." He gave her an even look. "You still keep your spare key under that fucking flowerpot."

She simply gaped at him. "Seriously?"

"I told you not to do that. It's dangerous. That's the first place any criminal's gonna look."

"God, Aidan. We're divorced! You can't just come in here like this and fix things up for me."

"I just did," he informed her.

Emma pushed her hair off her face, and let out a sharp breath. This conversation was going nowhere, fast. "You didn't come over here just to fix my light. So why don't you tell me why you're really here?"

"To talk," he said tightly.

Finally, the truth. "And this couldn't wait until I'm back at Wolfshead on Monday?"

"No." He removed the bit from the electric screwdriver and bent down to place it in his toolbox—a large metal affair that had been hidden by a hall table and the dark. Then he rose and crossed his arms over his chest again, waiting for her next move.

And there he was. Stubborn as ever. He wouldn't leave until

he got what he wanted, so she may as well get comfortable.

"I'm hungry. Are you hungry?"

He gave a nod.

"Well, come on, then," she said.

She hated fighting on an empty stomach.

It was strange, having Aidan in her kitchen once again. Even stranger to have him watching her while she moved around the small space. When had they last done this? She couldn't recall.

For a good chunk of their marriage, he'd always been working, never around to share the simple things with her. Go grocery shopping. Prepare a meal. Most nights she'd eaten alone in their empty place, wondering when he was going to come home.

First things first. "Would you like some wine?" she asked as she grabbed a cutting board and gathered up a few ingredients. She sure as heck needed some.

"I'll take a beer if you have one."

"In the fridge in the garage," she said.

While he went to find his beer, she poured herself a glass of pinot from an already-open bottle. After fortifying herself with a couple of nice, long sips, she pulled two defrosted chicken breasts from her fridge, thought for a moment, then pulled a third one out, just in case. The man could eat.

Despite the new research saying you shouldn't rinse your chicken because of the bacteria getting all over the place—or something equally awful—she did it anyway and patted the breasts dry with a paper towel.

From behind her, Aidan cleared his throat. "Can I help?"

"Sure," she said. "If you wash your hands you can make the salad."

He nodded and came over to the sink, his broad shoulders nearly touching hers as he laved his hands with soap.

"Here," she said, handing him a head of romaine.

He regarded the vegetable in his hand. "Do you remember that cabbage?" he said, a crooked smile forming on his face.

"Ugh, yes. I swear I haven't eaten it since."

"I don't blame you."

For Saint Patrick's Day one year, they had slow-roasted a

giant slab of corned beef. It was such an American tradition, not an Irish one, as Aidan had pointed out myriad times, but that didn't stop him or the rest of his family from indulging in the excesses of the holiday anyway.

She'd spent hours on that damned meat, and had served it along with boiled cabbage and homemade Irish soda bread. The cabbage had stunk up the whole house—a little cottage they'd rented in the Pearl District—and for months after the holiday she caught whiffs of that stinky cabbage in all the secret recesses of the place. It was the first and last time she'd ever eaten it.

She took another sip of wine and started in on the ginger-soy marinade for the chicken. Meanwhile, Aidan had cut off the base of the head of lettuce, then rinsed the sandy dirt away before giving the leaves a rough chop.

Aidan was large, but he'd always had a surprising elegance about him—he didn't lumber around, but moved gracefully, smoothly. Then again, he'd always been an athlete, and at one time, an elite one. His body was a tool for success, and he'd been paid to keep it in first-class shape.

He lifted up an arm to wipe his forehead with the back of his hand, and his shirt rode up, exposing a sliver of taut stomach. *Damn.*

Aidan glanced over at her, eyes questioning. Rather than admit than she'd been staring, she nodded approvingly as if she'd been only focused on his food prep, and went back to measuring out a portion of soy sauce. She doled out some olive oil to mix into the soy, then tossed in some salt and a healthy teaspoon of ground ginger.

Without prompting, Aidan had moved on to the cherry tomatoes, expertly cutting the tiny tomatoes in half, her paring knife looking downright small in his hands. In the early days of their relationship they'd actually talked. Shared their days. Made dinner together.

One evening they'd roasted a chicken, redolent with thyme and rosemary. They'd barely waited for it to cool before picking it apart in its roasting pan and eating the whole thing. He'd licked the succulent juices from her fingers, and they'd ended up making love on the kitchen floor.

About a year and a half into their marriage, she'd just quit making food for the two of them. He was never around to eat it anyway, and cooking for one seemed, well, kind of sad. So she'd started ordering takeout. Or getting those prepared meals at the supermarket that you just reheated. And she'd sit in their lonely little cottage, alone at the kitchen table, waiting—hoping—that he'd come home.

He rarely did.

The memories were coming fast and thick now, along with a huge wave of melancholy. Or maybe it was the wine on her empty stomach. Without realizing, she'd already drained her first glass.

She needed to stop thinking about this. And maybe drink more wine. She poured herself another glass and snared a garlic bulb.

"Can I share?" she asked, indicating the chopping board with her head.

"Sure." He moved over a bit, but it was still a tight fit. When she smashed the garlic clove with the flat of a knife, her forearm brushed his. Ignoring the lick of heat that coursed through her, she peeled the papery skin from the pungent clove and crushed it, then dumped that into the marinade, too.

She dipped her pinkie in to give it a quick taste. It was missing something, but she couldn't quite put her finger on what, exactly.

She shrugged and was about to give up when Aidan leaned closer, a finger hovering over the mixing bowl. "Can I taste?"

"Absolutely."

He dipped his finger into the sauce and licked it off. "A tablespoon of honey should do it."

"You think?" Aidan enjoyed food and was rarely wrong about flavor.

"Yeah."

"Okay." She rummaged around in her cabinet until she found what she was looking for and spooned some honey in, giving the marinade a good stir. "Now?"

Aidan tasted it again. "Good."

She did too. "You're right. It's better." She gave the marinade one last stir, then poured it over the chicken in the glass baking dish, making sure to coat everything evenly so that there'd be a taste of it in every bite. Then she shoved the baking dish into the oven and slammed the door.

"So what'd you want to talk about?" she asked.

Aidan cleared his throat. "I figured we'd start with you."

She gave him a sharp look to see if he was joking. "Me?" Not what she'd thought would be his topic of choice.

"Yeah, you," he said, not looking up. "With all the shit about Paddy's will and the company, I didn't even get to ask. How've you been?"

Making small talk with Aidan was…awkward. Then again, every interaction with him these days seemed to be, so she just went with it. "Okay, I guess."

"Why'd you leave your company?" He'd found a forgotten carrot in the crisper drawer and was now shredding it into tiny slivers, which fell in an orange curtain into the salad bowl.

She took a sip of wine. "It's complicated."

Aidan finished shredding the carrot and moved on to a cucumber. "I'm not going anywhere."

Emma considered this. He actually seemed interested, so why not tell him? "I liked Stroud & Thistle."

He gave her a look. "Really?" When they'd been together, she'd complained—more than once—about the company. There were weeks, especially in the beginning, when she'd have to drag herself to work. But as she got more senior, things had gotten better.

"Really. I did. We all have our good days and bad days, but I think overall, my time there was really positive. The people were great and the work was interesting."

"I'm guessing that because you left there's a *but*?"

She nodded. "But for the last year or so, I felt a bit limited. Like I was being held back from being my most creative self. It wasn't one thing in particular, no one project I can point to that was the tipping point. The dissatisfaction just kind of crept up on me." Kind of like the trajectory of their marriage. "Anyway, I thought if I went out on my own, I'd get to not only choose my own work—at least once I got established—but I'd have complete autonomy as to the way I ran projects." She gave him a small smile. "What I'm trying to say is that I thought it'd be fun."

"You were always good at what you did," Aidan said simply.

"Yes, well," she said, his nearness disconcerting, "things aren't going as well as I hoped. At least, not yet. Only a couple of clients have signed on to work with me so far. If business doesn't pick up soon…" She trailed off and shook her head.

"You'll be fine," he said, continuing to cut the cucumber into paper-thin slices.

"How can you be so sure?"

"You're not starting from scratch, you know what the hell you're doing, and you already have a couple of clients lined up. You're doing great."

"Right. Just FYI, one of my two clients is a toilet-bowl maker."

"I'm sure you have some brilliant marketing ideas," he said with a smile.

"Yeah. New tagline: Let It Flow."

Aidan let out a short bark of laughter. "See? You're on top of your game."

"I don't know about that," she said.

"I do," he said, sounding decisive. "You're a fighter. You always were. So you're going to keep fighting until your business succeeds."

"I like your optimism."

"I'm just stating fact. You're doing great."

"Now *that* is a matter of opinion."

He paused "You got a new job?"

"Yes."

"New house?"

"That too."

He nodded. "You're doing great." He finished slicing the cucumber, then wiped his hands.

"You didn't ask me about a new man," she said.

He snared his beer from the counter and took a long pull. "I didn't need to."

Baiting him wasn't wise, but she couldn't help herself. "I could have one, you know."

"But you don't."

"And how do you know that? Maybe it's Johann."

"The suit?" He laughed. "Nope."

Emma frowned. "Excuse me?"

"He's not your new man."

"And how do you know that?" she asked crossly.

"A new man would have kept you close. He wouldn't have walked away from you. And he wouldn't have let you out of his sight for a second, especially not around a man like me."

"Oh." She guessed he was right. Johann never would have left Sara alone.

But Aidan wasn't done. "Then there's the light."

Emma frowned. "How can *that* tell you whether or not I have a new man?"

"Easy. A new man would have been here already. He would have scoped out the place, kept it safe for you. He wouldn't have let you walk around in the dark even for a day. A new man would have been waiting for you at home. So," he concluded, "no new man." He paused for a moment, cocked his head at her. "The only question is why."

"Why what?"

"Why no new man?" Under his scrutiny, she felt herself warm. "A woman like you should have moved on by now. Found another man. Started having kids."

Now that hurt.

"Why haven't *you* started having kids?" she retorted.

They'd had the kid discussion numerous times. She'd always wanted them, lots of them, and sooner rather than later, but he'd wanted to wait—until he got over his father's death, until things at Wolfshead were settled, until, until, until.

Until she realized that maybe he really didn't want them at all.

It hadn't been the primary reason she'd divorced him, but it had definitely been a factor, mostly because the issue epitomized their entire relationship. She asked. He simply ignored. Their conversations were growing increasingly one-sided, and not just about the kids. About everything. And it hurt like crazy.

Aidan's gaze sharpened. "Having kids is serious business."

"So you've told me," she said, and took another sip of wine.

But he wouldn't let up. "You didn't answer the question. Why no man, Emma? Why no kids?"

He was picking at old wounds tonight, and damned if she knew why.

If she had thought that a new man could alleviate the ache inside, she would have jumped into dating with two feet. But just as she had with Mike, she'd turned down every advance she got. It wasn't that she didn't want to be with someone. It's that the only person she'd ever dated was Aidan, but she wasn't going to admit that to him.

"No time," she finally said.

It was a blatant lie, and she knew he knew it, because he was watching her a little too closely, the atmosphere charged.

To alleviate some of the tension, she flicked on the oven light and peered in. "I hope the chicken comes out all right."

He didn't relax, but at least he went along with her change of subject. "It's going to be good," he said. "You were always a good cook. I wasn't around a lot, but that doesn't mean I didn't appreciate it when you made dinner. You enjoyed doing it. I felt bad when you stopped."

Emma blinked. "I never knew you noticed."

"I noticed everything, Emma. Except I was too wrapped up in my own shit to do anything about it."

She wanted to ask what else he'd noticed, but that just seemed silly. Their marriage was over—it had been for a long time—and playing woulda-coulda-shoulda definitely wouldn't repair the damage. Wouldn't even make a dent in it, actually.

An uncomfortable silence filled the kitchen. Finally, Aidan cleared his throat. "The chicken'll take a while, so I'm going to clean up in your office, get the rest of my tools, and put the old light fixture in the garage so you can recycle it. Let me know when dinner's ready."

Emma managed a nod as he disappeared out the kitchen door.

The wind had finally brought rain, and it was pleasant to sit around her small kitchen table, talking and eating salad and chicken, which turned out to be delicious. With some more alcohol in them, conversation seemed to flow a bit more freely. They talked about work, family, even music. Emma had always had a thing for indie rock, and since Finn played electric bass for a local band, Aidan was pretty knowledgeable about the scene.

For a while, she caught the glimmer of the old Aidan—the young Aidan who stayed up all night listening to her vinyl collection, who made her laugh with a well-timed reference. She could almost forget that so much time had passed. That they hadn't been separated for so long.

"Finn's playing is getting really good. They're even talking about recording a demo," Aidan said with pride. They fought like animals, especially if they disagreed with each other, but Aidan was incredibly supportive and proud of his younger siblings and cousins.

"Is he still with Meyerston?"

Aidan shook his head. "He and the drummer moved on. They're with another band now, and I actually think they're better. They kind of have a Decemberists feel," he said, referencing another local indie rock fave. "You'd like them."

"I probably would," she admitted. She loved the Decemberists and had caught several of their shows over the last few years. None lately, though.

"He's playing at Rontoms in a couple weeks. It's a fun venue. Decent vibe, especially on Sunday nights. You should come."

"Maybe I will."

They were staring into each other's eyes—not wise at all. When Aidan's gaze warmed, when that look became too intense, Emma slid her seat back and stood.

"Are you through?" she asked, reaching for his plate.

"Yeah. It was great," he said, the spell broken. "I've been eating takeout for so long, I almost forgot what it's like to have a home-cooked meal." He reached for her plate. "Let me get this. You sit down."

"Okay." She sat, admiring the way he moved around her kitchen as he cleaned up, a trick he'd certainly never done before.

This was good. This was okay. If things had been like this before…well, she didn't want to go there. But the fact that things were like this now, she could live with this. Maybe this evening was the tipping point for the two of them, some kind of middle ground where they could coexist peacefully after so long at each other's throats.

"Thanks again for replacing my fixture," she said. "I'll actually be able to work tomorrow, which is good because I have a project due next Thursday."

He closed the dishwasher and lifted his chin in the direction of the dripping faucet. "I'll come back to take care of that next."

One drop. Two drops. Three, in a steady pattern. "You don't have to."

"Emma?" She turned to him. Met his gaze. "Yeah. I do."

She just shook her head. "Okay. I'll pay you with dinner."

His expression softened. "I remember that about you. How you want everything to be fair."

"I just think that people should be rewarded for their work. That they should get back what they put in."

He dropped into the chair right next to her, his gaze intense. "Why'd you stop fighting for us?"

She stilled, unprepared for his question. This was the first time they'd spoken about it. The first time he'd even acknowledged that there might have been a reason for her leaving him.

Unable to look at him, she rose and went to the sink. The soft drips echoed hollowly in the room.

It wasn't fair for him to tempt her like this, to show her the old Aidan. The one who cared. Who asked her about her day. Who wanted to do nothing more than talk to her and hold her. Who loved her with all his heart. The Aidan she'd loved before they'd gotten married and their relationship turned into an empty husk.

"I can't do this," she said.

Pretend everything is normal. Pretend I don't still want you.

"We're just talking, Emma."

She still couldn't look at him. No, they weren't just talking. If she wasn't careful, she was going to spill her soul.

She sensed his hands before they covered her shoulders, and when they did she hurt, so badly she could barely breathe. She closed her eyes against the onslaught of emotion—sadness, betrayal, all those wasted years she'd waited for him. Just him. To come home and hold her in his arms and tell her everything was going to be okay. That he loved her and he'd do anything it took to keep her in his life.

And in the silence of her kitchen, the sound of their breathing intermingling with the dripping of the faucet, she allowed herself to feel, after not feeling for so long. But it was too late. The past was in the past, exactly where it should stay. Because if she allowed it to come into the present, she was going to have her heart ripped out all over again.

She turned and he was right there, his big body so close to hers, crowding her, not giving her any space to think or to breathe.

With a finger, he urged her chin up so that he could look her in the eye. What she saw there was infinitely complicated. Sadness and regret and desire all wrapped up together—and then a glimpse of something more.

What could have been.

God, she missed him. Missed his eyes and his smile and his laugh and everything she'd clung to for so long that wasn't truly there anymore. She wanted to cry—for the lost time, for everything they'd thrown away.

"Thanks again for dinner," he said, giving her lips the briefest brush with his. "I'll see myself out."

He turned and left, but Emma stayed precisely where she was, listening to the thud of his boots on the wooden floor, the slam of the front door.

Then he was gone, thank God. Because if he'd stayed, she'd have done something very, very stupid.

Her skin was still tingling with awareness. She let out the breath she hadn't known she'd been holding. Slowed her too-rapidly beating heart. Went to drag herself to bed.

It was then she heard it. A knock on her front door, a soft rap that vibrated through her entire body.

Aidan.

The knock sounded again, echoing in the chambers of her heart.

Slowly, she walked down the hall, at once knowing what was going to happen but powerless to stop herself anyway. Her hand was on the knob, turning it, opening the door. Beyond the edge of the porch, wind whipped the crepe myrtle, and the rain fell in hard sheets, stinging the ground where it landed.

"I forgot my toolbox," he said.

Fate? Destiny? It didn't matter. He was here and he was hers. He'd always been hers.

And she was so very weak when it came to Aidan Phelan.

She took him by the hand, dragged him inside, and shut the door.

He turned to her in surprise, right before she pulled him down and pressed her lips against his.

CHAPTER 10

His mouth hot on hers, his beard scraping her face, and his hands, Lord, those hands, branding her skin wherever they touched.

Everything she'd been wanting so badly for the past two years.

"Emma," Aidan groaned, his breath feeding hers, and she wasn't sure if it was a moan or a plea. Probably both, because he was gripping her upper arms as if he was afraid that at any moment she'd bolt, pinning her in place while he took what he wanted, what she wanted to give him.

He pressed her back against the door, the hard wood barely grounding her as she gave in to the sensation of having Aidan's weight on her once again.

No, screamed her brain.

Oh yes, replied her body.

And then his lips moved over hers again, his tongue sliding in to stroke, and that internal war was completely forgotten as he took her mouth like he owned it, owned her. And in some way, he still did, even after all this time.

He'd asked her why there wasn't another man. The truth, the *real* truth, was that there hadn't been anyone else because she was still in love with him. That no one could measure up to him, despite all his flaws.

Aidan shifted, giving her more of his weight, and she pulled him closer still, wanting to feel him, touch him flesh to flesh. The contact she hadn't had in so long with anyone. Because when she'd left him, she'd left all of this behind, every ounce of physical pleasure wrapped up with Aidan.

Always Aidan.

He moved his mouth to her jaw, his facial hair sensitizing her skin. And when he nuzzled her neck and then bit in that secret spot that always drove her crazy, a shiver of unbridled want swept through her, pushing aside every emotion except desire. She shuddered in his arms, but he groaned and pulled away.

"I didn't come back for this," he said.

"I know." She cupped his face in her hands. "I want you anyway. Do you want me?"

"God, yes," he said.

She touched her forehead to his. "Then make me forget."

He let out a growl and then she was in his arms and he was carrying her to the back of the house.

Yes. He could say no to her in everything else, but not in this. Never in this.

Somehow, he knew exactly where to find her bedroom. He kicked open the door with his foot and practically dumped her on the bedspread. She tried to scramble up to her elbows, but he was already there, a big knee pressing into the bed, his large chest covering her as he pushed her back down and crushed his mouth to hers.

Tomorrow didn't matter. There was only tonight, with him.

She was going to regret this in the morning, she was sure of it, but as shivers coursed through her willing body, she couldn't find it in herself to care.

Even more so when he skimmed his hand down her chest and covered a breast with a huge palm. Her nipple hardened instantly.

"Aidan—" she said on a moan.

"You still light up for me like you used to," he said, urging her up to unhook her bra and shoving it up along with her shirt. "Guess that's one thing I never managed to fuck up." He muttered something else, but she couldn't hear it because all at once he had his mouth wrapped around her nipple, sucking on it like he wanted to devour it whole.

Oh God, the pleasure.

She'd missed this. Missed him like this, because in this one thing, they'd been compatible in every way. He liked giving it hard, which was just fine with her, because she liked getting it hard. It was a point of pride that she could take everything he dished out and still ask for more.

"Ohmigod," she gasped as he rolled his tongue around the tip, dragged it into his mouth deep, and sucked again. He worked her just the way she liked—expertly, a bit roughly, which only served to ratchet her pleasure up higher and higher.

When he had one nipple pinched and wet, he moved on to the other, giving it the same treatment while she moaned in bliss. At the same time, he slid one hand down to cup her ass, pulling her against his thigh, which he'd wedged between her legs.

"You like that?" he said, nibbling on her neck just below her ear. "My mouth on you? My hands on you?" He tightened his grip on her ass. "Tell me."

"I—" she started, then gasped because he'd gone back to the first nipple, which was now a heightened bundle of nerves. "I like it, Aidan." *Lie.* She loved it.

"Gonna work you," he said. "Gonna give it to you hard, and you're gonna take it."

Oh, she'd almost forgotten the dirty talking. Aidan was a master, and his filthy mouth had always thrilled her, made her crave him with more than touch alone.

And when he drew his thigh up, her core pressed against him. Shamelessly, she rubbed her softness onto his hardness. There was no give to him at all, something he took full advantage of by drawing his leg up a fraction more. An acute shard of pleasure sparked through her system.

"Oh God." She moaned and rubbed harder.

"Yeah, that's right. Move yourself on me. Take what you need. Get yourself nice and worked up so that when I get inside you, you're hot and slick and ready for me."

He continued tormenting her breasts for a while longer, softening her nipples with his tongue before pinching and rubbing them back to tight peaks.

"Gonna make you come now."

He unsnapped her jeans and tugged them from her hips, then kicked them away. And before she knew what he was doing, he'd pulled off her panties, too, and had buried his face between her thighs.

The first touch of his tongue on her clit made her jump. The second made her gasp. And the third made her moan.

His beard scraped against the insides of her legs, chafing her, just like it used to. *So damned good.*

"Jesus, Emma. You're just as sweet as I remembered."

"Aidan," she murmured, spearing her hands through his thick hair.

He worked her just as he'd promised, licking and stroking, adding a finger into the mix, then two. "Please," she said, her voice ending on a gasp as he twisted his fingers.

"That's it, wildcat. Beg for it. Beg for me."

He sucked on her clit and all at once she was there, coming so hard she thought her brain had exploded in her skull.

But he didn't let her down. Just kept her on a heightened plane of pleasure by toying with her, rubbing those two clever fingers inside her until she was panting again.

"Insatiable," he said with satisfaction.

"Please, Aidan. I need it. I need you. Now." She was babbling, and she didn't care. All she knew was that if he didn't get inside her this instant, she was going to combust.

"You still off the pill?"

She nodded. "Yeah." Her body hadn't reacted well to the artificial hormones, and even the IUD had side effects she couldn't handle, so she and Aidan had always used condoms. Once she'd gotten divorced and had stopped having sex, there'd been no reason to try anything new.

"I got it." Aidan reached over to pull a foil packet out of the pocket of his jeans, his abdominal muscles flexing with his movement.

Somewhere in the back of her mind, it registered that Aidan's carrying condoms around probably meant that he hadn't been celibate since they'd divorced. Hell, she'd expected it—a man like him could never be single for long. But at this moment it didn't matter. Tonight he was here, with her.

He sheathed himself, every magnificent inch, and in another moment was pressing against her.

"If you want me to stop, say it now."

She ran a hand down his arm. Looked him straight in the face and tilted her hips up in unmistakable invitation. "Don't stop."

"I've waited too long to fuck you again," he murmured, "to be inside you, to feel your body tight around me."

His tip was crowding against her opening. There was no room for rational thought. No room for thought of any kind.

"Need you, Aidan," she managed to get out. "Please."

His eyes darkened with pleasure, and then with a sharp flick of his hips, he buried himself inside her in one long thrust.

He moaned. She gasped, because Jesus, he was huge, her little-used flesh stretching around him even more tightly than she could have imagined. And the strangest thing of all was how well she remembered this most intimate of touches. Even in those times when she would much rather have forgotten, alone in the dark of the night, he was there. She held her breath, trying to imprint this on her brain forever, to make these sensations last.

He was barely breathing himself. "Forgot…how tight you are."

There was zero give, above her, around her. Inside her. "Forgot…how big you are," she said, squeezing her internal muscles around him.

"Damn, it, Emma—" he said, his face a mask of strain above her, and she realized how tightly wound he must be. "Just give me a minute."

She wiggled against him experimentally. "Move," she urged him.

"Not yet," he gritted out. "Trying to be gentle."

"I don't want gentle," she told him. "I just want you."

It was as if a switch turned on in his brain. He pulled out and slid back in, stretching her, forcing her to accommodate him, even as he bent a head to her nipple.

He was deep, so deep inside her, and it was almost as if they'd never been apart, the way he moved over her, touched her so intimately, instinctively knowing how to handle her.

"I need more," she begged.

"I'll give you more."

He speared one hand through her hair, and the other clamped on her hip, pinioning her for the taking.

"Yesss—" she hissed, and his lip curled in satisfaction.

"Gorgeous," he whispered, gripping her even more tightly. And then he was moving, powering into her so hard and so fast that she gasped, her pleasure inexplicably rising again.

He hit her sweet spot over and over, and yet he kept going, ramping her up at warp speed. It didn't take long for her to feel it, and when he sent her over the edge once more, she gasped and clawed at his back like an animal.

But he wasn't done, and apparently, neither was she. His thrusts were smooth and sure, as if he were determined to wring every ounce of pleasure from her body.

Only he had this power over her—the highest highs, the lowest lows. Groaning, he kissed her mouth.

"So fucking hot, Emma. I could watch you do that all night." He was slamming into her even faster now, leaving no room for anything except the pure, unbridled pleasure of being taken, and taken hard. "Come for me again," he demanded.

"I can't," she gasped, but he wouldn't let up. Just kept going, forcing her once again up that mountain, inch by deliciously torturous inch.

"You can," he growled, and because this was Aidan, he clamped a big hand on her thigh and lifted her leg to wrap it around his waist. This had the dual effects of drawing her even closer to him and changing the angle of his thrusts.

Pleasure swamped her, invaded all of her senses. She thought there was no possible way she could let go until he swept a thumb right over that sensitive flesh between her legs. She gave a hoarse yell as she was thrown over the precipice a third time, his triumphant laugh echoing hollowly in her ears.

And then he was powering into her and coming on a roar.

In one smooth move, he withdrew from her body and flipped onto his back. Dimly, she registered what he was doing—disposing of the condom, tucking her against him, and pulling her close.

He fingered her necklace, the one he'd given her so long ago. Then he smoothed the hair back from her face and kissed top of her head, just like he used to do.

Exhausted, sated, and dazed, Emma let him.

Her body was leaden, her brain completely fried. But as she drifted into sleep, she couldn't help but hope that maybe, just maybe, things would be different this time around.

CHAPTER 11

Emma woke to the sound of tree branches scraping gently against the eaves. The storm had quieted, but it was still raining, as evidenced by the soft pattering on the roof and plinking on the gutters. Thin light filtered through gauzy curtains on the window, muting the pastel colors of her room to gray. A quick glance at her bedside clock confirmed the hour was still early.

Her body ached in the most pleasant of ways, a tired but satiated ache. Just like old times. Except this was now, and she had new memories to make.

Only Aidan wasn't in bed. Emma propped herself up on her elbows, and a motion near the side of the bed caught her eye.

Aidan was crouched between the bed and the wall, head down, as he tugged on his boots.

Sensing movement, he lifted his head and his gaze met hers. "Hey."

"Hey," she replied, her voice still thick with sleep.

He bent down his head again to do up his laces. "Sorry I woke you up."

"It's okay." She yawned. "You don't need to go out for coffee. I have plenty here. Stumptown." He liked Stumptown.

"I'm not going out for coffee."

Suspicion began to bloom in her mind. "Where are you going?"

"Home, then Wolfshead." He didn't even lift his head this

time. Just finished tying one lace and went on to the next one.

"It's only five."

"I know. I have a bunch of stuff to get done."

"Can it wait just a little longer?" The mattress was still warm from his body, the sheets still rumpled from their night together. "Then we can go in together. Maybe grab breakfast on the way?"

He finished doing the second lace and stood up. "Can't, babe."

It was only two words. But all of the warmth left the bed. The room. Her chest.

He grabbed his wallet from the dresser and shoved it in his back pocket. Strode to the door, then turned back to look at her. "In fact, there's no need for you to come in. It'll just be me sorting some things. Boring stuff." He ran a hand through his hair. "So—I'll see you tonight, maybe, after I'm done? It'll be late, so you might not want to wait up."

Oh, she knew exactly what was going on here. Same old Aidan, same old tricks.

First of all, he hadn't planned to tell her he was leaving. If she hadn't woken up and caught him, he'd have just been gone, period.

No kiss. No promises. Not even a good-bye.

Second, and more importantly, he was back to making all of those stupid assumptions, pushing her out, pushing her away, just like he used to do. And that burned.

All of the anguish, the pain, the suffering from the last few years of their marriage came rushing back. The fighting. The sex. The anger. The heartbreak.

Make me forget, she'd begged.

Instead, she remembered. *Everything.*

She'd opened her heart, just for an instant, and he'd walked right in, except he hadn't changed. Nothing had changed, and once again, she was left to pick up the pieces.

What was it with him? Stubbornness? Hubris? Cluelessness? It didn't matter.

Things for her had never been clearer.

Once, she'd given herself to him so completely that she'd lost sight of who she was.

She couldn't do that again. She was older now. Wiser. She had to protect herself, guard her heart even better than she had before.

Because she knew with the utmost certainty that she wouldn't survive it being crushed a second time.

"Actually, tonight doesn't work for me."

"Why not?"

"Because." Emma sat up. Cleared her throat. Looked him straight in the eye. "Sleeping with you was a huge mistake. One that will not be repeated."

Aidan blinked, obviously surprised by her words. "I thought we were good together."

"No, we're not," she said, shaking her head. "We're *so* not."

"Yeah?" He uncrossed his arms, which only served to emphasize his chest. "Is that why I had you screaming my name?"

Evenly, she met his gaze. "We never had a problem in the bedroom department. It's everywhere else we have issues."

"What are you saying, Emma?" he asked slowly.

Naked, she rose from the bed. Pushed her shoulders back and tilted up her chin. He wanted her to lay it out? She'd lay it out.

"You broke into my house last night, to satisfy your curiosity, wanting to talk. So we talk. As usual, we have sex and *boom*. You think everything's fixed, all neat and tidy. Then you're up and out in the morning. Business as usual. But it's not like that for me. I can't go back to the way things were. I won't. Sex—no matter how incredible—isn't enough. I need more from you, and unfortunately, you don't know how to give it to me. You never did."

Aidan stood there, staring. When they were married, their arguments were fast and furious affairs. Both of them were pretty hotheaded, and along with the arguing and the tears, there'd been a healthy amount of passion—no surprise since they usually ended up in bed afterward, pounding it out.

But this was different.

Emma wasn't crying this time. She wasn't even shouting. Just telling the truth. A truth he clearly wasn't anticipating, from his expression of abject confusion. No doubt he'd expected to head back to Wolfshead on his schedule, drop back in when he felt like it, sex her up when he wanted, and disappear again.

Not. Going. To. Happen.

"What do you need?" he finally asked.

"A man who listens," she said patiently. "A man who takes

the time to figure me out. Someone who treats me like a partner in our relationship, who doesn't decide things unilaterally. Someone who doesn't try to control everything or sweet-talk problems away."

"I'm listening."

Sadly, she shook her head. "You had years to listen, and after all that time, you're still as oblivious as ever."

All of a sudden he looked very, very tired. He rubbed his forehead, hard. "Christ, Emma. I just woke up. Can you give me a minute to catch up?"

She had, too, but she refrained from noting it. "Sure," she said, flipping up her hand as if to signify the conversation was over. "Take a minute. In fact, take all the time you need. Lock the door when you leave. Put the key back under the flowerpot." She stepped closer and patted his arm. "And Aidan? I'm not doing this anymore, so don't come back. Ever."

By the time Aidan dragged his ass to Wolfshead later that morning, he felt as if he'd been run over by a steamroller.

What the hell had just happened?

Last night had definitely not been what he'd expected. Like he'd said, he hadn't gone there to sleep with her. Just talk. Find out why she still had such a hold on him even after all these years. But she'd offered herself up to him, and he damn well sure couldn't say no to that. He never could.

They'd had sex. Incredible, mind-blowing sex that only reminded him how good they used to be. How good they still were. And maybe, how good they could be again.

Only problem was that Emma was having none of it.

Going home to take a shower and change his clothes hadn't improved his mood, and what he saw in the lot didn't help, either. The Costas' van was once again illegally parked, this time practically blocking the side entrance to their warehouse. And because of that, their delivery guy hadn't been able to drop the boxes off close enough to the door. He'd left them there, twenty feet away. Now he'd have to get Dylan out here to drag them inside, which would probably mess up his schedule for his warehouse checks.

His temper getting fouler by the minute, he went up to the second floor, and immediately ran into Fiona and Brody, who were talking quietly on the catwalk. Fiona was a couple of years younger than his own mom, with a totally different style. While his mom was outgoing, Fiona was a lot more introverted, which was evident from the way she spoke and even dressed. She favored jeans and button-down oxford shirts, and she usually kept her long red hair pulled back in a gentle ponytail.

When she spied him, she gave him a concerned look. "Are you okay?" she asked. "You look kind of peaked."

"I'm fine, Aunt Fi," he said. "Just got a lot on my mind."

"Well, take care of yourself," she said, before turning back to Brody. "I'll have those numbers to you later, okay?"

"Thanks, Mom," Brody said.

As soon as Fiona was gone, Aidan turned to Brody. "Thought I asked you to deal with the Costas," he growled.

"What?" Brody looked surprised. "I did. At least, I thought I did."

"Then why's their van blocking our side door?"

"Shit, really?" He let out a breath. "Okay. I'll go back and have a talk with them again."

"Do that."

Aidan went to move past him, but Brody stopped him by stepping in his path and giving him a once up and down. "You look like hell. What happened?"

"Nothing. Emma show up yet?"

"No." Brody looked puzzled. "Why?"

"Just tell her to stay out of my way when she does."

Brody's eyebrows went up, and Aidan could almost see his mind whirring. "Oh, man, I knew this was going to happen."

"What?" Aidan shot back, not liking his cousin's expression.

"You know," Brody said, giving him a significant look.

Aidan snorted. "I doubt it." He tried to move past him again, but once again, Brody got in front of him.

"Uh-uh," he said, crossing his arms over his chest. "You don't get to weasel out of this so easy."

"Okay, know-it-all, you tell me."

"You tried to handle her and got your ass handed to you in return," Brody said, his voice smug.

Aidan simply scowled at him, which was clearly all the answer Brody needed.

"I knew it! Damn, that woman gets better and better. Did she tell you to shove it?"

"Not in so many words," Aidan muttered. The argument they'd had this morning had been brief, but effective.

"Well, in my opinion, you were playing with fire."

"You think?"

Brody ignored his sarcasm. "Get some coffee and pull yourself together. I'm off to deal with the Costas. And if Emma shows up, I'll let you know. Take your own advice and stay away from her. I need you whole today."

Aidan grunted at him and went to his office. Luckily, it was empty. Good thing, since he was in no mood to deal with anyone right now.

With great reluctance, he opened up the regulatory program again—the software that Brody had painstakingly walked him through just yesterday—and found that everything he thought he knew was all mush in his brain.

There was a strange twinge in the vicinity of his chest. Like heartburn, even though he hadn't eaten anything this morning.

Emma had dismissed him. As if he wasn't even worth the bother anymore. As if everything they'd shared meant nothing.

But although he'd been in denial for far too long, it had meant something to him.

When she'd asked for a divorce, he'd claimed to have been blindsided, but he'd known, even then, that he was lying to himself. She wasn't happy. Hadn't been for a while. Everyone saw it. Even him. Problem was, he had no clue how to fix it. He'd been wrapped up in Wolfshead and couldn't give her what she needed.

Clearly, he still couldn't.

He was such an idiot.

A woman like her—beautiful, smart, sexy—should have moved on ten times over by now. Whether she'd hooked up with anyone since their divorce, he didn't know, and he sure as hell didn't want to, but evidently nothing had stuck.

Maybe it was because she was still hung up on him, the same way he was hung up on her. And one thought kept repeating in his mind—even though she'd summarily kicked him out the door this morning, she still hadn't taken off that damn necklace.

Did that mean she still loved him?

The thought filled him with intense satisfaction.

Because if she still loved him, that meant he had hope that there was something left between them. Something that could be fixed.

Fate—or rather fate in the form of his irascible grandfather—had dropped her right back in his lap. Now that he'd talked to her, tasted her, *been inside her*, he knew with the utmost certainty that he had to have her back—in his bed and in his life.

He had his second chance, and he wasn't going to blow it again. But to repair the damage, he was going to have to be smart about his approach. Emma was no idiot, and he'd need to show her that he'd changed, for real this time. Figure out what she needed. Be the man she wanted him to be.

First things first; he needed coffee. Then he'd commandeer Brody and tackle the regulatory shit. And finally, too many years overdue, he'd figure out how to undertake the most important task of all: reclaiming his wife.

CHAPTER 12

Wind whipping her face, Emma leaned on the metal rail, pulled her baseball cap down a fraction, and looked out across the water. It had been a long time since she'd been out on her dad's boat—last fall, right before he'd winterized the vessel by dry-docking it for the season.

He'd insisted that she join him for his spring launch, and she was glad she had.

From this vantage point, the rocky Oregon shore seemed even more majestic, and she breathed in the damp, salty sea air. There really was nothing like being out on the water on a fine, brisk day.

They were motoring past Ecola State Park now. She could barely make out the tiny figures swarming Cannon Beach, but Haystack Rock stood tall and proud, as did the old Tillamook lighthouse—"Terrible Tilly" in local parlance—battered by wind and water, its decaying structure atop Tillamook Rock slowly, inevitably, being reclaimed by the elements. Pelicans circled overhead, their telltale beaks prominent against the misty sky, while black cormorants with their sleek necks perched on the rock, two, three, four in a group.

Her dad was at the wheel, his face etched in concentration. The waters were dangerous around here, so she let him alone while he navigated the treacherous shoreline. He was pulling farther out to sea now, a wise choice, since it was all too easy to get dragged by the current against the shore. Getting dashed to pieces against the rocks was not in her game plan today.

Today, all she wanted was to lose herself in the wild, to forget who she was and what she was running from.

Aidan had called her. Just once, and the message he'd left was brief. "Babe. We gotta talk," was all he'd said. Feeling too raw to deal with him, she'd simply ignored it.

But she hadn't deleted the message.

They were clear from the most dangerous part now, so Emma went to join her dad.

Dan Crandall smiled at her, his worn face looking a little fuller. He'd gained some weight lately, and his hair was salt-and-pepper now instead of the rich dark brown it had been when she was younger, but it was surprising how much the same he'd remained. He still had the same great sense of humor, the same crooked smile. And his brown eyes still sparkled with mirth and intelligence. Though right now what she saw in them was mostly weariness.

"Enjoying yourself?" he asked.

"Totally. Thanks for taking me out today. You sure you won't be missed at the store?"

"Nah," he said. "It's launch day. The guys understand."

Her dad lived in the same house she'd grown up in, and still owned the same hardware store. The "guys"—really a crew of grizzled old dudes who helped her dad out because they liked tools and doodads—were extensions of her own family. Emma had had a happy childhood, with plenty of good food, fresh air, family, and friends. And her dad had been a big part of that.

Growing up, she'd always thought of Daniel Crandall as unbreakable. He was a large man—just over six feet tall, with broad shoulders and a barrel chest who'd loved tossing around a football with Ryan and helping her train for her volleyball games. He'd buckled when his wife had died—they all had—and it had been a rough couple of years.

But he didn't break. He'd been a rock, holding her and Ryan aloft, never allowing them to sink into misery, forcing them to move forward.

When they'd come out of mourning, he'd stepped up, ferrying both Emma and her brother through the toughest part of adolescence in a tiny beach town on the Oregon coast.

But her dad looked different now. In the past few years he'd seemed to age more quickly. Now he looked way older than his sixty-two years, and a far cry from the fit, healthy man he once was. Every time Emma asked him about what he was doing to maintain his health, he'd given her excuses—things had gotten busier at the hardware store; he'd had less time to go on the long, rambling walks he loved.

Unfortunately, once he'd started on that downward health spiral, there didn't seem to be an end to it. Things started snowballing—his blood sugar, his balance—one issue after another, until it seemed like every month it was something new. He didn't seem that interested in managing his health care, and since Ryan was married to his job, Emma had taken it upon herself to keep track of his medicines and doctor's appointments. Given that her dad refused to acknowledge his disease, it was increasingly becoming an uphill battle.

"Are you okay?" she asked him.

Hands still on the controls, he nodded. "Now that we're out of those waters, yeah."

"That's not what I meant," she chided. "Have you been taking your medicine and checking your blood sugar the way the doctor said you needed to?"

"Uh-huh."

"And going to the physical therapist?" When they'd been at the boat launch, she'd noticed that his balance was getting worse. He'd actually teetered a couple of times and had to brace himself on something. But when Emma had asked him about it, he'd simply waved her off. Clearly, he wasn't that steady on his feet. And his shuffle was worrisome, especially because it seemed to be the new normal.

"Sure," he said, a little too quickly.

Emma pursed her lips, doubting that very much. Though his doctor had recommended PT, saying it would strengthen his muscles and sense of balance, her dad thought it was a waste of time. Ditto the pills—or maybe he just wasn't that interested in taking them.

Emma had pushed him time and again to count out his pills at the start of every week. She'd even bought him one of those little pillboxes with the days of the week on them so that he wouldn't forget, but he refused to use it, claiming it made him feel like an old geezer.

"Let me guess. No on both counts. Am I right?"

Her dad sighed. "I'm just so busy with the hardware store and keeping up the house. It's a lot to remember."

"That makes me really sad to hear." Emma put her hand on his arm and squeezed. "Your health should be a top priority. You're way too young to be like this." He started to protest, but she cut him off. "No, seriously, Dad. I can see it. Your energy is flagging, and you're not steady on your feet. I don't even want to know what your blood sugar is."

"I'm not young anymore," he said, bitterness in his voice.

"You have a disease, and without proper treatment, it's going to get worse. Should I call Suzi and Merv?"

"No, no," he said quickly. "They have enough to take care of."

The Richardsons had two high school–aged children, and in Emma's opinion, they'd already gone above and beyond to make sure that her dad was doing okay. Suzi checked in with him at least three times a week, and Merv often stopped by on his way home from work at the library, just to say hi and to have a beer.

"Okay, then you're stuck with me. I'm going to recheck everything when we get back to the house. Make sure you have the pills you need and you have your next PT appointment scheduled."

"Fine, fine," he said with a sigh.

"Look, Dad. I love you. I care about you. And if there's anything I can do to get you to step it up, I'm going to try it, whether that means counting out your pills like you're six years old or scheduling these appointments for you or pestering you until you're so annoyed you don't want to see me anymore."

Her dad glanced over at her. "You really want me to take care of myself?"

"More than anything."

"Just like your mother."

Her chest panged at the mention of her mom, but she forced a smile anyway. "Don't tell me she wouldn't be doing the same exact thing."

"She would," her dad admitted. "Even way back when I was running and taking care of myself, she always encouraged me to do more."

"Because she loved you," Emma said. "That's what people

who love each other do."

"Right," her dad said. They motored for a while longer, her dad clearly lost in thought. After a few minutes, he turned to her.

"Let's make a deal."

Emma narrowed her eyes. The last deal she made was with Aidan Phelan, and she had no idea how *that* was going to turn out.

"What kind of a deal?" she said. "Because if you want me to, say, work at the hardware store in exchange for you taking your medicine, then no dice." She'd done more than her share of shifts at the store, as had Ryan. She'd loved being with her family, but she'd hated the work. In her mind, there was nothing creative about selling zip ties or shovels.

"As much as I'd like to have you back home, I'm pretty sure you've moved beyond stocking the shelves with nails and placing reorders on garden hoses," he said, his tone wry. "No, what I'm talking about is an equal exchange. I take care of myself, if you take care of yourself."

"But I'm already taking care of myself," she protested. She wasn't model-thin, but she ate pretty well—not counting the occasional drink or doughnut—and she definitely got plenty of exercise from walking around the city all the time.

Slowly, her dad shook his head. "I see that sadness in your eyes, Emma. And I know the real reason why you wanted to get out of Portland so badly."

Emma stilled. "You...do?"

Her dad couldn't know about what she'd done with Aidan. There were some things a father should never have to think about— and his daughter having filthy, wild sex with her ex-husband was definitely at the top of that list.

"Sure, I do. I've known for a while what's been going on. I only wish you'd come to me. I could have helped you work through some things."

Not very likely. "Uh, sorry I didn't tell you."

"Well, we're talking about it now, so that's good."

She forced a smile. "Great. So, um, how much do you know?" A searing vision of her tangled up in the sheets with Aidan came to mind, and inwardly, she cringed.

"You don't need to be like that. I was there too, once upon a time."

Ew. As painful as it was to know her father was thinking about her having sex, thinking about her father having sex was even worse.

"Come on, Emma. It's not like I don't know how tough starting a new business can be."

"Oh, *yes*," she said on an exhale, relieved he didn't know the truth. "The business."

"And I'm sure that all that Wolfshead jazz hasn't been good for you, either, what with seeing Aidan again," he went on.

On that score, her dad was right. He'd been as surprised as she was when she'd told him about the share she'd inherited. At one point, he'd loved Aidan. More importantly, he'd loved Aidan for her.

When Aidan changed, he'd noticed it, too. Obviously, given that he'd pretty much stopped coming to family events. Both her dad and Ryan had supported her decision to divorce him, telling her that if she wasn't being treated like the amazing woman she was, it was better to leave than to be unhappy.

If they knew she'd slipped up and slept with him, she'd probably get an earful about self-preservation and pride. Not that she didn't deserve a lecture; she just wasn't ready to hear it right now.

"He's not giving you a hard time, is he?" her dad asked. "Because we can get Dean Narbeth to handle things if you're not comfortable." Dean was a lawyer and one of her dad's dearest friends.

"Doesn't Dean do real estate law?"

"Sure, but he'd make an exception for you. He went to law school, after all. He can handle a little wills and trusts work."

"Thanks, Dad. I appreciate that. But I'm handling things fine on my own."

Not quite the truth, but she couldn't have her dad worried about her when his health was already on the fritz.

"If you change your mind, let me know. And in the meantime, try to find time to relax. Go out with your friends. Maybe a date or two?"

What her dad was asking for was impossible. She couldn't relax, not with her new business and with all that was going on at Wolfshead. Nor could she go out on any dates when she was still in love with Aidan.

What she *could* do—something that was probably better for

her in the long run anyway—was to focus on the future. A future without Aidan Phelan. The sooner she figured out how to get over him, the better things would be, both personally and professionally.

"I don't know about the dating," she said slowly, "but I can do the relaxing and hanging out with friends."

"Oh, Emma," her dad said with a sigh.

"What?"

"Sometimes you're so much like me it's hard to look at you."

"Are you talking about the freckles?" she said teasingly. "Because there's not much I can do about them." Sara stayed out of the sun, while Robin turned a nice, toasty tan, but Emma had always freckled like crazy, no matter what she did.

"No, honey. I'm talking about hanging on," her dad said. "Long after hope is gone."

Emma bit the inside of her lip, doubly glad her dad didn't know about her tryst with Aidan. He would only be disappointed in her for being weak, and that's something she couldn't stomach. Not now, with everything else weighing on her.

And as much as her heart ached for herself, it ached for her dad even more. There was a reason he'd never remarried after her mom's death, and that was because he loved her. Would love her until he was in his own grave.

"Okay, I'll *think* about dating," she said, "if you take your medicine. And go to physical therapy."

Her dad smiled and squeezed her hand tighter. "Deal. Love you, Emma. And appreciate what you're trying to do."

Emma kissed his cheek. "Love you too, Dad. And ditto."

CHAPTER 13

"Well, well, well," Gabe drawled when Emma showed up at Wolfshead midafternoon on Tuesday. "Look what the cat dragged in."

"Hi, Gabe," Emma said, accepting his kiss. "Sorry I wasn't here last week. I had some family business to take care of." Not quite the truth, but *I was too much of a coward to show up after Aidan and I had hot sex* would probably shock even the typically impossible-to-embarrass Gabriel Phelan.

"I'm just teasing," he said, giving her waist a squeeze, and dropped his voice into a mock whisper. "Things were *really* boring without you."

"Oh? What happened?"

Gabe gave a shrug. "The usual. Nothing ever changes around here, that's for sure."

"Right." Which unfortunately included her. She clearly hadn't moved beyond her past—a fatal mistake when it came to Aidan.

Since he'd come back into her life, they'd had all the same tension, all the same fights…and all the same heat. It was how she'd ended up in bed with him, even though she'd vowed not to let him affect her.

Speaking of the man, he was coming down the metal staircase as he spoke with Brody. As soon as he saw her, an expression of unbridled heat flashed in his eyes, which he rapidly schooled.

Unfortunately, he wasn't fast enough, because beside her, she felt Gabe stiffen.

"Whoa," he said.

Whoa was right, because today, like every other day, the man looked *good*. Jeans skimmed down long legs; a Henley shirt stretched over a broad chest. Those cheekbones, slicing out prominently over his beard. A modern-day lumberjack with the strength to match.

And last Saturday night, she'd seen him naked.

She fairly itched to run her hands through his hair, to feel the bulge of his muscles under the pads of her fingers.

Without meaning to, she licked her lips.

No.

He and Brody came right up to them.

"Hey, Emma," Brody said, giving her a half smile. If he knew what had transpired between her and Aidan last weekend, he wasn't talking. Then again, Brody had always been a smart man.

"You're back," Aidan said without any other preamble. "For a visit? Or for good this time?"

Emma cleared her throat. "For good. And if you wouldn't mind, I'd like to have a word with you. In private," she added, intensely conscious of the fact that Brody and Gabe were staring at the two of them with considerable interest.

Once again, his eyes flared with heat. Whatever she was feeling, he was feeling it, too. This did not reassure her.

"Brody," he said, without even looking at his cousin. "Talk to your mom and get the books closed for March, okay?"

"Got it." Brody turned and practically vaulted up the metal stairs to the second floor.

"And Gabe?"

"Yeah?"

"Get on that project…the one you and I talked about last Friday."

"Are you sure you want me to—"

"Go," Aidan demanded.

Gabe muttered something and stalked off, ostensibly to do Aidan's bidding.

When he was gone, Aidan pointed up. "My office?"

"Sure."

"After you," Aidan said, indicating the staircase.

When they were inside, Aidan shut the door, but didn't lock it. Calmly, he walked over to his desk and sat down, elbows on his desk, a veritable picture of restraint. She didn't know why he wasn't jumping down her throat the way he usually did, but everything about this encounter was still stilted and strange and awkward.

"How are you?" he asked, his voice warm. Concerned.

"Fine," she returned.

"I was worried about you when you didn't call me back."

She chose her words carefully. "I'm sorry. I just wasn't prepared for…what happened between us. But I should have called you back. As an owner, I know it's my responsibility to let you know where I am. In the future I won't go off the grid—I promise." Good. Keep it professional. "I'm sorry about last Saturday, too. I think you know as well as I do that if we're going to keep working together, we can't sleep together again."

Aidan was still motionless behind his desk. There was a long pause before he spoke.

"Are you finished?" he asked.

She smoothed down her skirt. "Yes. Yes, I think so."

"Nothing else to say?"

"Not at the moment."

"Then it's my turn." He rose to his full height and stalked around the desk until he was standing directly in front of her. "I was with you all the way until the end."

"I'm sorry?"

"Apologize for not returning my call. Apologize for disappearing on me, but don't apologize for the sex. I'm not."

"But—"

Big, warm hands settled on her shoulders. "We're good together, Emma. I said that before and I'll say it again and again. The way you light up for me, *Christ*. The way your body was made for mine. I won't forget that. I can't. And I'll be damned if I let you apologize for something that's so fucking right."

But even as his words stirred up those emotions she'd tried to bury time and again, her heart sank. As she'd said, they may be right in bed, but they were wrong everywhere else. She'd put some distance between the two of them, tried to look at this from a clearer perspective. Separating out her feelings from the physical had blown right up in her face. Doing it again would mean disaster.

As if sensing her reluctance, he withdrew his hands from her shoulders and immediately, she felt the loss. "You need time. I get that. But Wolfshead's not going away, and neither am I."

"I'm not going away, either. I'm a part of this company, and I can't let you dictate what I do and don't do here. Don't get me wrong, I still think that what we did was a mistake. But that doesn't mean we can't work together," she continued quickly, ignoring his frown. "In fact, I'm hoping that we can move beyond what happened, figure out my role here in a way we both can live with. Can you get on board with that?"

"For now," he bit out, and she got the uncomfortable sensation that he was holding something back.

"So now what happens?"

"Now we start over." He sat on the edge of his desk and gestured around. "This place has too much baggage for both of us. So we get out of here. Talk. Just you and me without any of my brothers and cousins breathing down our necks. Figure out how to move forward."

"Where?" Because he if suggested her bedroom, she was going to have a hard time saying no.

"A hike. Just the two of us, up near Mount Hood. Sort things out, away from Wolfshead."

Emma shook her head. "You and me alone in the woods? Not a good idea."

"We need space," Aidan said firmly. "And it will give you a chance to tell me about your plans for Wolfshead. This Thursday. I'll take the day off. Just us, talking."

"That's what you promised would happen the last time," she said accusingly.

"Nothing's going to happen. Unless you want it to."

"I won't," she said quickly.

"Then nothing will happen. Do me a favor. Pull out that calendar of yours and check for me."

"I still think this is a terrible idea," she said. But when Aidan got like this, nothing would stop him until he got his way.

With a heavy sigh, she retrieved her cell phone from her purse. She'd put the ringer to silent as soon as she'd come into Wolfshead, and now she noticed she had three missed calls in the last fifteen minutes, all from Suzi Richardson's number.

Emma frowned. Suzi hadn't left any voicemail messages or texts.

While she was flipping back to her calendar, a message bubble popped up, indicating a call was coming in from the same number. Guess Suzi really wanted to reach her.

She glanced up at Aidan. "I think I have to take this."

He slid off the desk and motioned for her to go right ahead, so she clicked it on.

"It's Emma," she answered.

"Emma," Suzi said, her voice breathless. "I'm so glad you picked up. I've been trying to reach you."

The connection wasn't the best—crackly and hollow. "Are you okay? Where are you?"

"In my car. So sorry the connection's bad. I'm okay."

"Then what's going on?"

Aidan was seated behind his desk now, his gaze trained on her.

"It's your dad. He's had a fall."

Emma stiffened and sat up straighter. "What? When?"

"An hour ago. I've just left the local hospital, and—"

"Whoa, whoa, wait, back up," she said, gripping her cell phone tightly. "Start from the beginning."

"He was heading to the garage to get something—a step stool, he told me—and he tripped and fell."

"*No*," she whispered.

"Luckily, Merv was out walking Juniper and found him."

"How bad is it?"

"He broke his leg, and when Merv found him, he was actually passed out—we're not sure if it was from the pain or from him hitting his head. He had a pretty bad knock on his temple. We called 911 and the ambulance came to get him."

Her poor dad—afraid, alone. "Is he okay? Is he even awake?"

"Yes, he woke up before the ambulance came, but they have to do a CT scan and an MRI anyway. They're telling us it's likely he's going to need surgery."

"What?"

"The break is…bad, Emma. When I left him, he was in a lot of pain," Suzi said, her voice laced with tears.

She needed to be there. Now.

"Where are you? What hospital?"

"They're airlifting him to Salem. It's a better hospital, and they do lots of work like this. I'm in the car right now, but it's a long drive, and I'm worried that they'll take him into surgery before I get there."

"I'm coming. I'll be there as soon as I can." She only prayed she'd get there before they put him under.

"Hurry," Suzi said. She clicked off, and the phone went dead.

Okay, this was bad. Really bad. Her dad hadn't been doing that well to begin with, and this would only set him back even more. There were so many questions—would they have to put hardware into his leg? What about his blackout? What if he'd gotten more than a bump? What if he'd hurt his brain somehow?

And what about the diabetes? He was supposed to control the disease with medication and exercise, but now the exercise would be off the table for a good long while—until his leg healed. Would they have to increase his dosage? Put him on insulin?

There were way too many unanswered questions. She needed to get to the hospital ASAP. It was only 3:00 p.m. now. She could bypass most of the rush-hour traffic if she left in the next few minutes.

"Emma?"

She blinked, startled, then realized that Aidan was still sitting there, watching her intently.

"Emma?" Aidan said again, giving her a searching look. "What's going on?"

"It's my dad," she said, still numb. "He fell. Hurt himself badly. I don't know much more. He's heading into surgery, and he's there all alone. I have to go."

Aidan's expression hardened, but she ignored it. He wasn't her concern now; her dad was. Emma needed a plan, but she could barely think straight. Fifty miles. That's how far it was from Portland to Salem, and the helicopter was already en route. Would she even make it in time? It didn't matter. She had to get there.

With shaking hands, she put her cell phone back into her purse. She tried to jam the notepad in, but it wouldn't fit. Giving up, she tucked it under her arm and rose.

"I…I have to go. I'm sorry. We'll have to finish this another time."

"Emma, wait." Aidan rose too. "Where are you going?"

"To Salem."

"You're trembling. You can't drive in the state you're in."

"I have to," she said. "He needs me. I have to be there."

"Yes, you do," he said calmly. "I'll take you."

Emma shook her head. "But what about your work? The company…"

"Right now, this is more important. Just"—he stopped, picked up the phone, and started dialing—"just give me a minute to let the others know what's going on." He held up his hand while he barked something unintelligible into the line, then hung up and came around the desk. "Okay, I have one more thing to do. Promise me you won't leave until I get back."

She shook her head. "I have to go now."

"Emma—" he started, his voice calm. Persuasive. He wrapped his hands around her arms. "Just give me five minutes. Please."

Somewhere, deep in the recesses of her mind, it registered that Aidan had asked for something politely. "Okay," she whispered.

His gaze was searching. "You won't leave without me?"

"I won't leave without you," she swore.

"Good. Stay right here."

Still half in shock, Emma stood there and waited.

Aidan didn't take five minutes. He took three.

"I'm back," he said, steering her out of his office, down the metal staircase, and out Wolfshead's main door.

They didn't run into anyone on the way out, which was probably a good thing, since Emma couldn't have said one coherent thing anyway.

Aidan practically placed her in the passenger seat of his truck and nodded in approval when she put on her seat belt.

He went back around to the driver's seat, and set up his cell phone's map feature. "Are they taking him to Salem Hospital?"

"Yes."

He reached over and took her hand. Squeezed it. "I've got this, Emma. I've got you. The drive will take an hour. I wish I could make it go faster, but I want to get us there in one piece. Use the time. If there's anyone you need to call, do it. Does Ryan know?"

"I'm not sure."

"Call him," Aidan said, easing the truck out of the lot and onto the road.

Emma dialed Ryan's number, but he didn't pick up, so Emma left him a voicemail supplying the basic details of what she knew. She also texted him, but he didn't text back.

"No answer?" Aidan asked.

"He's probably in a meeting."

"Right. Don't worry. He'll call you back when he's free."

"'Kay."

"The app says there's no traffic, so we'll be there before you know it."

Aidan was at the wheel, his capable hands guiding his truck on the city streets and onto Interstate 5. For the first time in a long time, she let herself be driven, allowed someone else to take over the thinking for a while. Which was probably for the best, because her mind wouldn't shut off, thinking about her dad and how afraid and hurting he must be right now.

It was pretty much a straight shot from Portland to Salem, and soon enough they were pulling off the exit ramp of the highway. It didn't take long for Aidan to navigate the local roads to the hospital.

"You run in," he said, pulling up to the front entrance. "Find your dad. I'll park and join you when I can."

She nodded and hopped out of the truck.

Thanks to the helpful information desk staff who understood her garbled, frantic questions, she was pointed in the right direction and got to the OR waiting room without too much difficulty.

The place looked like a typical hospital waiting room. Upholstered chairs, a little worn, a little tired. Framed nature pictures on the wall, probably intended to be soothing to those worried friends and relatives waiting for countless hours at a time for their loved ones to emerge safely from the bowels of the hospital. Small groups of people sitting, mostly with dazed expressions on their faces, as if they didn't quite know where they were or how they'd gotten there. An information desk, lit by too-bright fluorescent lights, that seemed to be the hive of activity.

Emma was about to ask the nurse for information about her dad when Suzi came rushing up.

"Oh, Emma!" she said, giving her a huge hug. "I'm so glad you're here. Quick," she urged. "Talk to them. I think they're about to take him into surgery."

Emma turned to the nurse, a sad-eyed woman who looked like she'd seen it all. "I need information about my dad, Daniel Crandall."

"Hang on a moment," she said, typing something on a computer. "Looks like they're about to operate."

"Can I see him?"

The nurse shook her head. "No. I'm not supposed to—"

"Please," Emma said, her voice pleading.

The woman looked up at Emma's face. "After surgery prep has started, I can't let you back there…"

"I'm begging you," Emma said.

The nurse sighed. "… but I'll make an exception since you're the only family member here. Go through there," she said, pointing to a doorway, "and I'll meet you on the other side."

With the nurse's help, Emma found her dad just as he was being wheeled down a white-painted corridor, surrounded by three hospital workers in scrubs.

"Dad!" she yelled, racing to him. He was strapped down to the gurney, and his face was pale as a ghost's except for an awful bruise on his temple that had turned purple. His leg was in a splint— bruised from ankle to thigh, so clearly mangled beyond belief. God, he looked like he was in agony.

Not wanting to jostle any of the needles or tubes sticking out from her dad's body, she put her hand on his head and stroked gently.

"I'm here," she said. "I'm not leaving."

"Emma," he whispered, his voice laced with pain. "Sorry. So sorry."

Tears welled up in her ducts. Spilled down her cheeks. "There's nothing to be sorry about. Just get better."

"Talk…to…your mother for me," he said, grimacing with every word. "Tell her to put…in a good word…upstairs."

Emma nodded. "Yes, Dad, yes. I will. Love you."

The attendant looked at his watch. "We have to go."

Reluctantly, Emma stepped away from the gurney. The second she did, the attendants wheeled her dad away.

"This way, miss," the nurse said, indicating the way back to the waiting room.

Emma followed, now even more upset. She still had no idea

what was going on, had no information about the extent of the damage. All she knew was that her dad was in pain.

Suzi was waiting for her as soon as she stepped foot over the threshold.

"Were you able to see him?"

Emma nodded. "Right before they wheeled him into the operating room."

Suzi looked relieved. "Good. He was so scared—I didn't realize how much the man hated needles. He kept asking for you over and over again. Did they tell you anything about the procedure?"

"No. There wasn't any time."

"So you don't know anything? Not about his leg or his head?"

"No." Emma bit her lip, getting more upset by the minute.

"That's okay," Suzi said, trying to soothe her. "He's in good hands."

Numbly, Emma nodded. Not knowing was awful, and immediately her mind went to worst-case scenarios. Panic swept through her.

At that very moment, Aidan appeared in the doorway, looking strong and solid. She waved her hand to indicate her position, and he spied her immediately, walking those long legs over to where they stood.

"Isn't that your ex?" Suzi hissed, loud enough she was sure Aidan could hear.

"He drove me here," she whispered back.

"Oh."

Aidan moved forward, not taking his eyes off her. He was here to help, of this she was certain.

Because since that moment in the office when she'd gotten the call from Suzi, she'd seen the old Aidan, the Aidan she'd fallen in love with, generous and kind and yes, still stubborn, but his rough edges smoother, gentler.

"Did you find out what's going on with your dad?" were the first words out of his mouth.

"I caught him just before he went into surgery. He…he asked me to pray for him." Her dad was spiritual but not religious, so what he'd requested was as close as he'd get to prayer.

Gently, Aidan cupped her face in his hands. "Then that's what we'll do."

Tears welled up in the corners of her eyes. "I'm so afraid, Aidan."

"He's at the best hospital around. The doctors will take care of him. I can promise you that. And I will do everything I can to make sure that happens. You got me?"

He was gripping her face tightly, but it didn't hurt. Instead, she felt strangely at peace.

"Emma." His gaze was intent upon hers. "You got me?"

She licked her lips. "I got you."

"Good."

He released her face, but didn't let her go completely. Instead, he tucked her against his body, keeping her close, and turned to acknowledge Suzi, whom Emma realized was standing there, watching them closely.

"Suzi, right?" Aidan said to her.

"That's right. Hi, Aidan," she returned evenly, without any hint of animosity, for which Emma had to give her a lot of credit.

Suzi had witnessed the fallout of their divorce, and while Emma hadn't confided in the older woman the way she had her friends, she was sure she'd heard an earful about Aidan from her father. "Thanks for driving Emma here."

"It means a lot that you stepped up. Came all the way out here for him."

Suzi made a motion like it was no big deal. "He's a good man. He needed someone." She reached out and took Emma's hand. "And now you're here, too."

"Do you need me to stay?" she asked, looking to Aidan.

"You've done more than enough already," he said. "You should go. Get back to your kids."

"I don't want to leave Emma alone, but at some point, I need to," she said with a sigh. "Merv's at home right now, but Abby's got her dance performance tonight and it's at the same time as Justin's robotics team competition." She smiled weakly. "He's in the finals."

"I have things covered here," he said.

Suzi gave a nod. "Okay. I'll go. Take care of Emma."

They were talking about her like she wasn't even there, but she was too dazed to argue about it.

"You're in good hands." Suzi gave her a tight hug. "Dan's a strong man. He's going to pull through, I promise. Text me when he's out of surgery. And please let me know if there's anything else I can do to help, especially once he's home."

Suzi was being so generous, and she definitely couldn't afford to look a gift horse in the mouth. "Thank you," Emma said.

"Make sure you call me later to let me know how everything went," she said to Aidan. "My number's on Emma's cell phone, okay?"

"Got it."

As soon as Suzi was gone, Aidan pulled her over to a quiet corner of the waiting room and got her to sit down.

"It's going to be a while," he said. "So we may as well get comfortable."

"You don't have to stay," she said.

"Babe." He gave her an even look. "I'm staying."

"Seriously, you don't—"

"How are you going to get home?"

Crap. Her car was sitting in the lot at Wolfshead back in Portland.

"I'll figure something out," Emma said.

Aidan shook his head. "I'm staying," he said simply. He was looking at her in that way he did—that *there's no one else in the universe but you* way she hadn't seen in forever. "First things first. You look kind of pale. When was the last time you ate?"

"I...I think it was at breakfast." She'd skipped lunch by accident. No wonder she wasn't thinking clearly.

"Right. Then you need to eat," he said decisively. "I'll go get you some food."

"You've already done enough," she said, half rising. "I'll go get the food."

Aidan stopped her with a hand on her arm. "No. Stay." He tugged her back down.

"Please."

"I'm not trying to steamroll you. Just speaking the truth. You need to be here in case decisions need to be made."

He was right. "Okay," she whispered.

"Good. You take care of your dad. I take care of everything else. Including you." He gave her arm a gentle squeeze. "I'm going now. I'll be back soon."

He rose from his seat.

"Aidan?" she called out after him.

He turned back. "Yeah?"

"Just…thank you."

He gave her a brief smile, then dipped his head and was gone.

Emma was glad Aidan had insisted she stay, because while he was getting the food, the surgeon, a sharp-looking woman in her fifties, came out to tell her what was going on.

Her dad's leg had broken in two separate places, and they would have to insert a steel rod in order to stabilize his tibia, a painful but necessary procedure to ensure that his leg would heal properly. According to the doctor, this meant six full weeks of bed rest, followed by several months of PT.

They still didn't know the extent of the damage to his brain and wouldn't until they did the scans. On this, the doctor was optimistic. He'd quickly regained consciousness, and though he was in pain, at least he was talking lucidly before they'd put him under.

There was nothing else to do but sit and wait and worry. She texted Ryan some more. She talked silently to her mom, hoping that she'd pass on the message and prayed that her dad would make it through all right.

A short time later, Aidan came back carrying a brown paper bag.

"Any news?" he asked, sinking into the seat next to her.

Emma told him. Aidan paid attention, nodding.

"I'm glad you stayed."

"Me, too."

"Now it's time to eat. You need some food in you to keep your strength up for whatever's coming next." He reached into the bag, pulled out a sandwich, and handed it to her.

She took what he offered and began to unwrap the wax paper. "What is it?"

"Turkey and cranberry with lettuce and tomato. No mayo or mustard."

Her favorite, right down to the lack of condiments.

"Aidan—" she started, her eyes welling up with tears again.

"I told you I got you," he said. "Now eat."

Sniffing a little, she bit into the sandwich. It was good. Really good, and she finished half of it right away. She hadn't realized how ravenous she was.

"Babe."

When she turned to him, he cupped her jaw and swept his thumb out from the corner of her mouth. "Cranberry sauce."

"Thank you," she whispered. Her gaze dropped to the half-eaten sandwich on her lap. "I can't tell you how grateful I am that you're here. I know you're missing a lot of work right now, and, well, I just wanted to say how much I appreciate everything you're doing." Wolfshead needed him, his brothers and cousins needed him to be their leader, and yet he was here, with her.

"Emma?" She looked up to meet his eyes. "There's nothing more important than this. Family comes first. *Always.*"

There was nothing more important to Aidan than his family. It was why they'd split before—he had to choose, and he'd chosen them every single time.

She nodded sadly. "I get it."

He set his jaw, his gaze intense. "Wherever you're going in your head, forget it. Just let it go. I fucked up before, Emma. We both know it, and I've been paying for it for years. One thing's for sure—it won't happen again."

She didn't know what to make of what he was saying, not when she was already emotionally wrecked. It was difficult, almost impossible, to process. Her throat closed up, her eyes swelled once again, and she was in serious danger of crying.

"Aidan, I—"

"Now's not the time to talk. You need to stay strong and focused on your dad, not on this." He nudged her knee with his own. "Come on. Eat up. You need to make sure you're set so when your dad gets out of surgery you can go to him."

Emma swallowed past the lump in her throat. "Okay."

And then she did just that.

After another couple of hours—which seemed like an eternity—the surgeon came out again to announce that the surgery had gone well, and her dad was now in the recovery room, regaining consciousness.

"Thank God," Emma breathed.

"He'll be groggy," the doctor said to them. "But he'll definitely know who you are. You were the last person he asked for before he went under, and the first person he asked for when he woke up. Are you ready to see him?"

Emma glanced at Aidan, who nodded at her. "I'll guard the fort."

The surgeon smiled. "I can take you back now."

"Okay."

She followed the woman back down the corridor, this time to a recovery room where her dad's big body was laid out flat in a hospital bed. He looked even worse than he had before, mostly because of the drugged-out look on his face.

"Emma?" he whispered hoarsely.

"I'm here, Dad," she said, crossing the room to sit by his side. Gently, she took his hand.

"Throat," he croaked out, reaching toward his neck with his other hand.

She reached out and took that one, too. "Shh, it's okay. They had to use a tube when they did the anesthesia during the surgery. It'll be sore for a while. How's the leg?"

"Makes Columbia…feel like a massage."

Emma knew what her dad was talking about. Almost twenty years ago, they'd taken their boat on a road trip to the Columbia River. Ryan had been so excited to ride on the river that he'd rammed the craft right into a sandbar while their father had been trailing behind on water skis. Dad had broken his wrist and gotten a concussion. Mom had still been alive then, and she was more furious at Dan for letting nine-year-old Ryan drive the boat than she was at her son for getting into the accident.

"Oh, Dad." There was so much pain in his eyes. Despite her vow to keep herself together, seeing him hurting this much was just too much to bear. Wetness trickled down her cheeks.

"Don't cry, honey. Please."

She stifled a sob and pressed her hands against her face to stem the tide of tears. In another moment, she'd collected herself. "I'm not crying. I stopped, okay? I'm here for you."

"What the hell did they do to me, anyway?" her dad asked.

"They put in some fancy new hardware. A permanent rod of

steel to go along with that hard head of yours." She gripped his hand again. "Want to tell me what happened?"

"Went to the garage to put away the caulk. There was a leak in the guest bathroom—you know, that spot in the corner between the tub and the wall? I got up on the ladder a little too high. Shouldn't have gone up there, couldn't feel my feet that well. Last thing I remember is reaching for the top shelf. I must have fallen."

"Merv found you."

"I left the garage open, is why."

"Thank God, or you could have been lying there for days." She took a breath. "They tell me the foot numbness is a side effect of the diabetes—neuropathy, it's called, and it messes up the nerves in your feet. I thought it was your balance, but really it's been because you can't feel your feet. You should have taken your medicine, Dad." She hated lecturing him, but he needed to understand this wasn't something he could fool around with anymore. Diabetes affected way more than blood sugar, and he needed to know that.

"It was stupid of me…not to take my meds. Didn't want to deal with it. Should have."

"That's in the past," she said, almost starting to cry again before she pulled herself together. She needed to be strong for her dad. "You have a clean slate, starting now, okay? No more cheating and skipping pills. And when you get out of here and you're all healed up, you're going back to PT." She squeezed his hand. "Deal?"

He smiled, but it came out more like a grimace. "Deal."

"Good. Because nothing like this can happen again. I—I can't lose you too, Dad." Despite her best efforts, the tears she'd suppressed trickled down her cheeks.

Her dad gripped her hand. "You can't get rid of me that easily. You know that."

"I'm sorry, I'm sorry." She sniffed, wiping the tears away. "It's just that you scared me so much."

"I'll…try my best…not to do it…again."

His eyes were closing, his strength obviously fading.

"Go to sleep, Dad. And when you wake up, I'll be here." She kissed his hand. "I promise."

CHAPTER 14

The days after the surgery passed in a blur. Emma had temporarily moved into her childhood home, and she spent her time making trips back and forth from the house to the hospital to the hardware store, bringing supplies, coordinating her dad's care, making sure the business stayed open, and getting everything set up for when her dad was finally discharged.

He'd be out of commission for a while, and for the first month and a half, he'd barely be able to move at all. They'd set up camp for him in the living room on the first floor, so she'd moved his bed downstairs, along with a side table, and gotten extension cords so he could plug in his laptop and cell phone right by the bed. She'd also gone to the library and taken out ten books for him to read—all mysteries.

With Ryan's help, Emma had hired round-the-clock nursing care, at least until her dad was marginally mobile. It was a huge expense, but given that she couldn't lift her dad and there was no one else to take care of him, there was little choice.

Aidan had moved seamlessly back into her life.

He had to be in to Portland to deal with his company, but he'd been coming to visit with her almost every day. Most days he'd drive out after work, hand off the mail he'd collected from her place, take her out to dinner, make sure she had everything she needed for the evening, then drive back to Portland late at night.

She was grateful for his assistance, but she found herself even more grateful for his company. He didn't press her about anything having to do with Wolfshead or her share. Just focused on her and what he could do to make her life easier while she sorted out her dad's care. He'd been there when the hospital had released her dad, helping to carry him into his new room, and he'd been there when she'd informed the staff at the hardware store that she'd be taking over the accounting for a while until her dad got back on his feet.

In fact, their routine felt like the one they'd shared in college, at least the first year they'd dated—their days apart, their evenings together. Until he'd graduated and left to go on the road.

Right now her dad was resting downstairs, and Aidan was taking out the garbage while she finished up the laundry. So domestic. And weird, being in her dad's empty room.

She folded her dad's shirts and opened a dresser drawer to put them away. When she rearranged some of his other shirts in the drawer so that the piles would lie straight, something caught her eye at the bottom. Carefully, she slid it out from under the stack of shirts and picked it up.

It was an old photograph—one of her and Aidan at his first minor league start, back when he was playing Single-A ball. He was wearing his baseball uniform and a slight smile. His chest was puffed out in pride and he looked handsome. Invincible. Euphoric.

She'd been so proud of him that day.

Right after the picture was taken, he'd laughed, pulled her into his arms, and kissed her, a powerful kiss that had sucked all the air right out of her lungs. Then she'd sat in the rickety stands at some aging ballpark in Savannah and watched him play.

God, they'd been so young and happy and stupid, never knowing that three years down the road, life would wallop them upside the head with the deaths of Aidan's dad and uncle.

"That was a good day, wasn't it?"

She turned to find Aidan leaning on the door frame, watching her.

"You looked good without your beard," she said, glancing again at the photograph. His cheekbones stood out more prominently, his lips almost carnal.

"I'm so used to it now, I'd feel weird if I shaved."

Quickly, she slid the picture facedown on top of the dresser and placed a small stack of shirts into the drawer. "I was just putting away some of my dad's undershirts. He hadn't done his laundry in forever." Aidan didn't answer, so she kept stacking and talking. "I'm finding all sorts of things in this house, things I don't even remember keeping. Old airline tickets, a certificate from my first communion, photographs…" She shook her head. "I don't know why my dad kept that one. Probably got left behind when I…"

"…got rid of everything that reminded you of me?"

She shut the drawer and slowly turned back to him then. "What happened to us, Aidan? Why couldn't we make it work?"

It was foolish, getting all sentimental about a photograph. About the way things were. But somehow, with Aidan so close, she couldn't help it.

"Because I'm an ass."

"I was to blame, too," she said. "I didn't stay. Try harder to work things out."

An expression of infinite sadness crossed his face. "Don't say that."

"Why not? It's the truth. If I'd stayed, maybe we could have—"

"Stop," he said, his voice jagged. "Please, just…stop blaming yourself. It wasn't you. It was never you." The look on his face had morphed from one of sadness to one of absolute agony. She hadn't seen him like this since he'd buried the two men he loved most of all, and it hurt—God, it hurt so much—to see him like this.

"Aidan—" she said, crossing the room to touch him, to hold him, to take away his pain. To take away her own.

When she reached him, he simply enveloped her in his arms and held her close to his chest.

"I never deserved you," he murmured. "All the sweetness you bring to my life. And me, bringing you nothing but hurt."

She buried her face in his chest. "You brought me happiness, too."

"Not for a long time. You just gave and gave, just like you're doing now. I mean, look at you. Your dad's laid up and you're working your ass off, telling me that I'm the one who didn't screw things up between us. You've got to take care of yourself. Protect who you are. Even from me."

He pulled away from her and ran a hand through his hair. "Look, Emma, I want to make things right with you so bad, but this isn't the time. You need to focus on your family now. Take care of your dad. Take care of yourself. And when you're ready, we'll talk. Really talk, okay?"

"Okay," she whispered, looking up at him.

His gaze softened. "I don't deserve this. But I'm gonna take it anyway."

Then he bent his head down and kissed her, a soft, sweet, achingly gentle kiss.

All too soon he had pulled away.

And like always, Emma was left aching for more.

Late on Thursday afternoon, just as production was winding down for the day, Aidan strode into the distillery. He spied Connor crouching on the concrete floor near the still, a clipboard in his big hands as he peered at the gauges.

"I need a favor," he asked.

Connor rose and cracked his left shoulder, the sound reverberating in the hollows of the room. He looked down at Aidan. "Name it."

"Can you push off the barrel tasting until tomorrow?" Once a week, he, Connor, and Finn dipped into the whiskey barrels and took a taste to see how the flavors were developing.

It was part of the process, but he found he enjoyed the sampling for its own sake. It was an education, for sure—tasting every stage of the alcohol from its birth through its youth, and finally to maturity—a front-row seat to the complicated chemistry that went into the creation of a fine whiskey.

More than that, it was a chance to convene with his cousins, to keep his finger on the pulse of his product, and Aidan looked forward to those few minutes every week.

"No need to push it off," Connor said. "Finn and I can handle it solo."

Aidan shook his head. "I'm in. Just give me an extra day."

"Going to see Emma?" Connor asked.

"Yeah."

There wasn't a question in his mind that he needed to be there for her, make sure she had the physical and emotional support to take care of her dad and herself.

Because once he'd decided that he needed her back in his life, he found himself not just wanting to be the man she deserved, but craving it. It was high time he started living up to Emma's expectations. And if he hadn't made that abundantly clear already, he was going to by letting his actions speak louder than his words.

"Do what you have to do," Connor said. "But we got this. Besides, I already asked Finn to change his band rehearsal this week."

It wasn't in Aidan's nature to give up control. If he reworked his schedule, he knew he could get everything done. But the way Connor was looking at him made him rethink his game plan. He could let it go, just this once.

Aidan let out a breath. "Okay," he finally said. "Take care of it."

"Consider it done." Connor shoved the clipboard into its holder on the wall and crossed his arms over his massive chest. "So how's she holding up?"

"All right, I think. She's tough."

"Plenty tough," Connor agreed.

"She's got it under control." *Or thinks she does.*

"She does," Connor said firmly. "She always did. Sometimes more than you."

"Well, this time she has help."

Connor nodded. "I always liked her. Especially for you. Even though you guys met young, I always knew she'd grow into the kind of woman who could handle you. Be everything you needed and more."

Aidan let out a breath. "Just say it. She's too good for me, right?"

"I'd never say that," Connor said with a frown.

"You thought it."

Connor gave him a sage look. "What I thought was that she made you a better man."

"She tries to."

"Now you're getting the picture," he said, and Aidan swore he saw the hint of a smile underneath his cousin's beard. Connor clasped his huge hand on Aidan's shoulder. "Go take care of your woman."

"I will, man," Aidan said. "I will."

CHAPTER 15

Emma stayed with her dad for a full week after he got home from the hospital. The home care aide—a woman named Marjorie—was kind as well as competent, for which Emma was grateful. Marjorie made sure her dad took his medicine and was as comfortable as possible. Plus, she was a wizard around the house, which meant Emma could actually get some work done, which was good, because she had a couple of projects that absolutely needed to get finished.

She'd somehow managed to acquire two more clients, who'd hired her for small projects. Neither of them was a huge deal like the Younger Beverages account, but jobs were jobs, and she was happy to have something to keep her occupied when she wasn't helping her dad.

Emma had gotten word that she'd been invited in for a second-round interview with Younger the day before her dad had his fall. It had been difficult to prepare, given her dad's state, but she'd managed. The interview was coming up early next week and although she was stressed about it, being with her dad helped her keep everything in perspective. Like Aidan had said, there truly was nothing more important than family.

Emma finished making some notes on the Younger account, then glanced at her watch. Time for her dad's medication, which she would be administering, given that Marjorie was on her lunch break. She went into the living room, expecting to find her dad asleep, but he was wide-awake, pain clouding his eyes.

"Hi, Dad," she said, approaching him.

"Hey, honey," he said.

"How are you feeling?"

"You don't want to know."

"Hurting?" she asked, helping him to adjust the pillows behind his head so that he could sit up to swallow the pills.

"Yeah," he said.

"Let's get you feeling better, then." She apportioned out the correct medicine—painkillers first, then antibiotics, then diabetes medication—making sure her dad had plenty of water to swallow everything down. "Need to go to the bathroom?"

He shook his head tersely. "I can wait."

Most likely he was too embarrassed to use the bedpan in front of her, but she nodded all the same. "Okay. Marjorie will be back from her lunch break soon and I'll send her in then."

"Sure."

She pushed his hair back from his forehead in a soothing gesture. "You're doing great, dad. The worst stuff has passed, and it's only going to get better from here on out."

He grunted in response.

While her dad shifted to make himself more comfortable, Emma took the opportunity to get him fresh water, swap out the magazines, and throw away the copious amount of trash that had somehow managed to gather around her dad's bed.

"Feeling up for payroll?" she asked, holding up a manila folder with the paperwork inside. "I went through everything to make sure it all looks good, but it needs your signature."

"Later," he said, waving it off.

"Sure. I'll just put it right here." She placed the folder on the coffee table, now relegated to the side of the room so it wouldn't be in the way. "We'll deal with it this afternoon. If you're okay for now, I'm going to tackle the garage."

Emma figured that while she was home she may as well take the opportunity to clear out her dad's old junk. She'd already told Ryan her plan, and he was beyond thrilled—he'd been after their dad to get rid of his crap for years, but his pleas had fallen on deaf ears.

"It's not that bad in there," he said, sounding defensive.

"Dad," she said, trying to keep her tone reasonable. "I can barely squeeze in to do the laundry, and you have to park your truck on the driveway."

"Guess it is a little cluttered."

"A little cluttered" was putting it mildly. "I counted two broken TVs, and a bunch of electronic devices, not to mention a ton of sporting equipment that no one's used in a decade—and that's just what I could see." Undoubtedly, when she started digging, she'd find a lot more.

To Emma, her dad's fall was a real wake-up call, a chance to set things right before it was too late to deal with everything. She wasn't looking forward to the task, but her dad was a captive audience, and it was the perfect time to clear everything out in case something like this, or worse, happened in the future.

"Fine, fine," her dad grumbled. "Do what you want."

"Good," Emma said. "I'm going to pitch what I can and donate the rest. And don't worry. I'll save the receipts for your deductions." Her dad was almost fanatical about his taxes, something she understood all too well, since she was the same way. "And anything that's important, you'll have final say on, okay?"

"Sure, okay."

Excellent. She thought she'd get a lot more pushback from her dad, but his fall seemed to have mellowed him a little. Or maybe that was the pain medicine talking. His eyes had lost their bright fierceness and had gone a little softer—a sure sign that the opiates were kicking in. She felt a twinge of guilt that she was getting her dad to agree to her plans, especially in his current condition, but a thorough cleaning of that garage had been a long time coming.

"Emma?" he asked.

"Mmm-hmm?" she said, spying a tissue under the bed and reaching down to get it.

"He's been here every day."

Emma straightened and looked at her dad. "Yes. He has."

It wasn't as if it was a secret. When Aidan arrived each evening, without fail, he would poke his head into her dad's room. If he was awake, he'd give him a polite hello. If he was sleeping, he'd ask Emma to give him his regards. Her dad hadn't asked whether Aidan had been spending the night, nor had he asked what was going on. He'd been like that when she and Aidan had separated, too.

She'd just shown up at the hardware store one day in late spring, crying her eyes out. He'd taken one look at her tearful face and had simply embraced her. *What did he do?* he'd asked.

Nothing, she'd replied. *Absolutely nothing.* And that was the problem.

"I—" her dad started, stopped, then started again. "I'm the last person who should be lecturing you given, well, given *this.*" He gestured to his leg.

Emma rose. "But you're going to lecture me anyway?" she said wryly, trying to get him to smile.

He didn't.

"I'm no good at this," he said, shaking his head. "I tried to be like your mother, but she was always so much better than I was at telling you the important—"

"Dad," she said, interrupting him. "Just say what you want to say."

"Fine. I've seen the way he looks at you. The way he watches you. He wants you back, Emma, and I don't know how I feel about that."

She didn't either, but she kept quiet. No use telling her dad her own doubts about the whole situation.

"Two years ago, you came back to Cannon Beach with a broken heart. Now the man who caused my baby girl that much pain is back again. If it were only the Wolfshead connection, I wouldn't be talking like this, but there's more to it this time, isn't there?"

"Yes," she admitted. It felt strange to say that out loud, odd to articulate the fact that whatever it was—this simmering thing between the two of them—went way beyond mere attraction.

"What are you going to do?"

"I don't know." The absolute truth.

"That's what I figured." Her dad let out a breath. "Look, Emma, you were married to the man for three years, dated him for years before that, and you know that Aidan isn't a man who messes around. He wants something, he gets it, period. And honey? He definitely wants you."

At this, Emma took issue. She'd always been independent—it was probably why she'd stayed so long with Aidan even when she wasn't getting what she needed in return. "So you're saying I have no choice in the matter?" Emma said, her words coming out more sharply than she anticipated. "That he wants me and that's that?"

"Hardly. You're tough as nails, just like your old man," he said, grazing her cheek with the back of his hand. "So you call the shots. Figure out whether you want him or not. If you don't, tell him to go. If you do, well, then you'll figure it out. But you need to be in control here. He hurt you before, so you need to be careful. Because watching you go through that again?" He shook his head. "Well, that's something a father doesn't want to see once in his lifetime, let alone twice."

Emma looked at her dad's plain, worn face. Despite his pain, despite the fact that he couldn't even walk without support, her dad was protecting her. Her heart swelled with love for this singular man.

"I love you," she told him.

"I love you too."

She bent and kissed him on the cheek. "I'll let you get some rest while the meds finish kicking in."

Her dad nodded and closed his eyes. Quietly, she slipped from the room and shut the door. Once she was in the hallway, away from his keen gaze, she leaned against the wall, thinking about what her dad had said. *Be careful.*

But she wasn't. Unfortunately, when it came to Aidan, she just couldn't help herself. He'd come back into her life, bigger than ever. No wonder she hadn't been able to move on—she'd never let go in the first place.

She'd slept with him again, but that could easily have been explained away by the wine and the memories and the reminiscing. She'd even kicked him out in the morning when she realized he had no intention of changing. But the fact that he'd been there when her dad had gotten hurt, had stayed by her side and not left, had helped her while she went through one of the most trying times of her life, couldn't be discounted. There *was* something more, something she wanted very much to explore once her dad's health improved and she got back to her regularly scheduled life.

Whether he would stay or go then, she wasn't certain. But one thing she knew for sure—she wasn't through with Aidan Phelan, not by a long shot.

So she would proceed with caution, see how things developed. Time would tell whether he'd turn out to be different than he was before…or whether he was the same old Aidan he'd always been.

She prayed she was making the right decision, hoped against hope that she could trust him again. Because if things turned out like they did before, it wasn't just her heart that was going to break. It was going to be her soul.

CHAPTER 16

The sun had barely risen when Aidan got to the turnoff for his cabin in Parkdale. He was looking forward to that hike he'd promised Emma, and he could tell the day was going to be perfect for it. The early morning light filtered through the clouds, lifting his mood. Deliberately, he rolled down the windows on the truck, inhaling the scents of pine and damp earth.

As always, past and present came together the moment the cabin came into view in the clearing, two rustic stories filled with love and loss, memories and dreams.

How many days had he stood on the back porch and simply stared at the majesty of Mount Hood, which rose high in the distance? How many nights had he sat in the hot tub, the stars above his head, the mountain standing sentry?

Aidan's great-great-grandfather John had hewn many of the logs for the original place himself, which back then must have been quite a feat. He'd often wondered if old John Phelan had known then what kind of legacy he'd be leaving, or whether it had simply been wishful thinking on his part. Whatever the reason he'd chosen to build here, Aidan was grateful.

This was more than simply a cabin—this was home. Where he'd played as a boy, come of age with his brothers and cousins, and now escaped to as an adult. There was so much of himself wrapped up in this place, just like there was at Wolfshead. So many memories—good and bad—that were part of him.

After parking his truck on the gravel driveway, he unlocked

the cabin and went inside. At least one of his family members was up here every weekend, and sometimes even during the week, plus everyone pitched in to keep it clean, so the place felt warm and cozy, without any of that dank, dusty aroma he associated with rarely inhabited houses.

From the front, the place didn't look that large, but his dad and uncle had added on to the original 1,500-square-foot cabin so that it was now closer to 5,000 square feet. Inside, it had nine bedrooms, and a huge great room that connected to an equally large kitchen. It was rustic, to be sure, with exposed ceiling beams and an original pinewood floor that they covered with large throw rugs.

In the well-stocked pantry, he found several boxes of granola bars—Brody's favorites, likely remnants of his cousin's car-restoration vacation. Aidan was tossing a few into his backpack when he heard the telltale crunch of tires on the driveway and then the slamming of a car door.

He went outside to meet Emma. She'd parked her Outback next to his truck. Her hair was swept back into a high ponytail and *Jesus* what the hell was she wearing? A tight, long-sleeved athletic shirt and some kind of spandex pants that clung to every dip and rounded curve. When they were together she'd never worn clothes like that…ever…but they looked damned good on her.

Shoving back an inconvenient surge of lust, he leaned against the porch rail.

"Hey," he said.

"Hey," she responded, going around to the passenger side of the car and rummaging around.

"How's your dad?"

"Not much to report," she said. "He's still unhappy about the bed rest, but it's the only way he's going to heal properly. Ryan's there with Marjorie this week, which is why I was comfortable leaving him." Emma pulled out a small blue day pack and shut the car door.

"Have any trouble finding the place?"

"Nope," she said. "I remembered how to get here." She glanced up at the sky. "I think it might rain. Better get my poncho."

She popped the trunk, and he was treated to a perfect view of her ass. His cock swelled uncomfortably against his fly, and he shifted to relieve the pressure. He'd better be first on the trail, because if he had to stare at her butt for the entire hike, he wouldn't be able to get that far.

"Aha!" she said triumphantly, pulling it out and slamming the trunk. "I'll just pop this in my bag and then I'll be ready to go. Do you have a hike mapped out for us already, or do you need me to make a recommendation?"

"I thought we'd do Mirror Lake," he said. One of the more popular hikes in Mount Hood National Forest owing to its easy terrain, mild altitude change, and killer view of the mountain reflected in a glacier lake, it was usually pretty crowded. Hopefully the hordes wouldn't be swarming today. "But we could do something more challenging if you're up for it. Say Paradise Park or Cooper Spur?"

"No. I love both those trails, but Mirror Lake is great. And we can do Tom Dick and Harry Ridge if we're feeling it." The ridge would add several extra miles onto the trip. "Does that sound okay?" She shrugged on her pack and came over to the side of the porch.

Emma was just as beautiful in this state as she was in her fancy work clothes. She wore no visible makeup, though she'd never needed it to enhance her natural beauty. Freckles dusted her cheeks and the bridge of her nose. Her eyelashes were lush and dark, perfectly framing her brown eyes, and her lips were a deep pink. Gorgeous. He couldn't help himself from wanting her. Didn't even try to pretend he didn't.

His expression must have been a little too intense, because she tilted her face up, her gaze searching his.

"Are you *sure* this is a good idea?"

"Just talking, remember?"

"Right. Just talking," she said, but she didn't sound too certain of that. Not a surprise, given that every time they'd been together in recent memory, there was serious tension between the two of them.

He cleared his throat. "So do you have water?"

"A gallon," she said with a decisive nod. "Do you think I need more? It's not that strenuous a hike, but I have an extra CamelBak I can fill."

"Nope, that should be good. Even if we add on the ridge it'll be under six miles round-trip, and we're starting early." He shoved himself off the rail, locked the cabin door, and motioned to his truck. "I'm driving. Hop in."

Aidan popped in one of Finn's old band CDs and they talked as they rode, mostly about people they knew, family, and friends. It was a good thirty minutes to the park entrance, where Aidan flashed his rec badge, required of all visitors, but the time passed by pretty quickly. After another ten minutes, they pulled into the lot near the trailhead.

Without any issues, they gathered up their gear and started out. The trail was well maintained and wide, but he took the lead, mostly so he wouldn't have to stare at her ass the whole time. As he suspected, things were quiet this morning and they didn't talk much over the first couple of miles. Only a few hikers dotted the path, murmuring *good mornings* as they passed by. A couple of times he turned back to make sure she was keeping up with him. The climb had an altitude change of about seven hundred feet, and she was doing fine, so he kept going, listening every so often for the soft padding of her shoes on the dirt trail.

Then he caught his first glimpse of the lake.

Some of the cloud cover had burned off, and the still-snowcapped Mount Hood had come out, rising high above the circular lake. Stately dark green pine trees surrounded the water, and a mirror image of the sky, the trees, the mountain, and the snow was reflected in the deep blue of the lake.

Behind him, he heard a little gasp. He turned back to find that Emma had stopped, her mouth partway open, as she stared out at the majesty laid out before them like a picture postcard.

"I'd forgotten how beautiful this place is," she said.

"Same."

The last time Aidan had been here was right after he'd returned to Portland. Feeling angry and volatile, he'd dragged himself out to the cabin and up to the mountain. But despite the beauty, the hike had been tainted.

He'd handled everything so badly, not confiding in Emma, not even talking, really. He'd barely been hanging on to his temper by a thread, but that didn't excuse the abysmal way he'd treated her.

But that was part of the reason why he was here. To move forward.

Emma was still watching the lake, her beautiful face gazing out over the water. She breathed in deeply, and he did too, the air redolent with pine and damp earth.

"Do you want to go back?" he asked reluctantly.

She turned to him. Slowly shook her head. "No, I remember that there are some great wildflowers up the side of the mountain. I want to see them. And I could use the exercise. I've been cooped up in my dad's place for a while—not that I don't love being with him, but seeing him in so much pain is hard to take."

"Okay. We'll go on then. You need to be feeling good in order to take care of him, so you're my priority today."

Her eyes warmed in acceptance, and they kept going.

They skirted the water using the lake path, then bore right and kept walking up the trail. The elevation change was a bit more intense—another nine hundred feet—but the incline wasn't that bad. They went at a good clip, and after another forty-five minutes they emerged at the summit, the valley spread out below them.

This was surely one of the most exceptional vistas in the park. Down below, the verdant green of the trees was punctuated by the deep blue circle of Mirror Lake. Beyond the trees and the lake, Mount Hood stood in all its glory. Nature, unspoiled.

Despite the fact that he'd seen the view a hundred times, Aidan sucked in a breath. Next to him, he heard Emma do the same.

He'd forgotten how stunning it was. And how incredible sharing it with someone else could be. With *Emma*.

She was looking out over the landscape with an expression of wonder, and when she shot him a brilliant, grateful smile, he nearly became undone.

"It's beautiful," she said.

"Yes." And not just the view.

Emma took a picture with her cellphone camera, then pulled a sketch pad and pencil out of her pack, sat down cross-legged, and began to draw. From the rapid way her sketch was coming together, she'd let none of her talent slide.

"I thought you'd stopped," he said. Though she'd minored in art, she'd pretty much given that up to focus on her career, and he hadn't seen her sketch since well before their marriage started to crumble.

Emma didn't look at him, but he saw that her cheeks had turned a bit red. "I did. Then I started again."

"When?"

Her pencil was still flying over the page, stroking, shading.

"Remember all those weekends when you were at Wolfshead?"

"Yeah." All too well. Those endless days spent fighting with Grandfather. Those sleepless nights spent locked in his office, trying somehow, someway, to figure out how to convince him to see reason.

"Well, I missed you. So I'd go on these long hikes to get out of the house, clear my head for a while. And I'd be alone a lot of the time, so of course I didn't have to worry about pacing myself to get back to someone."

Emma wasn't playing a game of point-the-blame. Still, shame and regret intermingled, making his throat close up. He'd let her down. Left her alone time and again. No matter what he'd been going through, what he'd done was unacceptable. No wonder she'd left him.

Emma kept on drawing and talking, oblivious to his shame spiral.

"I started this project for me, but then I began posting my pics on social media. People liked them and it kinda snowballed. I got upward of twenty thousand hits per month on my accounts, and I enjoyed it, so I kept doing it, even after we got divorced." She was still sketching, her head down. "I was so lonely, Aidan. And broken. I can't tell you how broken I felt. Like I'd screwed up not just my marriage but my life because our relationship had fallen apart. I know it's dumb, and they're just numbers, but the external validation meant something to me." She shrugged. "I guess it still does. Otherwise, I wouldn't keep doing it."

Aidan stared, stunned. He'd never known. She'd kept this part from him because he'd been so wrapped up in his own shit he hadn't seen what he had right in front of him.

But he saw it now. The sheer strength of her. The willingness to see the good in everything. The ability to make lemonade out of lemons, each and every time. She deserved so much more than what he'd given her.

"I'm sorry." The words burbled up out of him, stoppered for so long. He was intensely conscious of the fact that he hadn't apologized. Not once during their separation and divorce. Things were too raw, and he'd been too much of a jerk.

She looked up at him, her mouth a little open.

"You didn't deserve that from me. Not then, and not now."

"So…are we actually talking about this?"

"Yeah." It was time.

"Then I want to know why." Her voice sounded small in the damp air. "Why didn't you talk to me? All I wanted was to be part of your life. And you just shut me out."

So many reasons. Aidan took a deep breath, searching for the right words to say. "I'd always wanted to play ball. From the first time I held a baseball in my hand it just felt right, you know?"

He looked away, out across the valley.

"There really is nothing like being out on the mound, the hot sun scorching your face, staring down that batter, knowing that one pitch could win the game. I thrived on the rush. And I'd be lying if I didn't say the attention I got was a rush, too. For me and my dad, it was something more. I craved that pride in his eyes, the honor I was bringing to the family. When I got drafted, he was so fucking proud, he told everyone who would listen that his kid was playing ball for the Mets." He turned back to her. "You remember him after my first minor league game?"

"Yes," Emma said, a faint smile on her lips. "He strutted around like a peacock."

"Mom told him to knock it off, but he could never get enough. He kept everything—clippings, articles, whatever. He was my biggest fan. He made me want to achieve on a whole different level.

"When he died and I came back to Portland, I knew I'd never play ball again, but I was still striving, wanting to show that my sacrifice had all been worth it. Wolfshead became my pride, my obsession…" *My punishment.* "I didn't want to be back here. I wanted to be out on the open road, playing ball. But my family needed me here. My mom needed me here." He stopped for a minute. Took a breath. "She's strong, but even she couldn't stand up to Paddy. No one could except me. He controlled everything and scrapped all of Dad's plans. And the whole reason I'd come home, my chance to prove myself, to show what I could do, was taken away. I was so fixated on reaching for that, so angry about what I'd given up, I lost sight of everything I'd gained. I turned into a bitter man, hating everything around me."

"Even me."

He sat down next to her, close enough so that their shoulders were touching. "I never hated you, Emma. You were the best fucking thing in my life, only I didn't even realize it. I look back now and remember how you were always there for me, waiting, supporting. And I crapped all over your love. You deserved more than I could give."

Her lips trembled. "Why didn't you tell me?"

"What good would that have done? I couldn't see what I was doing."

"I could have helped."

"And dragged yourself down with me."

"At least we would have been together. Instead, you just pushed me away." Her eyes were brighter than they usually were, and he realized she must be holding back tears.

He wrapped his arm around her shoulder and pulled her close. "I know. I shouldn't have let you go. Shouldn't have ever let you walk out that door and say good-bye. I've been living in hell these past couple of years, and it's because I don't have you in my life."

"I've been living in hell, too," she said, chin down now, voice muffled.

He cupped her jaw. Tilted her head to face him. "That's going to change."

"You say that and it sounds so good, but that's not reality. People don't just change."

"I do. I know what I want, Emma. And that's you. I'm going to make it my mission to be the man you deserve."

"I want so badly to believe you." She closed her eyes for a long moment, and when she opened them again, he saw that the tips of her lashes were wet. "But what makes you think it'll work now when it didn't work then?"

"Because we're both different people." He knew that now. "Stronger people."

She didn't believe him; he could see the doubt in her eyes. But that didn't matter. As long as she gave him a chance, he would prove to her that he was exactly what she needed.

The sky had grown darker, and the air was thicker. Rain was definitely on the horizon, and they were higher up, exposed to the elements. He grabbed her hand and stood, pulling her up with him. "Come on. I think it's time to go."

They hiked back down in virtual silence. As they reached the lake, it began to sprinkle, and by the time they got back to the car, it was a full-on downpour. Emma hadn't bothered to put on her poncho because it wouldn't have done any good in the torrent, anyway. Cold and soaked, they drove back to his cabin.

He pulled into the familiar gravel lot and stopped.

"Want to come inside until the rain eases up?"

She gave him a strange look. "Is that a line?"

"Only if you want it to be," he said easily.

She looked down at her wet clothes and held her shirt away from her body. "I *am* pretty wet." As if on cue, she gave a little shiver.

"I'll get a couple of towels so we can dry off."

They raced into the house, getting even wetter, not as if it mattered, given that they were already soaked to the bone.

"I'll be back in a sec," he said, heading to the linen closet.

When he returned, he found Emma in the great room, visibly shivering. He wrapped a towel around her shoulders and rubbed her arms briskly, trying to impart some warmth to her. It didn't seem to help, so he pulled the edges of the towel toward him and Emma along with it, wrapping her in his embrace.

"Feels good," she mumbled, burying her face in his chest.

She was small in his arms. Vulnerable. *His to protect.*

And he'd done a shitty job of it. If he could erase all the pain he'd caused her over the years as easily as her chill, he'd have given anything. But this was going to take time and patience, something that had never been his strong suit. Still, for Emma, he was going to try.

She'd nestled into him more now, and her body rubbing gently against his was sweet agony.

"How are you so warm?" she asked, her teeth still chattering.

"Babe. You know I run hot."

She half groaned, half laughed. "Bet you say that to all the ladies."

He took a deep breath, wanting her—no, *needing* her—to know. "There hasn't been anyone else."

She leaned back to look at him, her brow furrowing in confusion. "Are you serious? You're telling me that you haven't slept with anyone since we split?"

There'd been opportunities. Plenty. Women liked him—the big, bearded ex-baller. But he hadn't indulged. After ignoring them for a while, they usually moved on to Gabe, who was an easier target. Gabe hadn't minded. But for him, it meant his existence had been lonely.

He took a breath and told her the truth. "There's been no one but you, Emma."

Her eyes went huge then, and her lips parted. He'd never seen her look more beautiful, her hair dripping wet, her eyes dark, her lips red. Without thinking, he bent his head and touched his mouth to hers.

When he pulled away, she had a slightly dazed look on her face, a look he'd never tire of seeing.

She gave him an accusatory smile, layered with sadness. "This isn't just talking."

"No." Reluctantly, he drew back.

He wanted her more than he could express in words, but if they were going to do this, she needed to be all in. No regrets. No apologies. "Your lead, Emma."

Her expression changed, as if she were waging an internal war. For one agonizingly long moment, he thought it was over. That she was going to step away from him. Nod and say thank you for the hike and get back into her little station wagon and drive away again. He steeled himself, waiting for it.

And then a small hand snaked out of the towel, grabbed him by the shirt, and pulled him in. "My lead," she whispered, just before her lips touched his.

CHAPTER 17

For one single moment, Aidan froze.

Then he groaned and followed her lead, wrapping his arms around her once again and opening her mouth with his.

She was here, giving herself to him, and there was no way he could say no, especially not when her little tongue stroked against his, eliciting all sorts of memories of exactly how talented she was with that particular muscle.

God, she felt good in his arms, even chilled and freezing cold, and he wanted her, the woman he loved, who'd once loved him back.

He dragged his hand through her damp, thick hair and held her there, clasping her head so she'd have no thoughts of moving away. A sharp wave of wanting swept through him, intense and uncomfortable.

This wasn't new for him—this need for complete and utter possession. What was new was the uncertainty that she might not *want* to be possessed by him. He'd never doubted it while they were married. And when they'd had sex that night after dinner at her place, he hadn't even been thinking in those terms. He hadn't been thinking much at all.

But now he knew exactly what he had in his arms. An exceptionally brave woman. One who could have run, but was instead showing him that she trusted him.

He didn't deserve this, for so many reasons. He knew that. But he would take what she was offering anyway and then do everything in his power to earn it.

He kissed her deeply, thoroughly. She tasted of chocolate and oats, sweet and nutty and utterly intoxicating.

She kissed him back with equal fervor, clearly as into this as he was. Thank God.

She was warming up under his touch, but he knew exactly how to make her even warmer. He shoved the wet towel off her shoulders, ran his hands up the back of her damp shirt, and slowly peeled it from her body. She moaned and pressed into him, her nipples tiny stones beneath her bra.

Unable to resist, he palmed one generous breast and was rewarded with a gasp. When he rubbed his thumb over the tip, she moaned.

"Mmm…"

"Do you like that?" he whispered.

"You know I do," she whispered back.

"Then let me give you more."

With an expertise honed from years of practice, he unclasped her bra. He let that fall to the floor too, until she was standing there before him, her beautiful breasts bared to his gaze, his touch. And he would touch. Over and over again.

He kissed her mouth, ran his thumb over her swollen nipple. When he gave it a gentle pinch, he caught her moan in his mouth. He nibbled on her lips, then tilted her head to give him better access to her neck and that sensitive spot just below her ear—the one that drove her crazy.

Both hands were working her breasts now as he kept busy on her neck, and when he got to that secret spot, he twisted both nipples at once.

"Aidan, *please*." Her breathing was coming raggedly now, and she was clutching his shirt, bunching it between her fingers and squeezing it so tightly that the fabric around the back of his neck was pulling taut.

"Bedroom," he said, and swept her into his arms.

She kissed him all the way there, refused to let go of him even when he deposited her on the bed. She dragged him on top of her, wrapped a leg around his waist, and gyrated beneath him.

"I need you," she said. "Now."

Shifting his weight off her, he moved to the side so that her head was nestled in the crook of his elbow. Then he slid a hand right down the waistband of her leggings. With some tugging they came off, along with her panties.

She was gorgeous, the whole deliciously curved line of her. Full breasts, her small rib cage, her waist that flared out to generous hips, more than enough for a man to hold on to. She was thicker in the thigh, but he loved that she was strong, with visible muscles and plenty of padding, just perfect for a big man like him.

She lifted her head. "Aidan?"

"Just looking my fill of you."

In the earlier days of their relationship, back when they were still young and Emma was still relatively innocent, she'd been shy, ashamed of her body. Slowly, patiently, he'd drawn her out, told her how beautiful she was…and shown her exactly how she deserved to be worshipped.

Under his perusal her gaze warmed, and then she opened her legs, just a fraction. That gesture, that offering, took his breath away. She hadn't forgotten how much he loved to look. And to touch.

He ran his fingers down her side, skimming them over her soft belly, the slight bulge of her hip bone. Hands played over her thighs, swept down, then back up again.

"I never forgot," he said slowly. "How very beautiful you are."

She pressed her lips together, shook her head.

He started at her toes, kissed his way up her ankle, her calf, the inside of her thigh. She trembled when he gently opened her legs even more. And when he finally kissed the sweetest spot of all, just once, she shuddered in his arms.

He slid a finger inside her heat, rewarded when she moaned. He worked in and out, going deeper each time, making sure to drag his fingertips across that sensitive pad on the upper side of her walls. She moaned louder with each pass, fairly panting now. Good. He loved seeing her like this. On the edge of control, craving his touch.

He added a second finger, stretching her, preparing her, wanting her to feel only pleasure when he finally entered her body. He rubbed his thumb on her clit, and her hips came off the bed.

Continuing to stroke inside her deeply, he bent his head and drew her nipple deep into his mouth.

She came on a shriek, then shuddered and lay still.

Cupping her jaw, he kissed her mouth again, at first gently, then harder as she responded eagerly. Soon he was kneading those fabulous breasts again, and when she started twisting and moaning, he swept his fingers right through her folds. She was wet, soaking.

That and the glazed look in her eye were proof that she wanted him as much as he wanted her.

And he definitely wanted her. His cock was rock hard, pressing uncomfortably against the inside of his fly, raring to be set free.

But he wanted to play some more.

"Here's what's going to happen," he said, continuing to stroke with one hand, even as he started stripping with the other. "I'm going to touch you," he said, unbuttoning his jeans and easing down the zipper. "Then I'm going to make you come again. With my mouth."

"Oh God," she said on a choked gasp.

His jeans hit the floor, and then he was right back where he was before, poised over her, his gaze on hers.

A shiver coursed through her, and she grabbed his face between her hands to smash her lips against his, so obviously turned on. He nipped the sensitive skin on her neck, and Emma shuddered. More so when he flicked one erect nipple with his finger. But he got the most intense reaction when he licked that crazy, sensitive spot behind her ear.

He slid down her body until his mouth was directly above her waiting core. Wedging his shoulders between her thighs, he lifted one leg, baring her to him even more. And then he bent his head and tasted.

At his first touch, she nearly came off the bed, but he clamped down on her hips with his hands and held her still while he pleasured her. Her hands found his head, speared through his hair. But he wasn't going anywhere until he'd brought her up again, just as he'd promised.

He took his time, tasting, loving her breathy moans, loving her hands in his hair, loving the power she had over him while he worshipped her body.

Her sweet little noises were music to his ears, and she was so primed it didn't take long before she was almost there. Her breathing quickened, and the fingers in his hair tightened.

"Aidan," she gasped. "I need…I need."

"I know what you need," he said, and curled his fingers and sucked hard enough to send her flying. Her back arched, she cried out his name, and then she went boneless.

He kissed the inside of her thigh and when he looked up, she was looking down at him, her gaze fierce.

"Hang on." He jackknifed off the bed and went searching for a condom.

One of the benefits of being in his family's house was that he didn't have to search long. He pulled open the bedside table drawer and found a whole box of condoms, likely Gabe's, but at the moment he didn't really care that he was raiding his little brother's stash.

Sheathing himself, he settled between her legs. "Gonna fuck you now," he said, drawing her thigh up and easing his way inside. She welcomed him, wrapped her arms and legs around him to pull him closer, and Christ, being buried in her was the best feeling in the entire world.

He pulled out, then plunged back in. Emma's breath left her in a soft whoosh. And then she was kissing him and kissing him, like she couldn't breathe without him.

He settled on a moderate pace, angling himself to hit her clit with each downstroke. She tossed her head and moaned, even as she rocked her hips against him, urging him on. Her fingers scrabbled for purchase on his back, then finally settled on his lats which she gripped—hard—as he picked up the pace.

She had to feel this as much as he did, this undeniable connection between them that would never break, no matter how long they were apart, no matter how many years had passed.

"Oh, it's too much, Aidan. Too much."

"You can take it," he said, sliding back in.

Her head was thrashing back and forth now.

"No, no, I can't, I—"

"You can." He rubbed her clit with his finger, and she clamped down hard. She cried out, her back bowed, and then he was thrusting into her once, twice, and a final time, until he came, too, on a triumphant shout.

He withdrew as soon as he came to his senses, and wrapped her up in his arms, pressing her head against his chest. She was still shuddering from the aftershocks, so he ran his hand down her back, calming her.

When he drew back to check that she was all right, there was an astonished expression on her beautiful face. Her cheeks were flushed, her hair everywhere.

She looked up at him with a tremulous gaze.

"Some talk."

"Yeah."

"We always end up here, don't we?" This, said ruefully.

"Is that such a bad thing?"

"It's not a good way to move forward."

"It depends on your goals, I guess."

The corners of her mouth went down. "I guess. I don't want to talk about that now, anyway. Not when I feel this good." She nestled back in his arms and turned her face toward his chest, hiding her eyes from his gaze.

This was the start of something new between them, something better. They'd build their relationship from the ground up again and emerge stronger than ever before.

And as he lay there, holding his woman—because at some point he'd started to think of her as his woman once again—he realized that his goals had changed.

He was no longer content to wage a mere battle for her heart. He wanted more than that. He wanted everything she had to give.

And when he got it this time, he damned sure wasn't going to let her go.

CHAPTER 18

Stretched out before Emma from her vantage point on the gently swaying porch swing lay the misty green of the meadow, and beyond that, Mount Hood, tall and proud, still hazy from the spring rainstorm. Despite the fact that she was wearing only her stretchy top and panties, she was warm and dry thanks to a huge, fuzzy blanket, not to mention her earlier workout in the bedroom. She felt complete in a way she hadn't in the longest time.

Three fabulous orgasms would do that to a woman.

She dragged in a breath, inhaling the aromas of damp grass and earth. Maybe it would rain again. Maybe not. When she was up here, time blurred, and all that seemed to matter was the cadence of the weather, the rhythm of the season.

She'd been here for a day now, during which time Aidan had warmed her, fed her, and made love to her. It was idyllic—the kind of getaway she'd always hoped to have when they'd been together before.

In the early part of their relationship, back when she was still in college, she'd been so damn young, foolishly thinking they'd have all the time in the world to spend together. But there'd been his career, the endless travel, a different city every third night. And of course, she was focused on her studies and her burgeoning career. They'd never really had the life she'd envisioned.

Maybe it was her own expectations that had been lacking all along.

She thought she'd had everything figured out. But then Aidan came thundering back into her life in the most unexpected way, and here she was again, right back where she'd started.

It wasn't such a terrible place to be.

The object of her thoughts emerged from the house, wearing only a pair of low-slung jeans that showed off his amazing chest, a solid slab of muscle, gorgeously defined. Lots of professional athletes just let themselves go after they'd retired. Not Aidan. He looked as good as he had when they first met and he hit the gym almost every day. Better, even. Brazenly, she let her gaze sweep over his form.

He noticed and returned her perusal with a smile visible even under the beard.

Emma had never been the kind of woman to fall for a pretty face or a prettier body. Her dad had taught her that it was what was inside that counted, something she saw firsthand when her mom had succumbed to cancer. Even while the disease had ravaged her body, her dad had told her mom that she was the most beautiful woman on earth.

In her mind, what truly made a person worthy was how they acted and treated others. How they conducted themselves. How much grace they displayed under pressure.

But there was no denying Aidan's straight-up sex appeal.

Settling next to her on the swing, he wrapped a big arm around her.

"It's cold out here," he said. "Sure you don't want to come inside?"

"In a minute," she said, letting her gaze shift from the man candy next to her to the scenery. "It's just so beautiful."

"Sure is," he said, then kissed the top of her head.

Sighing, she melted into him. She'd have to think about everything later when she'd put some distance between the two of them. Because right now, nestled into Aidan's side in front of the most beautiful postcard picture in the world, she could almost pretend that things were like they were at the beginning, back when their relationship had been shiny and new.

"You sure you're okay? You feel pretty cold to me." He'd snaked his other hand under the blanket to rest on her thigh.

"I'm sure you'll warm me up," she said. "And the blanket's plenty cozy."

"Yeah? I'll make a fire for you anyway."

Emma laughed. "What is it with men and their fires?" The very first time she'd joined Aidan and his family at the cabin, the Phelan boys had nearly come to blows over who was going to make, stoke, and maintain the fire. Christine had settled everything by having them draw straws, and even then there were still some hard feelings about who got to play with the pretty orange flames.

"Not sure," he said with a shrug. "Something primal about it, I guess. Besides, it'll give me an excuse to chop more wood."

"Are you still doing that?"

"Connor's still the fastest, of course. Dylan still loves it, but is crap at it. Ed still hates it, mostly because he can't get the wood to line up exactly the way he wants. Gabe's surprisingly good for his size."

"And Brody and Finn?"

"Finn doesn't care one way or the other, and Brody would rather be working on his cars. Anyway, we're supposed to take turns, just like we do with the rest of the maintenance for this place. I don't mind it. Whenever I feel stressed out, burned out…whatever…I come up here, chop some wood. Keeps us supplied in winter and usually makes me feel a hell of a lot better."

She loved that her lumberjack of a man actually chopped wood. "I'm glad you do it. Plus, it fits with the beard," she said, reaching up and running a hand through its soft thickness.

"So you like it?" he said, his voice a rumble.

"It suits you."

He smiled with his eyes. "That wasn't a yes."

"It doesn't matter whether I like it. What matters is whether *you* like it."

"Still not answering the question."

"What do you want me to tell you?"

"The truth," he demanded.

She gave a mock sigh. "Fine, it's sexy, okay? Is that what you wanted to hear?"

"Yes." He bent down and captured her lips with his.

She leaned against him again. "I've missed this." The teasing, the ease with which they interacted. "How long do you think this is going to last?"

"What, the beard?"

"No. This. Us, not fighting. Just…being."

"Long as you want."

"I'm serious."

"So am I." He wasn't laughing. Not even a little.

She shifted in his arms to face him. "You're telling me that this is the new normal? That you're not just going to shut me out again and disappear?"

He grasped her jaw in a big hand. "That's exactly what I'm saying. You let me into your life again, and I'm giving thanks for that every day."

"More like you barged your way in."

Aidan shook his head. "You're just as stubborn as I am when it comes to the two of us. You let me in," he insisted. "And no way am I going to disappear, not this time."

"We can't go back to the way we were, Aidan. I get that," she said. "But I'm not really sure how we're going to move forward. We just can't erase the last few years."

"No, we can't." He looked into her eyes. Refused to look away. "I told you I fucked up before, not giving you what you needed from me. I won't do it again. What we have between us is going to last as long as you want it to. As long as you'll have me. I want to be the man who deserves you, and now I gotta put in the work to make sure that happens. I lost you once. I'm not gonna lose you again."

"So you're not leaving?"

"You're it for me. You always were. The real reason I never had anyone else in my bed, in my life, was that no one could compare to you." He brushed his lips against hers. "My wildcat."

The emotion of the past few days must have been too much, because inexplicably, tears welled in her eyes. "Aidan—"

"You gave me another shot at this, another shot at you, and I'm not going to screw it up. Not this time."

He kissed her for real then, a deep kiss filled with passion and promise.

Her arms went around him, and it was the easiest thing in the world to let herself be pulled under once again, to let her body take over instead of her brain.

Things *were* going to be different this time. She was sure of it.

After her mini vacation with Aidan, Emma felt refreshed and ready to get back to her regularly scheduled life. For the time being, she planned to keep making trips to Cannon Beach, but while Ryan was still with her dad, she wouldn't have to stay overnight.

Now she was back in Portland, having just had an initial meeting with a new client she'd somehow managed to sign while staying at her dad's. This one—a start-up with a product in the later stages of development—had hired her to redo their company branding after a disastrous first go-round with another marketing consultant. The initial logo for the company, Doctor Base—a health-care service that matched doctors and patients—had not so much resembled a lower-case *d* and *b* together as it did an erect penis.

Which was obviously unacceptable for so many reasons and had made the middle-aged CEO, a physician himself, turn as red as a beet when he'd explained things to her. The situation called for not only a complete rebrand, but some damage control, as well. Luckily, she had enough experience with the latter that she knew exactly how to get the old logo scrubbed from the web.

She'd just emerged from that meeting and was heading down Fourth Avenue when she ran into Enzo Voglia coming out of a building. All at once, she realized she was right outside the Younger Beverages offices. Grateful she looked completely professional—skirt suit, heels, hair pulled back in a twist—she offered a smile.

"Mr. Voglia. Good to see you again."

"Ms. Crandall, hello," he said, his brown eyes twinkling as he shook her hand. "Nice to run into you. Are you here for work?"

"Yes," she told him. "A new project. Very exciting." She decided to leave out the details of the penis-capade.

"Excellent. Well, you saved me a call. I wanted to let you know that we had an executive meeting earlier today where we decided on our final round picks for our new branding plan. We enjoyed hearing about your vision for Younger, and we'd like to have you back one last time, just to make sure that the fit is right."

"I'd be thrilled," she told him honestly. "Just let me know when."

Enzo nodded enthusiastically, which hopefully meant she'd appropriately expressed her own excitement. "My secretary will be in touch to set up a time. But the sooner we get you in, the better. Mr. Younger is anxious to begin work."

"I'm sure we can find a good time," she told him. "I'll look forward to hearing from your secretary. In the meantime, while I have you, is there anything else you'd like me to prepare? Anything else you'd like to see from me that would help you to make a decision?"

"I like your ideas, Ms. Crandall, and I believe our founder will, too. He's big on personality, huge on fit." He gave her a rueful smile. "I know that information might not be what you were looking for, but it's what I can offer right now."

"No, thank you. That's a huge help. I appreciate your consideration, and I look forward to taking the next steps with Younger."

"Excellent, excellent. Well, I must be going. I have a meeting at four and I can't be late for it. See you soon?"

"Absolutely. Good-bye!"

Emma walked another two full blocks before she let herself relax. "Yes!" she said, doing a fist pump once she was sure Enzo was out of sight and earshot.

Some passersby gave her strange looks and edged away, but she didn't care what they thought. She was flying high and wanted to share.

The first person she called was Sara. Unsurprisingly, she was put through straight to voicemail. Then she called Robin. Her friend picked up after the third ring.

"Hello?" Robin answered breathlessly.

"It's Emma."

"Hi, Emma! No, don't touch that!"

Emma stopped in her tracks. "What?"

"Oh, I'm talking to the girls. They just started walking."

"That's great, Robin, I—"

There was a crash on the other end of the line, and then "Chloe, no! You'll get an owie!"

Emma chuckled. "It sounds like you have your hands full."

"No. I mean, yes. Oh my God, they are into *everything*. Charlotte just put her hand in the toilet!"

"I'd better let you go."

"I want to hear all the deets, I swear. Just…call me in five hours. After the kids go down. Chloe, noooooo!!" Robin wailed. And then the line went dead.

And that was that. Though Robin sure didn't need to be

talking to her after the kids went down. More like she needed a glass of wine. Or three.

Still feeling flush and wanting to talk, she tried her dad's cell next. It went to voicemail as well, and she didn't want to call the house in case he was resting. No matter. She was heading over there later tonight and would tell him then. And Aidan she could tell later in the weekend when she saw him in person. Somehow she knew he'd be happy for her.

How strange it was to even think of telling him something— anything—about her life after being apart for so long. Even a month ago, he wouldn't have been on her radar of people to call, and now she found herself itching to share.

She wasn't happy about her dad's fall, but it had been the catalyst for change, at least in her mind. If Aidan could stick by her when everything was falling apart, then there was hope for the two of them.

And for their future together.

With Brody, Connor, and Gabe standing around him in the tasting room, Aidan held out a shot glass of whiskey to their guest.

"Taste this," he said to the man by the name of Wes Parsons, alcohol buyer for the Roberts Group, one of the biggest restaurant chains in the country that had originally been founded in the Northwest. These were sports bars with big-screen TVs that served wings and burgers and beer. Lots of beer. Including every existing Wolfshead brew.

Wes might look like a bro with his blond hair, blue eyes, and penchant for wearing Seattle Seahawks baseball caps, but he had a real knack for knowing what was going to sell…and what wasn't.

It was the reason Aidan truly respected him. And the reason he'd chosen to renew Wolfshead's distribution contract with the Roberts Group when it had expired a couple of years ago.

It was in some part thanks to that distribution deal that their beer had become a household name. Seven years ago, few people outside the region had heard of Wolfshead lager. But with Wolfshead beers on tap in every Roberts Group restaurant, they'd been able to expand out naturally.

Under their watchful gazes, Wes swirled the amber liquid

around in his glass and took a deep sniff before tipping it back. He needed to like this whiskey.

Wes had been such a great supporter of them in the past, they'd invited him to the tasting party a couple of weeks ago. Unfortunately, he'd been traveling, so he'd asked Gabe to get Wes in for a private tasting because Roberts was a big buyer. If they could lock down a distribution deal for their whiskey with Wes it would be a good thing.

Wes was still sipping thoughtfully, a look of concentration etched on his slightly florid face. After way too long, where the only sounds in the room were the faint echo of the clock ticking on the wall and their comingled breathing, Wes put the glass down.

"Who made this?" was his first question.

"I did." Connor spoke quietly but firmly. "And Finn helped."

Wes looked the big man up and down with a careful gaze, taking him in from the top of his bearded head to his steel-toed boots and everything in between.

"*You* did?"

Connor gave him a nod. "Took me three years to perfect the recipe and another five years to produce and age it."

"Well, I'll be damned." He held out the glass, looking at it carefully. Did the sniffing and tasting thing all over again.

Finally, he put the glass down on the tasting room bar with a *thunk*. "That is some good shit," he pronounced.

"Thanks," Connor said, his lips twitching under his beard.

"Tell me about your process."

His big cousin shot him a look, and Aidan nodded. *Talk*. So Connor talked in that deep, quiet voice of his—about tweaking his recipes, his methodology, and his craft. Wes seemed to be lapping it up, nodding and smiling, and Aidan gave a sigh of relief that Connor hadn't clammed up, the way he usually did with strangers.

"Amazing," Wes said when Connor was through. He turned back to the other men. "What's your price point?"

Financials. Brody would take over, and he didn't need Aidan's permission. Just jumped right in. "Thirty-five dollars a bottle."

"Wholesale or retail?"

"Wholesale."

"What were you thinking for retail pricing?"

"Forty-five dollars."

"I'll give you thirty dollars a bottle. But I'll take the whole run."

"You serious?"

"As a heart attack."

"We'll have to talk it over," Brody said, looking over to him.

Aidan nodded. "We expected to break even with our first run. Recoup our losses. Maybe even make a little back. We'll have to run the numbers. See if we can make it work."

"If so, you have a deal."

Brody nodded. "Good." He seemed happy. So did Connor. Everyone except for Gabe, who stood there with his arms over his chest, watching Wes closely.

"Been doing this job for years," Wes said. "This product is just as good as the big-name brands I buy for Roberts. Better, maybe, and it's definitely better than any other small-batch whiskey I've tried in the past couple of years. Those big brands are fine as mixers, and they're smooth as hell, but they don't have much flavor. There's just something about a good craft whiskey that does it for me. And for anyone else who's a connoisseur. There's a depth to it—a kind of rustic note those big boys lack. Yours has honey, and tobacco and—" He picked the glass up, took another sniff. "Butterscotch. Incredible. How many barrels do you have available?"

Connor spoke up. "Our first run was fifty. That's what you're tasting. Second run was 75. Next year, we hope to be on track to double it."

"Is it all as good as this?"

"Better," Aidan assured him.

Connor didn't say anything, but the corners of his eyes crinkled with pleasure.

Wes took another sip. "Hot damn, that's good stuff. It'd almost be lost on the shelves at Roberts restaurants, but at that price point, I'd be a fool to let it go."

"Why would you say it'd be lost on the shelves?" Gabe asked. His tone was careful, but Aidan gave him a look anyway. One that said *shut your mouth*. Nothing was going to blow this deal.

Wes studied his glass again. "This is a finely developed whiskey. Most of the guys who show up at Roberts's sports bars want the cheap stuff. Your whiskey does not taste cheap."

"So branding—"

"Matters less than price point. Which, based on that alone, I find it hard to believe that no one else has spoken for it. It may be your first product, but it's going to be a winner."

"We've had interest," Brody said quickly. "But we haven't made any decisions yet."

"In that case, let me sweeten the pot. I'll put down an offer for whatever you have—your full run, like I mentioned—plus options for future runs. At the same price point."

"We still need to talk it over, but why don't you have your folks draw up a contract and send it over? You're one of our greatest supporters, and we're excited to continue to do business with you."

That was Brody, the master at smoothing things over at exactly the right time.

Wes grinned. "Always enjoy doing business with you boys." He rose. "I'll send a draft contract your way later today. That'll give you some time to think things over. Connor? You walk me out. Want to hear more about your plans for the future."

Connor nodded and walked with Wes to the door.

As soon as they were gone, Brody smiled. "Well, that went well."

"Yep," Aidan said. "Knew it would."

"What are you two talking about?" Gabe said. "Did you not hear a word he said?"

"I heard that we're about to sell our entire run, and future runs, too," Brody said.

Aidan nodded. "Agreed. The product is good, and in one whole shot, we'll be done."

"Not done!" Gabe said, obviously exasperated. "He all but said outright we'd be selling ourselves short if we sold to Roberts. You know as well as I do that we have something special here. Do you really want jocks and bros to be drinking our whiskey?"

Aidan raised an eyebrow. "What's wrong with jocks?"

"Or bros?" Brody added. "Let's just call them what they are—customers."

Gabe took a deep breath. "What I'm trying to say is that while our beers may be a good fit for the Roberts restaurants, our whiskey is not. Just like I've been telling you all along, we need to aim higher, and we need to have a solid branding plan to match our product."

Ever-calm Brody spoke up first. "Let's be reasonable, Gabe," he said. "Selling our product to Wes would be a good move. It's guaranteed income with a known partner. Breaking even financially our first year in market is a solid goal."

"No," Gabe said, shaking his head. "It doesn't matter if we break even, at least while we get our footing. We need to think bigger than Roberts. How many people have to tell us that we have an A-plus product before you two start to understand that? In my mind, we shouldn't settle for anything less than the most exclusive clubs, restaurants, and bars."

"Exclusivity isn't what our dads built this company on," Aidan argued. "They started with everyday beer for the everyday man, and we've done our best to keep their vision alive."

"But this whiskey is a completely different beast, something I've been telling you from the beginning," Gabe shot back. "You're gonna throw all of Connor's hard work away if you sign that contract, or any other contract that doesn't take the brand where it should go."

Brody scratched his beard. "I'm not convinced we want to get all fancy."

"Forget getting fancy, and don't think about the short term. If we sold it for double what Roberts would pay—a price I think we can actually get—we might sell less at first, but we would be pitching ourselves to a totally different client base. In the long term, we could be making so much more, don't you guys see that?" Gabe looked at the two of them, trying to get someone—anyone—to agree with him.

"So this is about the branding plan I had you prepare?"

"It's crap, Aidan. But you either don't know or don't care."

"What I think is that it doesn't matter. You heard Wes. He says that price point's more important to him."

"But it shouldn't be to us. Why aren't you getting this?"

Aidan reached out and placed a hand on Gabe's shoulder. "I hear you, but I'm not budging on this."

Gabe shrugged him off. "But *why*?"

"Because this is the way we do business."

"This is a bad way to do business," Gabe said, running a hand through his hair. He didn't look suave and put-together anymore. He looked upset, a man pushed past his limits. "Damn it, Aidan, why can't you see what you're doing?"

Clearly, Gabe wasn't going to let up until he spoke his mind. Aidan crossed his arms over his chest. "What am I doing?"

Gabe shook his head. "All my life I've admired you. Wanted to be just like you. But your pride's gotten in the way of the man you are. You're stuck in the past, caught up in some kind of need to prove yourself just as good as Paddy. He was a bastard. We all knew it. Except you're worse, because you run things the same way only you won't admit it."

"Gabe, just stop," Brody said. "You don't know what you're saying."

"I know exactly what I'm saying, and I know what you're both thinking, but I don't care. Laugh at me all you want. Tell me I'm a fuckup like you always do. But you're wrong, and I wouldn't be any kind of man if I didn't tell you how I felt." Gabe turned to Aidan and gestured at him. "You're supposed to be our leader, except you're not leading. You're just dictating, expecting everyone to fall into line. Look, I get that Wolfshead was never your dream, but I don't know why everyone else has to pay for it." Gabe's face got hard then. "He's not coming back, you know."

Aidan stilled. *Shut up.*

"He's never coming back."

Shut your mouth.

"And nothing you do, not this stupid deal or doing things the way he wanted or following his dream, is going to make that happen. Dad's dead," Gabe said, his face getting redder and redder. "He's been dead for six years. So how much longer are you going to let his death affect everything around you and everyone you love?"

There was a shocked silence. Even Brody seemed at a loss for words. Aidan clenched his fists, willing himself to stay calm, not to murder his little brother, whose face had morphed from red into a whiter shade of pale as he realized exactly what he'd said.

"Get the fuck out of here," Aidan finally rasped, his temper at its breaking point.

Gabe shook his head and pushed past him, actually knocking him off balance. When he left, the exit door slammed hard enough to rattle Ed's fishing poles.

For several long moments, Aidan continued to struggle for control. He wasn't a dictator. He was just trying to do what was best for Wolfshead. Yes, he'd put his dreams aside to focus on his family in a way that none of his brothers or cousins had ever had to do. But they should be thanking him, not treating him like shit.

"Don't worry," Brody finally said, putting a comforting hand on his shoulder. "Gabe's just being Gabe. He'll come around. You'll see."

Aidan nodded and grunted, but he still felt unsettled. Was Gabe truly just mouthing off, or was what he'd said truth? For some reason, that disturbed him most of all.

Brody seemed to agree with him, and so had Connor, but what if he was wrong? What if they were just saying yes to this deal because it was the path of least resistance? Because they didn't want to fight with him?

One of the things Aidan always prided himself on was his ability to keep his family together under every circumstance, no matter how challenging—the death of their fathers, the reign of their grandfather, the shifting market. Now it seemed as if they were coming apart at the seams. And despite Brody's words about Gabe being Gabe, Aidan wasn't so certain his little brother would fall in line this time.

If their family started to splinter, there was only one person to blame.

Him.

CHAPTER 19

Rontoms was crazy busy by the time Finn's band went on at ten on Sunday night. Luckily, Aidan, Brody, and Dylan had commandeered a table inside hours ago for dinner and had simply stayed for the music.

A restaurant/bar with a huge back patio in the industrial area of East Portland, a few blocks east of the Burnside Bridge, Rontoms was a little more on the trendy side than Aidan typically went for, but tonight's crowd was mellow, a mixed bag of PDXers, most of whom were here for the music. Sound echoed beneath the soaring wood ceiling, and if the acoustics weren't the greatest, it didn't seem to matter to the people nodding along to the strains of Finn's indie rock band, Fire of Youth.

Aidan had pretty much everything he needed: his family by his side, a cold beer in his hand—Wolfshead lager from the tap—and a great show to enjoy.

Finn had the most sublime expression of happiness on his face as he took a solo, foot pounding out the beat, fingers licking over the strings of his bass guitar. He never dressed up for his shows—just went on wearing whatever it was he'd worn that day to work. Which made sense, because Finn was all about the music.

Dylan leaned over the table, his voice carrying over the sound. "He's good, yeah?"

Aidan nodded. "Damned good."

Every time he saw Finn play, his cousin seemed to get better.

Fire of Youth had a decent following, had played in several Portland music festivals, and was written about fairly often in local publications. The band had even been featured on NPR for a story about local bands, something Finn had been pretty proud of. So far, they hadn't broken out of the Portland indie rock scene...yet.

Aidan had asked Finn more than once if he would ever consider leaving Wolfshead to get serious about his music. But every time he asked, Finn shook his head and said, *no way, man.* Apparently, it was no hardship for him to make beer and whiskey at the company—he loved that as much as he loved playing bass. It was just another part of him—or at least, that's how he described it to Aidan the one time he'd pressed further.

Which was fine with him, because at this point, any one of the Phelans' leaving the company was almost incomprehensible.

At the next break in the music, Brody leaned over to talk. "Gabe stop by your office this afternoon?"

Aidan shook his head. "Nope." He hadn't even known his little brother had come by the warehouse. As far as he knew, Gabe had been MIA since they'd gotten into their fight earlier in the week, the one dark spot in life right now.

"He'll straighten out," Brody said.

"You think?"

"Yeah. Might take a while, though."

On that, Brody was right. Gabe had definitely gotten the Phelan stubborn genes, and he knew as well as any of them how to hold a grudge.

When Aidan was sixteen, he and the twins had teased Gabe about his new braces. Gabe, nine years old at the time, took issue with their ragging and refused to speak to them for a whole year, and nothing their mom or dad did could make him change his mind. If nothing else, he appreciated Gabe's commitment to making them suffer.

"I'm not worried about Gabe right now. I'm worried about you," Brody said. "You still haven't signed the Roberts contract."

Aidan took a long drink of beer and set the glass back down. "That's right."

"Having second thoughts?"

"I just wanted to look at it a bit more closely, check to see if any changes were needed. I mean, it is a different product, after all." Not quite a lie, but the truth was more complicated—that ever since Gabe's outburst, he hadn't been feeling as certain about the Roberts deal.

Brody didn't press for details. "Okay. Just wanted to know in case I need to readjust my financials for the board meeting next week."

"I'll let you know."

"Great," Brody said. "And while I'm prepping up the agenda, I meant to ask whether you're still planning on presenting the branding proposals?"

"Sure." If he could corral Gabe and get him to hand over what he'd already worked up. Not that it would matter too much. From what Wes had said, the same old stuff would do. So if he couldn't get Gabe's help, he'd do it on his own.

Brody nodded. "Good. I'm sure your proposal will be a slam dunk."

Aidan took a sip of beer. "And why's that?"

Brody shrugged. "Don't get me wrong. Emma's great. I love her. We all do, but her ideas aren't like ours. They never were—you remember when we were working on that IPA, I don't know, maybe five, six years ago? And she suggested that we do some hipster woodcut label or some shit like that?"

"Yeah." He remembered. He'd been the first to shoot her suggestion down when she'd brought it up at a family dinner. They'd ended up going with a hand-drawn label with an inside joke on it, much like every other label they did.

"It would have been a disaster. No one would have known it was a Wolfshead brand. Anyway, I'm sure she'll recommend something equally crazy for the whiskey."

Even though Brody was probably right, Aidan found himself getting defensive on her behalf. "Maybe," he said with a shrug. "Or maybe she'll surprise us. Like Wes said, branding doesn't matter as much, especially if we're going to sell to places like Roberts. So maybe we could go Emma's way."

Brody snorted into his glass.

"What?" Aidan demanded.

"You're funny, man. Real funny. I'm glad you got your sense of humor back. Like I said before, Emma is definitely good for you." And with that, Brody turned to say something to Dylan.

Before Aidan had the chance to really think about what his cousin had said, an electric charge went through him. Emma must be close.

Aidan flickered his gaze to the door and there she was, her hair swept back in a twist, her luscious form poured into one of those pencil skirts and a sweater that skimmed her curves. All thoughts of Gabe were forgotten, because as soon as Emma spied him, she smiled so brightly that people around her turned to stare at her beauty. But it was all for him.

He rose before she reached the table, bending down to give her a satisfying kiss, and getting rewarded when her eyes went all molten.

They both sat down, and she greeted the rest of the guys, who nodded their hellos.

When everyone had settled down, he turned to her. "What's up with you? How's your dad?"

"He's okay. He's getting stronger for sure, but still in a lot of pain."

"How's he doing with Ryan?"

"Well," she said, nodding. "He knows Dad and what needs to get done at the hardware store even better than I do. Ryan told me he liked being home so much, he's actually going to stay a couple of extra days."

"It's good for your dad to have company," Aidan said.

"I know. So when Ryan goes back to LA, I'll have to figure out a way to get back to Dad's."

"Don't worry about things here. I'll help you take care of your place, just like I did before, no matter how long you want to spend in Cannon Beach."

"Thanks," she said, sounding grateful. "I mean, Marjorie is doing an amazing job. She's really on top of him with his meds. And she never lets him wallow at all, which I know he secretly appreciates. But I still feel like I need to be there with him. Make sure he gets through this recovery completely and starts his PT." Emma stopped and chewed her lip. "I'm still worried about him, but everything else is going well. I don't think I told you this, but I got called back for a final-round interview for that big account I mentioned."

"Nice." He kissed her, long and deep. "I knew things would work out."

She pulled away and smiled. "They haven't yet. But I'm hopeful they will."

"They will," he said.

"I appreciate your confidence," she said, and rested her head on his shoulder.

He loved that sensation—of Emma leaning into him, relying on him. He'd been part of his family's life for a long time, but he'd forgotten how good it felt to be a part of someone else's life, to have them share their triumphs and even their failures with him.

"We need to celebrate."

"I already got something," she said with a smile.

At that moment, a waiter came over. "Who ordered the Wolfshead amber ale?"

"I did," Emma said, reaching for it. "Thanks."

"Great. Tab's closed out. Let me know if you need anything else," he said before walking away.

Emma grasped the neck of the bottle and held it up. "Cheers," she said, before taking a long drink.

Aidan watched her, half bemused, half surprised. "Didn't know you liked beer," he said.

She looked at him sideways. "I like beer."

"The whole time we were together, I don't think I saw you drink a single one."

"Times change," she said, turning to him fully and smiling.

He looked at her, so beautiful, so willing to let him in once again.

"Yeah. They do."

At that moment, Finn gave a lick of his bass, and the singer's smooth voice crooned into the microphone as the next song began.

And there, in the dimly lit room, surrounded by the people he loved, Aidan knew there was nowhere else he'd rather be.

CHAPTER 20

Aidan was acting different tonight, more like the old Aidan than ever, and Emma was feeling grateful for so many reasons. Her dad was on the mend, she hopefully was about to sign a shiny new contract, and she had the man of her dreams by her side.

So she drank her Wolfshead ale, listened to Finn play, and enjoyed the warmth of Aidan's arm around her shoulders, letting the whole place know that she was his. Because she totally was.

He'd met her on her terms, supported her with her work, with her family, and with her life. He'd finally, *finally* morphed back into the man she'd fallen in love with so many years ago.

And when the show was over and he asked her if she'd come back to his place, it was the easiest thing in the world to say yes.

It wasn't a long drive to his house, so she didn't have time to think about exactly where she was going. But when she saw the familiar blue siding, the gently sloping eaves of the cottage they'd shared in northwest Portland for so many years, her breath caught in her throat.

She'd been back once since they'd gotten divorced to pick up a box of books she'd left by accident. But they were starting again—wasn't that what he had said? And that meant staring down their past with clear eyes.

Aidan's truck was in the driveway, and the lights were on in the house.

She knocked on the front door—once her own door. Before she had a chance to dwell on the past, it opened.

Aidan stood there, backlit by the hall light, larger than life. "Hey," he said, fire in his eyes. "Come on in."

"Thanks."

It felt odd entering this house like a stranger, and she couldn't help but glance around. There were a few new additions—a coat rack by the door, for example, that housed his collection of baseball caps. But other than that, he hadn't seemed to have done much to the place.

He hadn't replaced the hall table or the photographs on the wall she'd taken when she left. And she knew that if she went into the other rooms she'd find the same thing—gaps, missing items from their life together, divided into two separate houses.

"You didn't really change anything," she whispered.

A wave of sadness suddenly swept over her, the lost years, everything she'd given up. And then Aidan was there, his hands warm around her waist. "Don't go there, Emma. Not tonight. Tonight's about starting over, remember? Babe? Look at me."

Slowly, she raised her eyes to his, and he smiled at her.

"I never wanted to admit it, even to myself. I didn't even want to acknowledge it in case it never happened. But I always hoped you'd come home to me."

"I did," she whispered.

"Yeah," he said. "You did."

"Because I love you."

For one long moment, Aidan looked stunned. And then he said the words she'd been longing to hear for so very long. "I love you, too, Emma. I never stopped loving you."

Her heart swelled, and she reached for him, just as his lips crashed down on hers.

"God, I've missed you," he murmured.

"Show me," she said.

Aidan's eyes darkened in pleasure, and he simply picked her up, hoisting her against his body without a moment's hesitation. She wrapped her arms and legs around him, and then he was carrying her down the hallway to his room—their room—kissing her the whole way.

His hands on her ass, his mouth on her neck, the hard length of him between her thighs.

Yes. This. Flying and falling at the same time, lost in the here and the now with this one man, the only man.

"I've wanted this for so long," he rasped.

"Yes, Aidan." Because this was what she'd wanted. What she'd always wanted.

Then she was on the bed and her clothes were off and his hands were everywhere, followed closely by his mouth, touching and tasting *everything*, making her writhe with need. Under his touch, every square inch of flesh became an erogenous zone, but when he buried his face between her legs, she almost wept with the pure pleasure of it.

"Love the way…you light up for me," he said, in between tasting her.

Aidan wasn't going slow, which was just fine with her because she was already there. One last well-placed lick and she went off like a rocket, exploding into a haze of tingling sensation.

"God, Aidan," she gasped, trying to catch her breath as the warmth subsided. "That was…" She blinked. "That was amazing."

When her eyes focused, she realized he was sitting there, watching her. Carefully, he pushed a strand of hair away from her face. "You're so fucking beautiful."

"You make me feel beautiful," she admitted. "You always did."

"Because you are. Inside and out."

Before she dissolved into tears, she shifted under him and placed a hand on his chest. "Your turn."

A slow smile formed on his face, and he willingly flipped onto his back with the slightest pressure.

She took her time reacquainting herself with every inch of his body, and he kept still under her perusal.

And peruse she did.

He was magnificent—the corded muscle of his arms, the soft underside of his beard, the large expanse of his chest. She licked one flat nipple, then the other, loving the way he gasped and clutched her head, holding her there while she nibbled her way across and down to that throbbing mass of flesh between his legs.

He was hers, all hers, and she just had to taste.

But it had been a long time, so she started out slow, a gentle lick here, a little suck there. He moaned a bit, but didn't move and simply let her explore.

When she'd gotten him nice and wet, she wrapped her hand around his base, her lips around his tip, and sucked. He'd always liked it a bit rougher than she would have anticipated, but over the years he'd taught her what pleased him. Her skills were rusty and it took her a few strokes to get everything right, but she finally found a good rhythm, swirling her tongue around the underside of his tip with each pass, gripping his shaft firmly with her palm.

"Yess," he hissed. "So fucking good. Oh, Christ, Emma." He buried his hands in her hair, using it as leverage to guide, not force.

She took as much as she could, working her mouth over him the way he liked. His breathing grew ragged, and his moans grew louder, her cue that she was doing everything right. It didn't take long until his fingers tightened on her scalp.

"Inside you. Now."

He tugged again and reluctantly, she pulled off him with a pop. "You are inside me," she said. She'd meant to play it off as a joke, but Aidan must have taken her words literally.

Cupping her face in his hands, he pulled her up to him and kissed her, a deep, long kiss designed to make her forget everything that had come before, a kiss filled with hope and promise and something she'd never dared to dream about—a future with Aidan Phelan.

"You're inside me, too," he whispered.

Before she could respond to that, he was getting on the condom and pulling her down onto his cock and *oh my God* he felt even bigger in this position, but that didn't matter because it was good, so good.

"Yes," she moaned, her head falling back as he filled her completely, rubbing inside her in all sorts of new places.

She lifted herself off, just a fraction, then slid back down. Then she did it again, loving the power she wielded, the control she had over this big man.

"Work yourself on me, yeah, like that," he murmured, using his hands to guide her hips.

She leaned slightly forward, which allowed her a bit more leverage, made the slide and glide a hair faster.

He groaned at the increased friction. "Fuck, yeah. Ride me, wildcat. Take what you need."

She needed everything, so she kept rocking, feeling his grip tighten on her hips, watching his face contort into an expression that was half pain, half pleasure. Passion and need, love and regret, past and present, all melded together into the brightest, most acute sensation.

At that moment he met her gaze and it was then she knew—they were connected by far more than just their bodies.

He possessed her, body and soul.

"Love you, Emma," he said.

"Love you, too, Aidan," she said. *Always.*

Then his thumb was on her clit and that pressure was all it took for her to tumble over the edge into oblivion. She shouted his name, and he shouted, too, as he followed her over, his body straining, every muscle magnificently taut.

It was all she could do to hold herself up. She collapsed on top of him, and gently he rolled her off and tucked her against his body.

Surrounded by the scent of him, the feel of him, she went to sleep.

CHAPTER 21

The third and final round with Younger Beverages transpired in the same place as the first two meetings—in Younger's downtown office. There weren't just the seven executives this time, however. Burt Younger himself was present, listening with what Emma hoped was great interest.

She walked through her presentation smoothly and calmly, acknowledging the fact that she'd already gone through the same material twice before, but trying to keep it interesting and fresh. Since she'd had lots of practice by this point, it went well, and she found herself feeling remarkably Zen about the whole thing. Either they liked her or they didn't—and no amount of polish would disguise who she truly was and what she could offer the company.

From what she understood, it was down to her and one other party. Regardless, they'd be making a decision soon. With a smile, she finished out her presentation and waited for the questions and discussion to ensue.

Enzo Voglia spoke first. "I've seen you speak three times, Ms. Crandall, and each time, your message gets stronger and more on point."

"Thank you," she acknowledged. "I've done a lot of research into this company and the space, and I truly believe that my suggestions would help get the company where it hopes to be."

"I have one question for Ms. Crandall," a man said. Emma turned. It was Burt Younger, watching her carefully. He looked exactly like his picture on the back of the packaging—lean and wiry, with deep lines in his weathered face, the product of dozens of multi-kilometer, multiday runs through some of the most inhospitable places on earth.

"Yes, Mr. Younger?"

"Call me Burt," he said.

"Burt." She smiled. "What is your question?"

"What's your favorite Younger Beverage product?"

"Easy," she said. It wasn't a question she'd prepared for, but she didn't have to think too hard. "Original tonic. Raspberry flavor. Though I have to say, I recently took the new protein goo in peanut butter on a hike and loved it."

"You hike?"

"Avidly." Though she was on the curvier side, she was in excellent shape. "I've started hiking all the P2000s." Oregon peaks with prominence of two thousand feet or higher. "You better believe that I bring along Younger products to help me along the way."

There was silence in the room. After a too-long pause where Emma wasn't sure whether she'd nailed her answer or completely blown it, Burt Younger smiled. "Raspberry is my favorite, too," he said.

There were several more questions, which she answered with ease, having gone over everything before multiple times.

"One last question for you, Ms. Crandall," a woman named Jennifer Trawley said. "You gave us a list of graphic designers you were considering using for the new logo. Would you mind going through them again?"

"Of course not," Emma said. "Let's see, Kim Umber, Lyle Jaxon, and Ansel Hardt would all make my short list. I have a few others I've used over the years, but for this project, I think any one of these three designers would do a great job, Kim Umber in particular. She's local, and has done some amazing work in the beverage industry. I'm continually impressed with how everything she does looks so timeless. She'd be a good match for what Younger is going for—clean and modern."

"I'm working with Mr. Hardt on another project," Jennifer said conversationally. "I like his stuff, but I'm not sure it's right for us. When I mentioned our new branding project to him, he showed me some of his other work—including the new Wolfshead label."

The smile froze on Emma's face. "Label?"

"Yes…the new whiskey that's coming out later this year. Very impressive."

"Are you sure it was the Wolfshead label you saw? I mean, we haven't officially hired anyone yet."

Jennifer shook her head. "I saw it with my own eyes—definitely Wolfshead. Very manly. Very rustic. Looks just like the Wolfshead beer labels—you know, that hand-drawn rugged stuff?" She laughed. "Goes along with the whole lumberjack vibe I get from those guys. Not my style, but they're the real deal, so I guess it works for them."

"Yes, yes, I agree," Emma said, even as a sick, clawing feeling began to form in her stomach. "Even though what I think Younger would want is slightly different from what Ansel usually handles, I still think he's an amazing designer and would rise to the challenge. But my top choice remains Kim Umber, for the very reasons you mention. So getting back to the Wolfshead label, was what you saw a mock-up?" she asked, doing her best to keep her voice neutral instead of edging into hysteria. "Because as far as I know, we're still considering alternate branding plans for that whiskey."

The woman thought for a moment. "No, no. He told me the contract was signed, sealed, and delivered. Pretty sure what I saw was the final product. Ansel even told me that the whiskey had already been spoken for, too—that they'd sold the lot of it and that the branding was just window dressing." She narrowed her eyes. "Don't you, ah, work with them now? Isn't this something you should be on top of?"

Emma's face was beet red now, she was sure of it. All seven members of the executive team—plus Burt Younger—were looking at her strangely.

"Oh *yes*," she lied, covering as best she could. "*That* label. I must have been thinking of the branding for that new ale we're doing later this year. We'd floated some similar ideas for that one." She laughed, and it sounded fake to her own ears. "I agree with you, though. Very manly and rustic. And spoken for, yes. Already all spoken for." She cleared her throat. "So, do any of you have any additional questions for me? I'd be glad to answer them."

There was more silence, except this one was filled with a negative kind of tension, as each one of the executives continued to stare at her. Her face got redder, the sick feeling radiated outward, and she shoved back the nausea. She couldn't throw up, not here, not now in front of this very important prospective client. It would just make her look like an even bigger fool.

"Okay, well, if you think of something later, please feel free to get in touch…" she said, trailing off.

More silence. Jennifer coughed into her hand, and a few of the others shifted in their seats, making them creak.

Emma's shiny printed copies of her PowerPoint presentation and crisp folder looked faded and sad on the table. She desperately wanted to snatch them back, shove them in her bag and tell everyone she'd made a huge, huge mistake in coming. But she forced herself to sit there, that fake smile on her face.

She sat there in agony for several long moments until Enzo once again took control over the meeting.

"I think that concludes everything, Ms. Crandall," he said. "Thanks again for coming in to chat with us and share your ideas."

"My pleasure," she murmured.

"As you know, we're almost done with the process," Enzo said. "Our next step will be to make a decision as to who we're going with, and then, of course, we'll have to run that decision by our board before everything is finalized. It could take a while, so if you're banking on the work starting soon, we hope you're not disappointed."

It was at that very moment that she knew she'd lost the account. There was no way they'd hire her after that giant foul-up. The fact that she didn't even have a handle on the branding of a company *that she owned?* Unforgivable. Fatal.

"Right." Emma nodded. "Of course."

How she sat there with a smile on her face and got through the rest of the meeting she had no idea, but the next thing she knew they were all shaking hands and saying good-bye and then she was out in front of the office building on the street downtown.

Emma waited until she was two blocks away to lose her shit. First she leaned against the side of a perfectly innocent hotel right on Sixth Avenue. Then she dropped her briefcase by her heels and ugly-cried for a full ten minutes.

Once she'd gotten that out of her system, she moved right on past embarrassment, motored passed betrayal, and settled on anger.

How *dare* he?

Aidan had told her they were going to prepare their proposals and vote before deciding on direction. They'd made the deal weeks ago. Shook hands on it, even.

Then he'd gone behind her back to hire Ansel, thinking she'd never find out. And he'd sold all the whiskey already? There hadn't been any vote. It was already a done deal. All the Phelans surely knew it.

Everyone except her.

She was the outsider once again, except she'd willingly walked into it. She'd let Aidan back into her life, back into her *bed*, and he'd repaid her by lying to her face and tricking her into thinking that her ideas mattered. That she mattered.

She was such an idiot. How could she have been so blind and stupid?

She'd known that Aidan had the power to rip her heart out—again—but she hadn't counted on how terrible she'd feel.

She loved him, and he'd repaid her by making her look like the biggest fool. If what he'd done had only affected her pride, she could have walked away. After all, she'd done it before. But it wasn't just her pride on the line—it was her livelihood.

Deliberately, Emma wiped her eyes with her hands. She'd already wasted too many tears, too many *years* on what might have been. Starting now, she was done, completely—with Wolfshead, with the Phelans, and most definitely with Aidan.

Forever.

CHAPTER 22

Surrounded by his family, Aidan stood in the rickhouse at Wolfshead, surveying the damage. Splintered wood and seeping casks lay in a heap on the floor, emitting the overpowering aroma of fine aged whiskey. Ten of their first-run barrels—which constituted five years of work, easily a hundred thousand dollars of sales, and countless days and nights of arguing—were gone, evaporated into thin air. His family's sweat, blood, and tears had gone into making those barrels.

There really was only one thing to say.

"Fuck."

He'd raced over the moment he'd gotten word from Dylan that something had gone wrong in the rickhouse. When he'd arrived, he'd found them there—his mom, his aunt, and all his brothers and cousins, everyone except Gabe, who was conspicuously absent.

"What happened?" Brody asked.

"Broken rack," Dylan said, indicating a cracked beam that seemed to be at the epicenter of the mess. "Far as Ed and I can tell, this was the break point."

"We both inspected it just last night," Ed said tightly. "Signed off on it around six p.m. When I came in this morning, I found it like this. I'm so sorry."

"You didn't do anything wrong," Dylan said, putting a comforting arm around his brother's shoulders. "I looked at it, too. Thought everything was okay."

Ed shook his head. "It was my responsibility."

191

"Dude, the rickhouse is my domain."

"But safety's my thing."

"Sometimes these things just happen," Brody said, trying to de-escalate things, as usual.

"Right," Dylan breathed. "I'm just bummed that it was the bottom rack that broke. At least they rolled right instead of left. We could have lost more if the falling barrels had taken out the next set of racks, too."

"Dylan's right. It could have been worse," Christine said.

"Worse than losing ten barrels?" Aidan said. "That's a hundred grand on the floor, not to mention the fact that we spent years on that whiskey. It's irreplaceable." Realizing what he'd just said, he glanced over to Connor, who simply stood there, silent. Almost everyone had expressed their opinion, but since he'd arrived Connor hadn't said a single word. Just watched the dark liquid in puddles on the floor.

"This goes way beyond losing product," Brody said. "You know as well as I do that we still owe taxes on this stuff, whether we sell it or not."

"We can take this as a loss," Fiona said, piping in, "but we still have to pay up in the end."

Connor was still staring at the destruction. Finn walked over and looked up at his brother. "We'll make new stuff, Con. Better stuff."

The big man met his gaze, nodded once, then walked out of the warehouse.

"Oh, shit," Brody said, smacking his forehead with his palm. "I almost forgot about our distribution deal. What are we going to tell Wes?"

"And what are we supposed to do with this stuff? Clean it up?" Ed asked.

"Leaving it here's a hazard for sure," Dylan said.

"Should I call the insurance company?" Fiona asked.

Everyone had their faces turned toward him, looking to him for guidance, for leadership. He couldn't let them down.

Taking a breath, he started. "Don't touch anything. Call the insurance company first. They're probably going to want to come over and take pictures. Catalog the damage. Aunt Fi, you can do that now."

"Okay," she said, and went to make the call.

"Next, let's open up all the doors and windows. We need this place aired out so no one passes out from the fumes."

"I have the east side," Ed said.

Dylan nodded. "I'll take the west."

"Check the rest of the racks after you're done. We don't want a repeat of this."

"Got it," Dylan said as the two men went off to do their work.

"Next, let's figure out what we need to do to report this loss to the government. Brody, can you tackle that?"

"On it," his cousin said, and disappeared.

"Finn, you know what got destroyed, right?"

"I have every single barrel logged."

"Great. Pull those records up. We'll need them, and any other info you have about those ten barrels. Work with Brody and your mom. Get them the info they need."

"Will do."

The only ones left standing there were him and his mom.

"What can I do?" Christine asked him.

"Keep us all organized," he said. "Write down everything we know about the accident, and the steps we're taking to contain it. It'll serve as a timeline and a working document if something like this happens again."

"I can do that," she said. "But what are you going to do?"

Aidan set his jaw. "I have a phone call to make." He needed to let Wes know what happened.

Aidan went back to his office, cutting through the parking lot and vaulting up the metal staircase. Ulysses greeted him at the door with a whimper.

"Can't take you for a walk right now," he said, stepping into his office.

It was then he realized that he wasn't alone.

Emma was there, facing away from the door, looking out the window. She turned when he entered and opened her mouth to speak, but he cut her off before she could get a word out.

"Emma," he said tightly as he moved toward his desk. "This isn't a good time."

"Oh?" she said, raising an eyebrow. "Shall I come back when

it's convenient?"

There was snark in her tone, but he was too focused on dealing with the aftermath of the accident to deal with her right now. "Yeah. I'm busy." He riffled around the papers on his desk until he found what he was looking for—Wes's business card.

He pulled his cell phone out of his pocket, but before he could dial Wes's number, Emma plucked the phone from his hands.

"What the hell, Emma?"

"Right back to your old tricks, I see," she said, eyes glittering fiercely.

He took the phone back. "I don't know what's up your ass right now, but I can't talk. We had an accident."

Emma stiffened. "An accident? Is everyone okay?"

"Ten barrels of whiskey got destroyed."

"But no one was hurt?"

"No."

"Thank God," she breathed.

"It'd be best if you got out of here. We have a lot of cleanup to do."

Emma went hard all over. "Are you serious? I'm part owner of this place. Shouldn't I be here to help?"

"I have it under control."

"Oh, I'll just bet you do."

Sighing, he slipped the phone back into his pocket. Clearly, she had something she needed to get off her chest, and he had no choice but to listen. Engaging with Emma was not on his to-do list right now, but he composed his face into a blank mask, crossed his arms in front of him, and waited for her to speak. He was not prepared for the next words out of her mouth.

"You're a liar."

Aidan blinked. "Come again?"

"You. Lied. To. Me."

"About what?"

"About everything," she said. "Which really sucks because I thought we'd settled things after everything we talked about, after everything you promised me you'd do."

His head was buzzing with whiskey fumes and stress and phone numbers. "What, exactly, did I lie about?"

"Everything!"

"Emma—" he said, his voice a warning.

"Fine. You want specifics? How's this: you hired a graphic designer for the Wolfshead whiskey label." She crossed her arms over her chest, daring him to deny it.

Shit. "How did you find that out?"

"During my third-round pitch meeting for Younger Beverages. Ansel's name came up. He showed the label to one of their execs."

"Why the hell would he do that?"

"So you *did* hire him!" she said, eyes glittering with anger. "I've never been so mortified in my whole life. Realizing that they all knew more than I did about a company I'm supposed to be working for—a company I own!"

"Ansel should have kept his mouth shut," Aidan gritted out.

"Don't you dare put the blame on him!" Emma snapped. "You're the one who went behind my back, making me look like a complete idiot in front of a prospective client." She shook her head, as if she couldn't believe what was happening. "But what I don't understand is why? I thought we had a deal."

"We did," he said quickly. "We do."

"Then why hire Ansel?"

"Timing," he told her, the answer he'd prepared way back when he'd first asked Gabe to take charge of the project, just in case anyone came asking. "It takes a long time to get a label approved, and I wanted to get a jump on it."

Emma shook her head. "Ooh, sorry, no, you get an *X* for that answer. If you were concerned about timing, you'd have said so outright. You wouldn't have even bothered to go through the whole 'let's prepare proposals and vote' deception."

"We've worked with him before," Aidan offered.

"*You* have. Not me. If you really wanted it to be fair, you would have waited. Try again."

There was no way he was going to win, not with Emma giving him the stare-down while he was already half-distracted in damage-control mode, so he opted for the truth. "We already sold the whiskey. Branding doesn't matter."

Emma looked stunned. "What?"

"To a reputable group we've done business with before."

"So it's true," she muttered. "I didn't believe it. I *couldn't* believe it." She whirled on him again. "When were you going to tell me this?"

"I don't know. Soon? Anyway, this whole mess with the barrels may screw up the deal anyway. Which is why I have to make this phone call." He pulled his phone out of his pocket again, but she didn't get the hint to leave.

"So you sold the whiskey, and you didn't even think that this would be something I'd need to know?"

Aidan sighed. "Look, I know you, Emma. I know your work. You're great at what you do. Amazing, even. But we both know your style just isn't right for Wolfshead."

"You haven't even seen my proposal yet!"

"It doesn't matter what it is. It won't be what Dad and Uncle John would have wanted. They had a really specific vision for the future of Wolfshead—a vision that I plan to do everything to achieve. And your kind of branding doesn't match up."

"You think I have no concept of the vision for the company?"

"Wolfshead isn't fancy or elegant. It's rough and unrefined." Aidan strode to the door and flung it open wide. The noise from the machinery on the factory floor filtered in, underscoring his point. "It's messy and filthy and raw every single day."

"And I'm not."

"No," he said bluntly.

"So you're saying that without even hearing what I have to say, without even seeing the branding proposal that I spent a month painstakingly working on, you'd just reject it out of hand, not because it isn't great, but because it doesn't fit in with the forty-year-old vision that your father and uncle had for the company?"

"When you put it like that, I guess the answer is yes."

Emma blinked a couple of times, really fast, then looked up at the ceiling. "God, I really am an idiot."

"No you're not," he said, but she wasn't listening.

"I thought you were the man I needed," she was saying to herself. "The man I deserved. But you're the same guy, aren't you? Shutting me out. Doing what you want, just like you always do."

He was fast losing his grip on the situation. "I never promised you perfection, Emma."

Emma gave him a look of infinite sadness. "See, that's the

thing, Aidan. I never wanted perfection. All I wanted—all I ever wanted—was for you to hear me. To listen to me instead of rejecting everything I say out of hand. To give me a say, a voice. To love me the same way I loved you."

"I do love you."

"No." She shook her head. "Because loving someone, *really* loving someone, means that sometimes you make compromises. But that's not the kind of man you are. I get that now. Except I'm not the same woman. I haven't been since I left you."

"You still love me," he said, grasping for the right thing to say and failing miserably.

"Yes," she said calmly. "I do. But I need more from you than what you can give. I need real change, not the illusion of change. The real truth is that I don't have a say in anything in your world. I never did, and I never will because you just can't let me in. Not when things really matter." She blinked again. Held her head up high. "You've messed with my business, but worse, you've messed with me. You didn't promise me anything, Aidan, but I'm making one to you right here, right now: I can't do this. I won't. Not anymore." She put her handbag onto a chair, pulled out a thick stack of papers, and tossed them onto his desk.

"What's that?"

"The final draft of my branding proposal."

"What am I supposed to do with it?"

"Read it. Throw it away. Let Ulysses shred it for all I care." She jerked her bag back onto her shoulder. "I'm done. No, wait." With visibly trembling hands, she unclasped her necklace—*his* necklace—and tossed that onto his desk, too. "*Now* I'm done."

He could have called out to her. Grabbed her and kissed her and made her forget everything she'd just said. Started over again and made her understand that he still loved her.

But he didn't.

Instead, he just stood there as she walked right out of his life. Again.

It took Ulysses whining at his feet to snap him out of his stupor.

He scratched the dog behind his ears, handed him off to his mom, who was passing by, then turned to the problem at hand.

First, he tossed Emma's proposal onto the desk and pocketed

her necklace so he wouldn't have to look at it. Next, he picked up the phone and called Wes. Then, he spent the next eight hours dealing with his family, his employees, and his company, managing the situation as best as he knew how.

And later, when he'd done all the damage control he could, when the insurance people had come and gone and the cleanup had begun and the phone had ceased ringing, Aidan sat alone in his dark, empty office nursing a beer.

Fuck, it had been a long day, and it would be an even longer night because he'd be sleeping alone.

Every muscle in his body aching, he rose and went to the window. Beyond the dimly lit parking lot, beyond the highway, the river rushed by, dark and silent from his vantage point, ever flowing, ever moving forward.

Emma was right.

Nothing had changed. Especially not him.

CHAPTER 23

Seven days after the accident, things had mostly gotten back to normal at Wolfshead. The broken barrels and the spilled whiskey had been cleared away, and the factory was humming once again. They needed to fill out a ton more forms to start the insurance claim process. While they had no idea how long it would take to get resolved and didn't expect the insurance company to cover the whole loss, Brody told them that anything they got would help to mitigate their financial damages.

As far as managing their physical damages, Connor and Finn had been hard at work, doing their best to speed up their output to replace the ruined whiskey. Instead of a run of 150 barrels, they were instead going to shoot for 175 without compromising on quality. Connor had been optimistic they'd be able to achieve that, and morale on the production side seemed high.

Brody was still working through the financials with Fiona, and Ed and Dylan had systematically gone through each rack, layer by layer, to ensure they were solid. Nothing like that was ever going to happen again on their watch. As soon as Gabe found out about the accident, he'd returned to work, offering to pitch in to do anything he could to help. Things were still strained between them, but Aidan hoped in time that would change.

Yes, everything was running smoothly. Except him.

Since Emma had stormed out of his office, he hadn't been the same. It had been easy to chalk his attitude shift up to the strain he was under in dealing with the loss of the whiskey, but he knew it was more than that. Even as he threw himself into his work, he got frustrated far too easily, and his temper was on a knife's point at all times. When he was at work, he did his best to keep it together, knowing that his entire family and company were relying on him to get them through this crisis.

When he was alone, things got worse.

It was like the days and months after he'd gotten divorced the first time, except a hundred times worse. Because this time he knew exactly what he'd lost. Then someone would say something that reminded him of her, or he'd catch a glimpse of a woman with brown hair, and everything would come rushing back to him.

Brody poked his head into his office. "Hey, you good?"

"Yeah," he answered, same as he always did these days when anyone asked.

Thank God Brody took him at his word, because his cousin simply nodded. "Good. It's getting late, and I'm heading out. I need to do a print run for the financial statements down at the all-night copy shop, and they start to get really busy around eleven."

"The meeting." Truth was, he'd forgotten about the board meeting in all the chaos. He also hadn't prepared anything. Gabe had dropped his proposal off, but he hadn't looked at it. Nor had he written his state-of-the-company speech. "What time does it start?"

"Ten a.m." Brody cocked his head at him. "You sure you're okay?"

"Yeah."

"Okay, well, if you need anything, just holler. 'Night, Aidan."

"'Night."

When his cousin left, Aidan went searching for Gabe's proposal. It was on his desk somewhere—that he remembered. But where? He thumbed through a couple of stacks of paper and opened up his desk drawer.

There, right on top, was Paddy's letter, the one he'd tossed inside weeks ago after returning from the lawyer's office.

So not what he wanted to deal with right now.

He shoved the drawer closed and redoubled his search, almost toppling a couple of ultra-huge stacks from his desk in the process.

And that's when he found the proposal. Not Gabe's. Emma's.

Printed, but with handwritten notes in her perfectly tidy script in blue ink in the margins.

Fuck. When it rained, it poured.

Viciously, he shoved the proposal aside and put his head in his hands. He was going to keep finding bits and pieces of Emma everywhere, he just knew it. Her name on a paper on his desk, her scent on his pillows, the toothbrush she'd left in his bathroom.

She wasn't going away. Not this time.

Removing his head from his hands, he slowly pulled the proposal back so that it was directly in front of him. Emma wasn't going to come to the board meeting, he was certain. But he may as well read what she wrote, get over it so he could throw it away and try to move on with his life.

Flipping the first page open, he began.

Unsurprisingly, she'd been thorough. Her branding plan included a brief history of the company—a history he hadn't thought she'd known. Gabe had probably told her, which rankled. *He* should have been the one to tell her. Explain his family's history, bring her into the fold.

But of course he never had.

He scanned the intro, the general stuff, her philosophy. Fussy, fancy, not Wolfshead at all.

Exactly what he'd expected.

And then he saw what came next. Not only had she prepared a branding plan, complete with self-drawn logo and color scheme, but she'd edged into marketing territory, showing Wolfshead's place in the craft distilling market and projecting potential sales based on pricing.

Aidan found himself reading closely, very closely. What she was saying made sense, especially in light of recent developments. If they tried to sell the whiskey at the originally-agreed-upon price to Wes and the Roberts Group, there's no way they could break even, but if they upped their price point by at least twenty dollars, thereby placing the whiskey into a different playing field, they could make it work. Of course, Emma had laid out an entire pricing and marketing plan that reflected this.

His brain began to whir. If Wolfshead followed her plan, it might take longer to make the sales, but they'd end up more than covering the whiskey they'd lost…and then some. It was just as Gabe had said, but until Aidan had seen the numbers combined with the branding and marketing in Emma's plan, he hadn't realized how intelligent the idea actually was. And the way she'd positioned the brand, focusing on exclusivity, it could be that losing product—thereby making their first run even rarer—could help them get ahead in the long run.

Hot damn. Maybe this could work.

This was exactly what she'd told him before, but why hadn't it made sense in his brain?

Because you're fucking stubborn.

Because he couldn't see that there was any other way of doing things. But here, laid out before him, was a road map to saving the distillery arm of Wolfshead.

He needed to call Emma. Share his excitement. Tell her what a genius idea this whole thing was. He pulled out his cell phone and actually dialed the first few digits of her number before he stopped and put the phone back down.

She didn't want to talk to him. She was done, remember?

Despair washed over him in a powerful wave. Without her, he was nothing. The company, his family, even the damn whiskey he'd fought so hard and so long for meant little without her by his side to share in the glory.

Not for the first time, he realized exactly what he'd thrown away by ignoring her. He'd done something stupid by going behind her back and hiring Hardt, but even the business wasn't really where he'd messed up. That he'd done by not trusting her, by not letting her into his life in every respect.

He'd underestimated her, just like he underestimated everyone else around him. And now that he finally understood what he'd done, it was too late. Not with Gabe—his brother would come around eventually; he always did. But things with Emma were over for good.

If only she'd never come back into his life at all. Then he wouldn't have to deal with these feelings of anger, of impotence, of failure.

Fucking Paddy. Why had he done what he'd done at all?

Slowly, he opened the drawer. His grandfather's letter sat there, taunting him.

Without thinking, Aidan lifted the letter and broke the seal.

As soon as he unfolded the paper inside, he immediately recognized Paddy's spidery handwriting. His eyes grew accustomed to the script, and slowly, he began to read.

Dear Aidan,

If you are reading this letter, then that means I am no longer on this great green Earth. I had a good run, but the Good Lord has called me home to be with Mary.

By now one of the Lewises should have read to you the provisions of my will, which states that you, along with each of your brothers and cousins, are to receive one equal share of Wolfshead. You should also be aware that I have left one equal share to your ex-wife, Emma Crandall Phelan.

Because you are the man I know you are, I strongly suspect that you must be very angry about this. You must be asking yourself why I divided up the company I was so set on keeping to myself and why I deliberately chose to bequeath a share to a woman who is no longer part of our family.

My answer is this: because of you.

But let me back up, because my explanation will make more sense in context. My grandfather, may he rest in peace, came west to escape his crushing poverty. He ended up settling in Portland, which is where he founded Wolfshead with only $20 to his name and a handwritten recipe for beer in his pocket that had been handed down to him by his own grandfather, Jack Phelan of County Cork. I watched him work himself to death at the age of 61. When I took over the company, I vowed that I would continue in his legacy to make Wolfshead the greatest craft beer on the West Coast.

I see so much of myself in you, Aidan—my strengths and my weaknesses. I see that same stubborn Phelan streak, that tenaciousness that kept this company going through Prohibition and through the Great Depression, in the way that you hold on to your ideals. Your brothers and cousins follow you without question, and you understand the meaning of sacrifice as no one else in this family does. Except for me.

I learned too late that by making Wolfshead my life, I alienated myself from you and everyone else I loved. My late wife

Mary, long dead before you were born, was the one to instill in me the idea that there are things worth more than pride, than making your mark. Sometimes, as Mary used to say, the most important thing in life is to be that someone for someone else. I became a husk of myself after Mary died. If I could, I would have given up my stake in my own company for even one more day with her. You had that kind of love, Aidan, and I watched you let it slip through your fingers.

In struggling to show your worth, you have put the company above everyone else, including yourself.

I am not so full of hubris as to think that your divorce was all my doing; I am aware that you are your own person. But I cannot help but think that it was, in part, because I pushed you too hard. Because you sought, whether consciously or unconsciously, to emulate my leadership.

The truth is that I left the share to Emma in the hopes that you would understand that she is the one for you. That your happiness does not reside within the confines of this factory, but extends far beyond its walls. That your future isn't just grain and mash, but in flesh and blood. In her.

She is wise, Aidan. And she is worthy. I have never seen you so happy as you are with Emma. Happier than any second of time you spent at Wolfshead. Even happier than you were when you played baseball. When she left you, all the light you had inside left with her.

Don't wait to figure out that you need her until the years have passed you by, until all you are left with on your deathbed are regrets and dreams of what might have been. For once, follow your heart instead of your head.

This may not be what you want to hear, least of all from me, but it is the truth, something you should appreciate, if nothing else. Whether you take my advice or not, it is my sincerest wish that above all, you should be happy. Breathe, Aidan. And live your life, hopefully better than I did.

Yours always with my love and respect,

Grandfather

PS In the event that you should wish to purchase Emma's share, I have expressly written into my will that this is not to be allowed. Lewis has made it so, and it cannot be undone. —JDP

Aidan read the letter twice more before he shoved his seat back and rose.

He found himself on the catwalk on the production side, high above the factory floor. The space was silent and still, the ghostly echo the only hint that a few short hours ago the place had been a hive of activity.

This was his life. Would be his life until he died.

He'd spent years making his peace with that. But along the way, he'd turned into a replica of the man he swore he'd never emulate.

But he'd turned out just like him, pushing aside everyone who loved him to achieve what he thought were the best goals. The only goals.

Now he felt stripped bare, laid out, as he realized exactly what his closed-mindedness had cost him. He thought back to all the times that one of his brothers or cousins, or even his mom or aunt, had tried to steer him in a different direction than the one he was dead set on going.

What other opportunities had he thrown away? What else had he pushed aside as being unworthy because he was too stubborn to listen?

He was full of shit.

And what's worse? Everyone had known it all along but had let him get away with it because they loved him.

Paddy had known, too. Had seen what was happening and been powerless to stop it.

And Emma. She'd loved him, and he'd done nothing but push her away. He'd thought he was being so honorable, so true, when he'd come back into her life. But without even realizing it, he'd lied to her, just as he'd lied to himself.

It was too late for him and Emma, but he needed to make amends all the same, to prove to himself that he was the man he always thought he'd grow to be.

Slowly he walked back into his office. Placed Paddy's letter on top of Emma's proposal, and looked at the two of them there for a long minute.

Then he pulled his phone out of his pocket and made the most important phone call of his life.

<h1 style="text-align:center">CHAPTER 24</h1>

The day of the board meeting dawned sunny and cloudless—a rare enough occasion that Emma had to look outside twice before she actually believed it to be true.

She dressed carefully in a navy-blue pantsuit with a cream-colored shell, one she would never have dared to wear in the rain for fear it would get ruined, but was perfect in better weather. Crisp and lightweight, tailored and professional—it skimmed rather than hugged her body and spoke volumes about her mind-set: she was done.

Done trying to force herself somewhere she clearly wasn't wanted. Done trying to pretend as if Aidan valued her half as much as she valued herself.

After confronting Aidan in his office, she'd gotten into her car and driven straight to Cannon Beach, where she'd remained for the past week. Her dad was the one who'd encouraged her to finish what she'd started and end it clean.

Her dad was right, so she'd resolved to go the board meeting today. Sit through hours of legal and business discussions. Present the branding and marketing plan she'd worked so hard to prepare. Wait for the inevitable *no* she was sure to get from Aidan and his family.

And then announce that she was going to sell back her share of Wolfshead to the family.

Because if she couldn't be a partner with them, if they didn't treat her like an equal, then she didn't want to be there at all.

It was time she started looking toward the future instead of staying mired in the past.

Before Aidan had come back into her life, she'd actually had a game plan that didn't involve him, and it was time to follow through. She'd use the money from the sale to bolster her burgeoning business, and earn clients who actually appreciated who she was and what she could bring to the table.

Emma slipped on her pearl stud earrings and a pair of navy heels to match her suit. They gave her a few extra inches of height— not that it would make a ton of difference, but today, she needed every advantage she could get if she was going to make it through the meeting.

She arrived at Lewis & Lewis's offices in downtown Portland not a moment before it was absolutely necessary, as the very last thing she wanted was to see the Phelans—any of them—before she had to face them across the boardroom table.

A small, blond secretary greeted her in the waiting area, a tentative smile on her face.

"They're all in there, Ms. Crandall," she said. "The Phelans and the two Mr. Lewises, waiting for you to start. If you'll follow me."

She led the way back to the conference rooms, every moment bringing Emma closer and closer to her date with destiny. Emma breathed through the knot in her stomach, willing it to go away. She desperately wanted to flee, but she forced herself to keep walking forward, one step at a time. She had to go in. Finish this for good.

The secretary stopped in front of a door, the same conference room she'd been in before. How fitting that she would end this thing with Aidan in the very room where it had started up again. She clutched her valise in her hands, barely remembering the plan. Present, sell, leave. Right. She could do this. She *had* to do this.

The secretary had her hand on the doorknob, and now she was turning it. Time seemed to stand still.

"Good luck," she whispered, just before she pushed the door open and Emma stepped inside.

Eleven heads immediately swiveled to stare at her, but she was conscious only of Aidan. He had trimmed his beard so it lay neatly against his jaw, and had ditched the Henley and jeans for a well-cut suit. She was sure she'd seen him wear suits when they were married, but the last time she had any image of him wearing one in her mind was from their wedding day.

There was some irony in that somewhere, she was sure.

There was one empty seat at the table, directly between Christine and Gabe. Conscious that everyone was still staring, she crossed the room and sat down.

Lewis Junior, a man who looked almost identical to his father with the same bald spot on the top of his head, harrumphed. "Excellent. Well, now that we're all here, we can begin. As the corporate counsel for Wolfshead, I now call this meeting of the board of directors to order. We have several important issues to discuss today."

Lewis spent almost an hour walking through several legal issues that pertained to the new distillery arm of the business. It was kind of interesting, and she found herself paying attention, even though she knew it wouldn't be relevant to her after today.

Resolutely, she refused to look at Aidan. He would only distract her from what she needed to accomplish, and she was done with distractions.

At one point, he gave the state of the company in his role as CEO. Just to be polite she turned his way, looking at him, but not really seeing him. Then she made a critical mistake.

When he finally ceded the floor to Brody, her gaze rose to his eyes. Lingered for a few moments too long. The heat she saw there completely floored her.

"I'm sorry," he mouthed.

She shook her head. *No.* This wasn't the time or the place. As if she hadn't made it clear the other day that it was too late for them. That it had been too late for a long time.

After what seemed like an eternity of each Phelan talking about their respective part of the company, they took a quick break. Aidan immediately stepped outside with his mom. They stayed in the hallway for a long time.

"Want a snack?" Gabe asked, pointing toward the side table laden with pastries and jugs of coffee and hot water.

The Voodoo doughnuts did not tempt her at all this time—not even her favorite maple-bacon. She chose some lukewarm tea, which she gulped down as Gabe kept talking.

"I'm excited to see what you're going to propose. I'm sure it'll be great. You have such an amazing style. Need any help getting set up?"

"No, I'm good." She glanced up and met his gaze. "No matter what happens next, I just want you to know that I appreciate everything you've done for me over the past few weeks. Truly. I'll never forget the kindness you showed me."

"What's with the fatalism?" Gabe said, giving her a quizzical look. "You make it sound like you're leaving or something."

She was about to tell him that yes, she was leaving, when Lewis Junior made another harrumphing sound.

"Time to resume," he said.

Emma took a deep breath, arranged her presentation materials just the way she wanted them, pushed her chair back, and stood.

When she raised her gaze, all eyes were on her.

At some point, Aidan and Christine had slipped back into the room, and he watched, along with everyone else. Her hands trembled, but she took another deep breath and focused. When she spoke, her voice didn't waver in the slightest.

"As you may be aware," she began, "Aidan and I made a deal. Each of us prepared a branding proposal, proposals that we will share with you today. Afterward, you will all vote for whichever one you find more compelling." She cleared her throat. Looked around the room, at this family in which she'd never truly belonged. She wasn't one of them. And she never had been.

When she'd started this whole endeavor, she'd told Aidan that she would speak her mind, whether he agreed with her or not. And that's exactly what she intended to do. This was a tough crowd. They absolutely would not agree with what she was going to say, but she was going to say it anyway, because that was who she was.

"My proposal is simple: bring Wolfshead squarely into the twenty-first century by focusing on what makes it unique. Craft beer is having a renaissance. So is craft whiskey. Wolfshead needs to be branded in a way that speaks to the family history, as well as carries the Phelan name into the future."

No one spoke. It seemed like no one even breathed.

Emma went on. "This may not be what you want to hear, but the current brand is tired. You want timeless. By re-creating this company as one steeped in history but that is on the cutting edge of the craft spirit movement, you are injecting fresh life into Wolfshead now and for the future. In my opinion, the company needs a complete branding overhaul from beer to whiskey to image. With this whiskey launch, you have the power to change the way consumers see you, and potentially to expand even beyond what you originally conceived. Paddy couldn't see it, but—and please forgive me for saying this—neither could your fathers. Yes, they wanted to distill spirits, but they were looking backward, to your great-great-grandfather's dreams. You have the opportunity to look forward, starting with your branding.

"I have taken a long, hard look at the company, what you currently stand for, and who you are. There are so many things to love. The fact that it's family-run and has been for five generations. The fact that you were at the forefront of the craft beer movement, and are now reinventing the company as a fine distillery, as well. These are amazing qualities. But in trying to buck your grandfather's stranglehold on the company, in trying to hold on to your fathers' legacy, you've forgotten that you are the next generation with your own story to tell. That story is powerful. This is an authentic Northwest company. You have been here for a very long time. The old way of doing things was great, but you're doing something completely different now, and your branding needs to reflect that. You can do that while at the same time paying homage to your past.

"I didn't hire anyone. I didn't prepare anything fancy. I just used web-based software to draw up several renderings of what I think could be a strong direction for the brand to take."

She opened the manila envelope on the table in front of her and removed a stack of papers, which she passed out to the Phelans and the two Lewises. Then she gave them all a moment to examine what she'd prepared.

She'd worked hard on her vision. In the center of the first logo was a print of an alembic still in black and white, with the words *American Rye Whiskey* in a clear, clean font just below. Above the still was her version of the new Wolfshead logo. She'd used all capital letters in a supermodern font, and had drawn a stylized image of a wolf above the name. Just like in the original logo, the wolf had his mouth open and his head tipped up, howling at an unseen moon.

Thanks to the unusual shape of the still, the whole label had a retro, steampunk-y vibe to it. It could have been created in 1840,

1940, or 2040. It was fresh, but timeless.

She'd done another rendering of what she thought would be a great beer label and had chosen their summer ale as an example for her mock-up. In the center of the logo was a color picture of Mirror Lake drawn by a local artist. Below the picture were the words *Summer Ale* in a different, funky font, and above the picture, just like on the whiskey label, was a new-but-different Wolfshead logo she'd designed just for the beer. This one was much more casual, with the *W* capitalized but the rest of the letters in lowercase. And the letters were rounder, less blocky.

Comparing the two labels together side by side, it was evident they each had a different visual aesthetic, but were complementary enough for someone to connect the beer and the whiskey with the same company.

"You can play around with the font and the layout, but you get the general idea. Future labels can feature other aspects of the distilling process—the grain, for example, or the mountain spring where you get the water used in the recipe. But the logo would remain, ensuring brand continuity. Obviously, if you were to go with something like this, you would hire a professional graphic designer to do the final label."

The room was as silent as the grave, but she noticed that everyone was transfixed by the mock-ups she'd done.

"Now if you brand in this way, you'll be able to raise the price point considerably. Catering to the whiskey bars, the exclusive clubs and restaurants, and the established liquor stores in the area with your craft label and brand will allow you to raise the price to closer to forty-five or fifty dollars a bottle. Not only would that elevate your brand, but I've run some rudimentary numbers with the barrels you have left, and I believe it would allow you to break even, despite the loss of the ten barrels. Maybe even put you in the black, depending on how many bottles you're able to eke out of each barrel. Especially moving forward, it would be possible for the whiskey to be a self-sustaining arm of your business sooner rather than later. I've prepared some charts to show you how this could work."

Emma switched on the projector and calmly walked them through the numbers, as well as the rest of her branding and marketing plan.

When she was through, she paused, took a deep breath, and

looked around the room. Everyone met her gaze, except Lewis Senior, who was examining his notes.

"Do you have any questions?"

No one spoke. Time to wrap it up. For good.

"With this rollout, you have the chance to make your mark on the world of distilled spirits and ultimately, to elevate the Wolfshead brand. It's your choice as to what to do, but I would urge you to think long term and not status quo. Thank you for your time."

Again, there was dead silence as Emma gathered up her papers and sat back in her seat.

Gabe immediately leaned over. "Nice job."

In response, she gave him a nod and clasped her hands in her lap, not wanting anyone to see how much she was shaking.

Aidan was up next. He rose from the table, seemingly larger than life. It was almost unbearable to watch him, knowing that he was about to decimate her ideas. Rip her apart. Bravely, she tipped her chin up, refusing to let him see her cower.

Deliberately, Aidan opened the manila envelope and pulled out a piece of paper. "I had Ansel Hardt do a mock-up for us." He handed it to Brody, who examined it closely. "Pass it around. Take a good look."

As the drawing made its way around the table, there was nodding and murmurs. When she finally got hold of it, she studied it for a while. It looked really similar to the current beer label. A huge, howling wolf took up most of the center of the logo. It was definitely very rugged and very masculine—exactly what the woman at Younger had said—and would definitely not appeal to a huge portion of what Emma hoped would be their target demographic. On the positive side, the logo matched what they already had in place for branding, so if they went with that, they wouldn't have to change anything else and the product would appeal to those who already enjoyed Wolfshead products.

But in her mind, it wasn't enough. Not with that gem of a whiskey they had on their hands, and especially not since the accident. They'd be selling themselves short if they went with the status quo—this she knew for certain.

Ah, well. She'd tried her best. Done what she said she was going to do. After Aidan spoke, they'd vote, her proposal would lose, and then she'd announce that she was selling her share. She only had to get through a few more minutes and she'd be done with the Phelans.

The picture had finally made the rounds. When it got back to Aidan, he picked it up, examined it closely, then put it on the table directly in front of him.

"As you can see," he said, "not much is different. I figured that we'd take our existing brand, expand it out to encompass the whiskey, and be done with it. And why not? It's exactly what Dad and Uncle John wanted to do, and if it was good enough for them, I figured it'd be good enough for us."

More noises of assent.

"Gabe and I spent weeks working on our proposal. He didn't want to, but he did a great job on it anyway. I could go over all of it, but to be honest, it's more of the same stuff we've always done. Market to the distribution channels we know, that we're comfortable with, that already love our beer. Don't change anything. Lowball the price and sell it all. I hired the same graphic designer, was prepared to fight to the death to keep things the way they were, the way our fathers wanted, and then do you know what I realized? In doing that, in keeping everything the same, I'd turned into Paddy."

Brody spoke up. "You're not Paddy."

Aidan shook his head. "In some ways, I absolutely am." There was muted grumbling, but he held up his hand. "No, hear me out. Paddy was constantly railing at us not to change the status quo. Not to change *anything* about the company 'If it ain't broke' is what he always said, and I fought so hard against him for so long that I didn't realize that's what I was doing—trying to keep things exactly the way things were because of my own stupid pride."

Emma glanced over at Gabe. His mouth was half-open and he was staring at his big brother in shock. Probably because he'd never heard Aidan speak like this. To be honest, neither had she.

But Aidan wasn't done. "When Emma first told me about her ideas, I was more than skeptical—I was downright dismissive. After all, the Phelans have done things in a certain way for over a hundred years." He ran a hand through his hair. "I started out this process with my head up my ass. I was so convinced that my way was the right way to do things that I lost sight of everything, including what Dad and Uncle John were trying to do. Paddy thought everything they did was too risky, too bold. Well, guess what? They lived like that and they died like that—trying to impart their vision on Wolfshead. I was so caught up in that that I refused to be bold myself.

"I refused to see that the company had changed, by making that whiskey, by keeping our fathers' legacies alive and moving Wolfshead forward. You changed, too. The only one who didn't change was me.

"I could say that the accident was the thing that made me see reason. That losing a chunk of our initial run and realizing that there was no way the numbers could work if we sold to the Roberts Group was the reason I'm doing an about-face on this. But really, it was Emma—with a little help from Gabe—who showed me where I'd gone wrong. They're both right. The company is doing something different and amazing and timely and modern, and we need a brand that will reflect that. It's time I stopped living in the past and started looking toward the future."

He picked up the folder in front of him and held it up. "I insisted that Gabe help me prepare this stupid proposal. It was wrong to do it, and all I have to say is, Gabe, you were right, and I'm sorry. Sorry to all of you for pushing something that clearly isn't right for Wolfshead. I'm not selling to the Roberts Group. We need to take the company in another direction." And then, to Emma's shock, he ripped the folder right down the middle. "This is shit. Which is why I'm casting my vote for Emma's design and branding proposal."

Before Emma could process what had just happened, to her right, Gabe stood and placed a hand on her shoulder.

"I'm voting for Emma's proposal, too," he said, smiling down at her. "Glad you finally came to your senses," he said to his big brother.

Christine was the next to stand. "I vote for Emma's proposal," she said, placing her hand on Emma's other shoulder.

"As do I," Fiona said, rising next to her sister-in-law.

The remaining Phelan men looked at one another, then back at those family members who were standing. Brody stood. "I'm for Emma. I think her proposal's genius."

In turn, the rest of the men rose, each casting his vote for Emma's proposal. And then, somehow it was her turn, and someone was calling her name.

Gabe and Christine urged her up, and without really even

hearing what she was saying, she cast the final vote for her own proposal.

"It appears as if the selection is unanimous," Lewis Junior said, scribbling something in his notebook. "Wolfshead will go in a new direction and use the proposal that Emma has set forth."

Gabe was the first to let out a whoop. He embraced her in his strong arms. "Welcome back to the family," he said into her ear. She smiled and hugged him harder.

Then everyone else had to have their turn, starting with Christine and Fiona, then each Phelan man. She got a warm embrace from Brody, a fist bump from Finn, a slap on the back from Dylan, a stiff hug from Edward, and the gentlest of all hugs from Connor, who held her in his arms as if she were a breakable object.

The only one left was Aidan.

"Go to him," Gabe urged.

But Aidan stepped forward before she could move. Stood there staring at her for a long moment, during which time the only thing she heard was the rush of blood in her ears.

Finally, he spoke. "I've been a fool."

"Yes," she found herself agreeing. "You have."

"I know there's no way I can make amends for the way I treated you, for the mess I've made of your business, but I tried. This morning, I spoke with Younger. You'll be getting a call from them later saying you got the account."

Emma blinked. "What? How?"

"I told them the truth. That I purposefully kept you in the dark and went behind your back to hire Hardt and that you knew nothing about it."

This did not compute. "But…but how did you even know who to talk to?"

"Burt Younger is a good friend of mine. After every race, he has a Wolfshead ale to celebrate, and we're actually one of his sponsors. We keep him supplied in beer, and he acts as an unofficial ambassador."

Whoa. But wait. Aidan had tortured her, made her to understand that her opinions meant nothing. She crossed her arms over her chest. "It can't just be that easy. That you fix your mess and then we skip along our merry way."

Aidan flinched but kept talking. "You were right, Emma. You

were right all along. I shut you out. I didn't listen. All because I thought I knew what was best. I'm a stubborn ass, I wanted my own way, I was stupid, selfish, and you deserve so much more than me." He took a breath. "I know I have a lot to learn about us, about how to include you and keep including you in every aspect of my life, but I swear if you give me another chance, I won't screw up again. And if I do, I'll have many people to tell me that I'm out of line. But you have to give me that chance. Don't walk away again, not from me. Not from us. Not from—"

"Stop," she said quietly. "Just…stop."

Aidan shut his mouth.

"You're right," she said slowly. "You screwed up big-time, and you really don't deserve me." The look on his face was one of agony. "But here's the thing, Aidan: I love you. I can't stop loving you. So there's that."

"So…you want me back?"

"I never wanted you gone," she whispered. "I just wanted the Aidan I fell in love with."

"I'm here," he said. "And with my family as my witness, I promise I'm never going to let you down again."

"You might," she said truthfully. "But if you do, I want you to own up to it, not steamroll over everything to make it fit what you think is best."

"I can do that," he said slowly. "And if you let me back in, I will do my best to be the man you need. The man you deserve, now and forever."

How long had she hoped that he'd acknowledge his own fallibility? How long had she waited to hear these words and know that he meant them? Tears welled in the corners of her eyes.

"Oh, Aidan—"

She reached for him and he reached for her. And then his arms were around her and he was kissing her and kissing her and everyone was cheering and she was crying and Aidan was murmuring something against her lips and squeezing her tight.

Emma should have been mortified that all of this was happening directly in front of his family. Until she realized that they were her family, too. It was only fitting that he'd embrace her in this way, with his brothers and cousins and mom and aunt watching. She was part of the fold; now and going forward she felt with certainty she'd never be excluded again.

"If you don't mind," Lewis Senior interrupted, "we have a board meeting to finish."

Aidan lifted his head, leaving her momentarily bereft. "We're adjourned," he growled, and when his lips touched hers again everything else faded away until it was just the two of them there alone. Together.

CHAPTER 25

They all ended up heading back to Wolfshead and settling the rest of the business in the brewery's tasting room. Although Dylan declared it was never too early to start drinking whiskey, everyone else rejected that notion, and so beer it was.

And standing there at his tasting bar at his company, drinking a fresh, chilled glass of lager, straight from the tap, surrounded by his woman and his clan, Aidan had never felt more at peace.

The company was his, and their future was bright, thanks to the woman he'd almost lost—but won—again.

Aidan wrapped an arm around Emma's shoulders and looked down into her beautiful face. He truly didn't deserve her, nor did he deserve this extra chance he'd been given with her, and he'd be damned if he wasted it this time around.

He kissed her again, just because he could, loving the way she leaned into him.

"I was thinking," she said, after pulling away, "about going to visit my dad this evening."

"I'll come with you," he said.

"Really?"

"Sure. I know you'll be checking in on him a lot more these days, and I'll be right there with you."

She gifted him with a brilliant smile that lit him up from the inside. "That'd be amazing, Aidan. Thanks."

He merely shook his head. The look on her face—a complex mixture of joy and gratitude—hit him right in the gut. He should

219

have been doing this kind of shit long before now, if that was the reward he'd get.

"I got bad news, bro," Ed said, all seriousness. "The Costas are back to their old tricks. Their van is blocking our loading bay again."

"So we'll send in the peacemaker," Aidan said with a shrug. Nothing was going to put him off his mood. Not when he was flying so high.

Brody sighed and placed his beer down on the bar. "I'll go take care of it."

"Thanks, man," Aidan said, as he exited the building.

When things had settled down and the rest of his family had gone back to work, Aidan found himself alone with Emma.

"What's going on in that mind of yours?" he asked, noticing her worried look.

She put her beer down. "It's just that I'm not really sure how this is going to work."

"It'll work the way we want it to work."

"I have a house," she said. "And a life that doesn't include you right now. I'm not sure how to weave it all back in without going back to what we were."

He took her face in his hands. "We're never going back to what we were."

"Promise?" she asked.

"I swear it. You're in. Anything that matters, I will be talking to you about, whether that is for the company or for ourselves."

She closed her eyes. "You don't know how long I've waited to hear you say that."

"Too long."

"You're saying it now."

"Yeah," he said, and brushed her lips with his. "I am." He grinned. "We'll take it slow. As slow as you want," he promised. "I need to prove to you that I'm not the same man I was, and I know that will take time. Keep your house and I'll keep mine. For now."

"But we can have sleepovers?" she asked, a sly smile on her face.

He couldn't help from smiling, too. "Every night if you want."

"I want." And the look in her eye—so sultry, so full of

meaning—took his breath away.

"I want you, Emma. All of you. I want to marry you and raise a family with you." Something she'd always wanted, and now he did, too, because her dream was his. He took a breath. "I know it'll take time before you agree to wear my ring again, but in the meantime, will you wear this for me?" He pulled out the "forever" necklace, the metal still warm from his pocket, and placed it in the palm of her hand.

Emma looked down, then back up at him. She blinked furiously, a sure sign she was close to tears. "Yes," she whispered. She tried to do the clasp, but her hands were too shaky. "Help me?"

"With pleasure."

He took it from her, clasped it around her neck, then kissed her again, this time long and deep.

She gripped his wrists. "Things are really going to be different this time around, aren't they?"

"Because of you."

"I love you, Aidan," she said, her words coming out in a breathless rush. "I never stopped loving you. Even when we were apart and I thought there was no chance of us getting back together. And I know that makes me weak and pathetic and—"

He cut off her protestations with a kiss. "You're not weak and pathetic. You're the strongest person I know. And what your hope and love makes you, Emma, is mine. And I will make you mine again, claim you publicly for everyone to see. But I won't do it until I'm convinced that you see the man I am. Because I love you, too."

"Please," she whispered. "Kiss me again."

And there, in his tasting room, he kissed her, knowing that he would never, ever let this singular woman go again. No matter what obstacles they had to overcome, she was his and he was hers.

This time, forever.

ABOUT THE AUTHOR

Elisabeth Barrett lives in the San Francisco Bay Area and spends her days teaching, editing, writing sexy contemporary romance, and enjoying time with her sometimes-bearded husband and three spirited children. She is constantly perfecting her home-work-writing juggling act, but in her free time she loves to hike open space preserves, grow orchids, bake sweet things her husband won't eat, and sing in grand choruses.

www.elisabethbarrett.com